MOTHERS

# MOTHERS AND TRUCKERS

By IVANA DOBRAKOVOVÁ

Translated by Julia and Peter Sherwood

JANTAR PUBLISHING
London 2022
www.JantarPublishing.com

First published in Great Britain in 2022 by
Jantar Publishing Ltd
www.jantarpublishing.com

All rights reserved.

First published in Slovak in 2018 as *Matky a kamionisti* by
Marenčin PT, Brarislava

© 2022 Ivana Dobrakovová
Translation copyright © Julia and Peter Sherwood 2022
Foreword copyright © Anna Gács
Cover design Davor Pukljak, frontispis.hr

The right of Julia and Peter Sherwood to be identified as translators of this work has been asserted in accordance with the Copyright, Design and Patents Act, 1988.

Sections translated from Pier Paolo Pasolini's poem 'The Scream' ('L'Urlo') on p. 150 are quoted from the translation by Stuart Hood in *Theorem* (Quartet Books, 1992). Lines from the poem 'La Ricchezza' ('Wealth') are quoted from the translation by Stephen Sartarelli in *The Selected Poetry by Pier Paolo Pasolini* (The University of Chicago Press, 2014).

No part of this book may be reproduced or utilised in any form or by any means, electronic or mechanical, including photocopying, recording, or by any information storage and retrieval system, without written permission.

A CIP catalogue record for this book is available from the British Library
ISBN 978-1-914990-11-3

This translation was made possible by a grant from SLOLIA committee,
the Centre for Information on Literature in Bratislava, Slovakia

# CONTENTS

Introduction by Anna Gács
THE SHORT STORY SISTERHOOD ... 7

# MOTHERS AND TRUCKERS
## by Ivana Dobrakovová

| | |
|---|---|
| FATHER | ... 15 |
| IVANA | ... 31 |
| OLIVIA | ... 99 |
| LARA | ... 153 |
| VERONIKA | ... 203 |

INTRODUCTION

# THE SHORT STORY SISTERHOOD

For a couple of weeks at the end of 2017, half the world was discussing a 20-page long literary work. Kristen Roupenian's 'Cat Person', an unassuming story about the intricate hierarchies of dating that appeared in the *New Yorker* triggered a rapidly expanding conversation that engaged critics and ordinary readers, and native as well as non-native speakers of English. There occurred something that we had long thought lost: a single literary work seemed to unify the reading public. One can regard this perplexing phenomenon not only as the celebration of Western literary tradition and its role in forming the way we think about ourselves, but also as the victory of a somewhat neglected literary genre in this tradition: the short story. We know many literary career trajectories in which a single novel brought its author immediate literary fame and landed her incredible publishing contracts, yet it is rather unusual, if not totally unheard-of, that publishing a single short story could do the same. Beyond the merits of Roupenian's writing and the sensitive timing of its publication – at the climax of the #MeToo upheaval – this 'literary sensation' also attested to the growing significance of the short story as a literary genre in recent years. In its two-century-long history, the modern short story has played an important role in the work of many great prose writers, from Poe to Atwood and from Dostoevsky to Ulitskaya. Even though short stories might seem to be more accessible and digestible for many readers than novels, they have often been marginalised, conceived of as appendices to the famous novels responsible for their authors' success and canonisation. For a long time, the novel has been exalted as the truly representative genre of prose: a literary form capable of grasping a historical period in all its complexity and of depicting a tableau of society through its byzantine network of protagonists. From this perspective, the short story has often been referred to the realm of the private, the small-scale. As Frank O'Connor famously suggested 60 years ago, rather than a true hero, short stories tend to feature a 'submerged population group'. It is not at all unlikely that this characteristic of the genre, its tendency to offer alternative perspectives to great narratives, is the very reason for its recent ascendancy.

Though the Nobel Prize in Literature does not necessarily correspond with the judgement of either the reading audience or literary professionals at any particular time, it is still symptomatic in some sense that, in 2013, Alice Munro was the first to win the prize for an achievement comprised solely of short stories. And it may be no mere coincidence that, two years later, the posthumous republication of *A Manual for Cleaning Women*, a collection of short stories by Lucia Berlin, turned its author, who had by then been dead for more than a decade, from a niche writer into an international brand in a matter of months. These cases also point to a notable impulse in the history of the genre that has gained impetus in recent decades. Utilizing the short story's association with non-dominant experience, many women writers have moulded it to their own dispositions and used it to revise traditional representations in various ways, from rewriting ancient fairy tales, through the documenting of women's daily drudgery, to the analysis of the politics of the household.

Ivana Dobrakovová's darkly humorous short stories bond with this heritage in many respects. Just as in her previous short story collections, in the five stories in *Mothers and Truckers* she again focuses on the private sphere and micro-society, on family relations, love affairs, friendships, small-town communities. Dobrakovová was born in Bratislava when it was still part of Czechoslovakia; she lived through the collapse of state socialism and the break-up of the country as a young child, she inhaled the economic and political optimism of the first years of democracy as well as the disappointment that was soon to follow, and she moved to Italy as a young adult gaining first-hand experience of the newly enlarged Europe. While she includes elements of all this in the historical and political background of her protagonists, they crop up only as occasional hints. The first story in the volume, *Father*, for example, recalls a familiar East-European male prototype, a well-meaning but weak man pursuing naïve and hopeless economic enterprises, while struggling with alcohol and mental problems. And the very last story, *Veronika*, takes us to post-communist Slovakia at the time of the dissolving borders, yet the vision of a borderless world is more the product of the narrator's bizarre imagination than reality: she compensates for her rather dull life in Bratislava by spending most of her time sex-chatting with and daydreaming about men – truckers, farmers and the like – from around the world.

At the core of each short story, all narrated in the first person by a range of women, there is the protagonist's struggle for mental control. In *Father*, we soon discover that telling the story of the father serves a therapeutic purpose: the narrator tries to locate the roots of her own mental instability by recollecting his decline. Ivana, the heroine of the second story, is on psychiatric medication to keep her borderline mental disorder under control. She introduces the reader to her tangled daily life, in the course of which she tries to seduce a celebrity intellectual by pretending to be a writer. As the story slowly unfolds, a traumatic childhood secret surfaces from sparse flashbacks: a brutal episode from her horse-riding days, which could be worked into the 'great novel' she lies that she is writing. (This is just one example of how Dobrakovová's omnipresent irony permeates her heroines' otherwise tragic or petty fates – a character who shares her forename is a novelist in her own daydreams, yet what we end up with is 'only' a short story reporting on her fiasco). Other characters who do not explicitly suffer from mental illness also seem to have difficulties maintaining their composure and functioning in the required manner, which is sometimes reflected in their fear of literally falling apart: Olivia, a middle-aged teacher in Turin, Italy, suffers from a recurrent dislocation of the shoulder, and says, '[s]ometimes I imagine that I will fall apart completely inside, my joints slackening for good and refusing to do their job, that I will turn into a pile of bones floating loosely around my body and eventually beginning to force their way out through my skin, gouging holes in it.'

Everything we learn about these five women and the world they inhabit is filtered through their troubled minds – this narrative mode, too, goes back a long way in the history of the modern short story. The creation of a literary world entirely through the distorting subjective perspective of the narrator appeared in the first half of the nineteenth century, the best-known early examples being Gogol's *The Diary of a Madman* in Russian literature, and Poe's *The Tell-Tale Heart* in the United States. But of course, today's readers cannot be as confident as their nineteenth-century predecessors still could be in distinguishing the subjective from the objective, the disfigured from the unspoiled, and Dobrakovová does not go out of her way to help us in this respect. By focusing on the mental processes of her protagonists, sometimes almost in a stream-of-consciousness manner, she offers us five sensitive portraits written with an abundance of empathy, down to the most ironic details.

The short stories in *Mothers and Truckers* are also linked by the lyricism of Dobrakovová's style, as well as a wealth of recurring motives. Rhapsodic thoughts are conveyed by a carefully crafted language that breathes together with the narrators. The length of sentences changes constantly from a few words merely registering facts to page-long, impassioned tirades. This language can create cathartic moments even at the most unexpected points – one of the most memorable being the description of the birth of a foal, a beautiful moment of hope after Ivana's distressing confession.

Some of the motives weaving through the stories are reinforced by literary-cultural references scattered throughout the volume. For example, overtly or covertly, Dobrakovová invokes many of the representations of mental distress from Sylvia Plath through Roman Polanski to Robert Altman. And Pier Paolo Pasolini – a literary evening based on writings by the notorious Italian director acts as the gravitational force for two very different women in two different short stories, the prim, sexually inhibited Olivia, and Lara, a mother of two, whose unexciting family life turns out to be a cover for sado-masochistic sexual adventures. But it is not only the web of cultural references that creates parallelisms and hidden connections between the narrators. The most striking motive that appears in all of the short stories is the looming figure of the mother. All five women have this in common: the suffocating presence of their imperious, querulous mother(s), who 'spreads like mildew around the window. She devours everything that happens to find itself in her way. Overpowers it, suppresses it. She's everywhere' (*Olivia*). While the five narrators in the five stories, despite all their parallelisms, have distinct features, the mother who appears in each of the stories seems in every case to be the same character. Seen by the daughters as a figure of almost mythical proportions, crippling them, condemning them to an eternal childhood, the mother figure creates another kind of kinship between these troubled, somewhat pathetic, sometimes heroic, often comical, and even more often loveable women. She makes them secret sisters, their ties running through many a year and many a mile.

Anna Gács, Budapest, 2020

# MOTHERS AND TRUCKERS

By IVANA DOBRAKOVOVÁ

# FATHER

Let me start with a random image, I'm not saying it's particularly significant, it's just something I've heard others talk about, although I don't recall it myself. I'm sitting on the sofa next to my sister in the living room, we're watching a fairy tale on the TV. My sister is four years older than me; she might be around six at this point, I'm not quite two, our dad is in the kitchen. We live on Castle Hill, near Mudroňova Street, in Bratislava's most upmarket neighbourhood, with a shiny Ford Cortina in the garage, a fireplace in the living room, and a view of Austria from our balcony. Both my parents are working so I've been going to a crèche for a year now.

My mum comes in from work, exhausted, lugging bags of shopping, and finds the following scene: her older daughter has snot dangling from her nose down to her knees, so at least she can't smell that her little sister Svetlana has shat herself, her nappy overflowing. And my dad, yes, he's there too, in the kitchen, fast asleep, his head on the tablecloth, a bottle beside it. A bottle of something. No need to specify, you get the picture.

There's just one detail worth mentioning. Dad didn't live with us. He often dropped by during the week and spent the night in the flat, but his permanent residence was elsewhere, in a village south of Bratislava, not far from the Hungarian border, by the gravel lakes where we used to swim in summer. After my parents got married, my mum, already pregnant with my sister, was planning to join him down south, but there was the flat in the loveliest part of Bratislava, the fireplace, the view and all, so she changed her mind at the last minute and didn't move down to the village by the lakes after all. Perhaps my aunt, Mum's sister, had something to do with it because she had never stopped laying into Mum, saying 'those people will never accept you as one of their own, you'll be forever a foreigner among them. And to add insult to injury, you'll have to live with your mother-in-law. Take my advice'. And Mum did. But then Dad put his foot down. This was where his home was. That was all there was to it. To cut a long story short, they didn't live together. Not in the early years, at least. Until Dad's health deteriorated.

I don't really know what to say about Dad in those early years. He had a bald spot. I loved that. I used to call it 'ring o' roses'. I wished I had a ring like that on my head too. One day, I remember that moment very clearly, I found a pair of scissors in a sewing kit and cut a hole into my hair. I proudly went to show it to Mum. I forget how she reacted, but I do remember her telling the story to all and sundry later on. A family legend.

I also recall the village by the lakes. In Bratislava, Dad had a job at the Technical University but back home he was a peasant, a farmer, bare-chested, always with a spade in his hands, a hoe, a rake or a hose. When I was little, I thought his garden was enormous, a real kingdom where I could clamber onto trees, fall into a well, and get all sweaty in the greenhouse. I was astonished to learn later on that Dad's garden was just a fraction of the original farm that had belonged to *Nagypapa*, my granddad, before the communists nationalised it. Apparently, it stretched all the way to the lakes. Wouldn't it be wonderful to be able to jump into the water straight from the garden, to have horses and not just the chickens and rabbits that my grandma, *Nagymama*, used to keep!

We used to go down there at weekends and spend entire summers by the lakes. Nagymama was still alive, speaking more or less only Hungarian, shouting *kiskutya* at the local mongrels, stuffing me and my sister with pancakes, which I'd love to say were the best in the world but, to be honest, I can't remember what they tasted like. She and her son tended the vegetable garden, a small farm of sorts. She used to grow seedlings in the hothouse and sell them at the market. In the early days, Mum tried to make herself useful and learn a thing or two from her mother-in-law, but she soon realised that her sister was right. It was a waste of effort. She could never do anything right by her, *istenem, hagyj, ne segíts,* for heaven's sake, leave me, don't help. Nagymama chased her away from the seedlings almost as if she were a mongrel who'd sneaked in through a hole in the fence. Until Mum eventually decided she'd had enough, too. And that she would focus solely on the flowers in the front garden, and the ornamental trees and shrubs. Later she went as far as to claim that she'd rather get a divorce than push a wheelbarrow full of seedlings to the market.

Dad liked to travel and to take photos on his trips. In his bedroom there was a cupboard full of yellow envelopes with photos that I often rummaged through. Dad was capable of taking twenty pictures of the same rock through a bus window, of shooting three rolls of film of a blurry Niagara Falls. Dad had no talent for photography whatsoever. I also came across some pictures showing Dad in the company of some peculiar women wearing garish make-up and clothes. It wasn't until much later that I was able to put my finger on it – they looked vulgar. These are the only pictures that show him, embracing strange, vulgar women in various sleazy dives. The rest are just landscapes.

On his travels Dad met lots of foreigners he would later invite to come and visit him in the large two-storey house he built soon after the fall of communism, right next to Nagymama's traditional cottage. In the summer, Dad rented out rooms to holidaymakers who were keen to splash around in the lakes, and sometimes also to his foreign acquaintances. One summer I went to a football match with one of these foreigners, a young man called Pancha, from Peru. Or rather, we set out for the funfair on the far side of the lakes but let ourselves be swept along by the crowds streaming towards the football stadium. He spoke no Slovak, I spoke no English, we communicated by gestures. In fact, we spoke only once during the whole football match, which we both found boring. Pancha pointed to my shoes and said 'pretty, nice'. I could just about understand that. Afterwards, it was hard to explain why on earth we had ended up at a football match.

My sister loved to pull my leg. Once she told me that the lakes were created by people spitting. The area had been dredged for gravel some time ago, leaving a pit so ugly that no one walking past could help but spit in it in disgust. And so, gradually, over the years, it collected. The spit. I didn't believe her but found the idea truly repulsive. To be fair though, I ought to mention that she also taught me how to dive off a bridge. And to turn somersaults under water. The two of us used to swim to an island and Dad would swim with us. Mum likes to tell the story of how I once got lost by the lakes. I was four then. It was time to go home and Dad and my sister had lost me from sight. So they went home. Once there, Dad said to Mum, 'don't worry, she'll turn up on her own'. And sure enough, before Mum had time to faint, I came back.

For Dad, patriarchy ruled. The only reason Nagypapa had married Nagymama was that she was the hardest-working labourer on his farm and once she became his wife, he no longer had to pay her. Dad had adopted this attitude and he enjoyed saying that a woman's job was to work the fields and when she got tired, she should take a rest by doing the housework . But as I've mentioned before, Mum had put her foot down early on because of the seedlings and Nagymama's nitpicking and hand-wringing, and all she did was rest by doing the housework in the big house.

Sometimes Mum would make strawberry jam. Dad would praise her. In his own peculiar way. He said it was almost as good as the jam you get in the shops.

He was very proud of his hardscrabble childhood and of the education he had achieved solely thanks to his intelligence. When he was born, Nagypapa and Nagymama were living in a shed in the middle of the garden, without electricity or running water, just compacted earth for a floor, with a well close by, everything made of wood. Every summer, on his own initiative, Dad would work through all the maths exercises in his textbooks for the school year ahead and was then desperately bored in class. Later he went on to study at the university in Prague. He already had quite a serious drinking problem in those days. Once he got so pissed that he was literally legless and couldn't make it back to his hall of residence. But he applied logic to solve the problem. Since the pub was on a hill and the halls of residence at the foot of the hill, he simply lay down on the ground and rolled all the way down to the door of the hall.

After Dad graduated, Nagypapa showed him a notebook in which he had jotted down all the expenses he had incurred to put him through university. He didn't ask for any of it back, he just showed it to Dad so that he should know how much his son's fancy ideas had cost him. Mum says Dad never forgave him for that.

*  *  *

What do I know about my parents' relationship? The less the better? To be on the safe side? Mum must have seen something in him. But what exactly?

She said that once Dad had told her, in the presence of other people, that she was not only intelligent but also beautiful. It must have been quite a statement, an exceptional compliment for her to cherish the memory of it so much. To want to share it with me.

He had always had a drinking problem, which is why, as long as I can remember, I always thought of it as something inseparable from him, a part of him that was meant to be that way. Just like his illness. There's no point trying to figure out which came first, the chicken or the egg, what was the cause and what was the effect: his unstable mental state, the age-old proclivity to drink, the genetic predisposition to both that got all mixed up, reinforcing each other until they came to form his very essence.

Nevertheless, some episodes do stand out.

One night, Mum, at the end of her tether, dragged us out of bed. 'Girls, get up, go and tell your *Apuka* that we live one floor higher up'. My sister and I staggered out into the stairwell in our pyjamas, drowsy with sleep. We didn't understand what was going on. We found Dad one floor below, persistently ringing our neighbour's doorbell even though the neighbour was standing in his open doorway trying to stop him. With great difficulty, the two of us then helped Mum haul him upstairs and into our flat. I don't know when exactly this happened. Or how old I was at the time. My sister was still at the same school as me, so I would have been in the third form. One of the first incidents of this kind, to be followed by many more. It felt bizarre. Like a bad dream. Like a night-time escapade foreshadowing my eventful youth.

That stain has remained to this day. In our fancy block of flats. Complete with a garage, fireplace, and a view of Austria. And the stain. In the lift. The lift might be about forty years old now, it has no internal doors. It's one of those where you can see the floors pass by. One night, Dad was coming home, pissed as a newt, and wanted to lean on the wall. He leaned his head against the floor passing by. He hit his forehead, drawing blood. Leaving a long dark brown stain between the first and second floors.

He started spending more and more of his nights with us in Bratislava. His boozer of choice was Albrecht's. He'd spend entire afternoons there, just across the street from my classroom window. Sometimes I would catch a glimpse of him. Leaning on the windowsill, I would watch as he walked to the pub. Of course, I never said to anyone, 'hey, look, there's my dad'. Not even to my sister. Her classroom was on the second floor, but its windows faced the other way. Out in the street though, I ignored him on several occasions. He'd be walking towards me and I'd continue straight ahead, glassy-eyed. Eventually he'd grab me by the shoulders and make me face him. Later on, at home, I overheard him complaining to Mum that I didn't acknowledge him and was ashamed of him. But that wasn't the case yet, not back then.

It was around this time that my sister joined him. Actually, it must have been later, after she started secondary school. She didn't literally join him, just followed in his footsteps. Occasionally she ended up at Albrecht's but more often she hung out in other dives with her pals. The Albanians. That came as a real blow for Mum. First her husband, and now her daughter, too. One night my sister came home in the small hours, covered in dreadful make-up, purple eyelids and purple lips. Mum started to thrash her, shouting that this must never happen again, but my sister was so good at defending herself, so quick at sticking out her sharp elbows that in the end you couldn't tell who found the thrashing more painful. I wept as I watched. Apuka slept through it all like a baby.

My sister went from bad to worse. She began running away from home. Without a word, she'd just up and go. Mum and I would then trot down to the police station and ask them to start a missing person search. Oddly enough, I have a very clear memory of these visits, of skipping down Hlboká Street without feeling at all anxious. Even though I must have been old enough to realise the gravity of the situation. Sometimes my sister would disappear for days on end. Once she made it as far as Prague. The police did nothing, my sister would always turn up of her own accord.

* * *

I believe it all started with the goat. One summer's day, when we came home from the lakes, Dad announced that he was going to buy a goat. Nagymama was no longer alive and as my sister, by then sixteen, had different interests and different problems, so the only one who loved the idea of a goat was me. Me, the child. Mum couldn't understand: what goat? why a goat? Of course, Dad had a logical justification for it. He was fed up with having to mow the lawn so he thought he'd stick a stake in the grass, tie the goat to it, and lo and behold, the goat would graze, eating all the grass within reach. While I was happily skipping around the kitchen, tears welled up in Mum's eyes and she slammed the door shut screaming, 'it's either me or the goat'.

So that was the end of that story. No goat.

Sometime later it was the turn of a pony. I loved that idea too, but only until Dad revealed his business plan. I was supposed to walk around the garden with the pony, it would be a great draw for other children, a real goldmine. I stared at him in disappointment. I had thought the pony would be mine and mine alone, that he was going to buy it for me. Because he knew how I loved horses. I absolutely rejected the idea of treating it as a way of earning a few pennies. That might have been the first time that I stood up to him.

At this point Dad became rather obsessed with money. He kept telling us how much he was going to make, what was profitable and in what way, what we needed to do and what we ought to invest in, how much we'd get out of it. He was good at maths, we never doubted that, and yet, for some reason, his schemes never worked out. Instead of making money, Dad kept spending and losing it, he'd be in the red more and more often, having to borrow, unable to manage on his salary, making no contribution to the household.

But all along there was also something else. Something I started noticing with greater clarity at that point.

Dad's stinginess.

This thought came to haunt me later on. I was horrified that one day I'd be as stingy as my dad. Because stinginess is hereditary, you see. It's a genetic predisposition, I'm quite sure of that. Being stingy is not something you choose to be deliberately. You're stingy if you automatically quicken your pace when you're in an underpass and see someone selling *Nota bene*, the homeless people's magazine, you're stingy if you wonder if it's really necessary to buy all your friends and family a Christmas present. And you can't help it. Every now and then you make an extravagant gesture. You give someone a present out of the blue. Just like that. As if you simply wanted to make them happy. As if you just happened to think of them. But in fact, you're trying to fool yourself. So that you can tell yourself, 'me, stingy? No way, didn't I once give so and so a present?'. While at the same time you're drawing up a mental list so that you can tick off so and so, no need to give so and so a present for a good while. Because so and so has had plenty. Who do they think they are?

The seeds were sown a long time ago. 'You shit through all the loo paper.' This was the leitmotif of our childhood. Dad used to tell us off for making him buy loo paper all the time. Why couldn't we make one roll last a week? The fuss he would kick up! 'We need to save money,' he'd shout. My sister and I were convinced he did it on purpose. That he picked on loo paper specially to humiliate us. There were other household items that we went through. Soap. Washing powder. Tissues. Deodorants. He wasn't bothered about any of those. But he went to town on loo paper. Why the hell should he keep buying more loo rolls?

Pocket money was also an issue. We had an agreement. Dad was supposed to give me twenty crowns a week. Except that he always forgot. It was always up to me, to drop a hint on a Monday night. Could he be so kind. Pretty please. And then I'd have to watch Dad get his coat and fumble for his wallet with trembling hands. Watch him as he took out a twenty-crown note with the utmost reluctance. And handed it over to me. In the slowest of motions. As if he hoped I might change my mind. Take pity on him. He'd never look me in the eye. He evidently found the whole situation unbearable. I came to loathe this weekly ritual so much that, after a while, I took to helping myself to twenty-crown notes from his wallet. When Dad was asleep. Hung over. He never noticed.

Even though he did keep detailed accounts. He tried to work out what was better value, walking around town on foot or taking the bus. If you walk everywhere, you save on bus fares. It's a no-brainer. On the other hand – you wear out the soles of your shoes! More than by standing on a bus holding on to the handrail. And shoes don't come cheap either. Dad kept track of everything in his notebook. Two years' worth of research. I forget what earth-shattering conclusion he came to. All I remember is that there was a period when he forced my sister and me traipse around town on foot, ignoring our protests and whining about our sore feet.

It was while he was still living by the lakes that he began rummaging through the rubbish. He would never refer to it that way, of course. What do you mean, rubbish? It was all excellent, usable stuff. A broken computer keyboard. A battered wash basin. Part of a children's slide. And so on. The heap of junk in the garden kept growing. Waiting for him to fix the stuff up. But it didn't all come from rubbish bins. He got some of the stuff as a present, or rather, bought at knock-down prices from his drinking pals. The ones who called him Molecule. On account of him being a teacher, a scientist. Obviously. Molecule was a brilliant business partner since his stinginess went hand in hand with a kind of greed. When he saw a special offer, something at a discount, there was no stopping him. And so, one day, he brought home two hundred identical postcards of his village by the lakes, three bidets (presumably to wean my sister and me off loo paper altogether) and twenty rolls of film past their sell-by date. They made wonderful vintage photos.

And then he lost it. Completely. He found a new use for the films. One morning he decided to go to Prievidza. God knows why he picked that town, of all places. I will never know. In a word, destination Prievidza! Dad had no money, but he had his rolls of expired film. He managed to convince the bus driver to accept them in lieu of paying for his ticket. He made it to Prievidza, to the bus station. What happened there we learned later from a police report. And from Dad's jabbering. Or rather, Mum learned it. I only heard about it from her some time later. Dad had walked to the town centre and gone to a supermarket for a bread roll and salad, cod salad probably. He had sat down by a fountain to eat it. And that's when he noticed that someone was sending him signals. It was the tobacconist. Opening the shutters of her kiosk, she used the reflections of the sun to send signals to him, my dad, Molecule. He was absolutely sure of that. She was trying to tell him something. Something vital. He finished eating, cleaned out the remains of the salad in the plastic pot with the last bit of his roll, stood up and walked over to the kiosk. And the minute he saw her, it happened. It was love at first sight. And he knew that she was in love with him too, that was what she was trying to indicate by means of the solar reflections. Suddenly everything started to make sense. To Dad, I mean. A surge of energy and happiness engulfed him. That was it. 'I'm so happy we've found each other', he said to the tobacconist. She didn't understand, to her it made no sense, but Dad wasn't fazed by that. Maybe she was just shy. To stop her being shy, he decided to show her that he had long shed all his inhibitions. And he proceeded to shed his clothes. He undressed and jumped into the fountain. Now everything began to make sense to the tobacconist. She called the police. And they took him straight to the loony bin. That's how Dad landed in hospital for the first time.

My memory of the second time is clearer. I was fifteen. I was at secondary school but I didn't have a difficult adolescence, I was interested in cinema, in Hitchcock, Truffaut, I was into fantasy and was trying to survive physics and chemistry classes intact. My sister had left by then and Dad was spending more time in our flat than by the lakes. He was slowly climbing out of depression, on long-term sick leave. And then, all of a sudden, he got it into his head that I had to be confirmed. He started going to mass himself, insisting that he'd always been a believer, just like Nagymama, and what a disgrace it was that his fifteen-year-old daughter had not yet been to first communion or confirmation. I made it very clear to him that I had no desire for either. But of course, Dad didn't care what I thought. He went to the church to sign me up for religion lessons and asked the priest how soon it could be arranged. Luckily, it never happened because one day, during mass, the priest had to order Dad out of church after he stood up in the aisle and started snapping pictures of him. Back home Dad justified his behaviour by saying he was merely documenting religious life in the Church of the Holy Trinity.

But that wasn't the end of it. Dad came to believe that he was communicating with God. He only confided in me, he didn't tell Mum. I was at a loss as to what to do with this information. Should I pass it on? Grass on him? In the evenings, Dad would reveal God's grand designs to me in the kitchen. He started calling himself 'God's little finger'. As he uttered these words, he would raise his little finger in the air as if about to take a sip from a teacup. I had never really understood what these God's designs were all about. Maybe Dad didn't understand it either, but he seemed to be rather well informed about a number of things. For instance, he once told me how many years I had left to live. He had calculated it exactly, to the day. With God's help. The day I would die. Then he revealed to me how long my sister had left. And finally, Mum. Never a word about himself. I found he was off the waggon again. Although in a less conspicuous way. He was more secretive about it; he no longer went to Albrecht's. He drank at home. Like a housewife, a closet alcoholic. Then he started scribbling something in his notebooks. And then he vanished.

We found him in the house by the lakes. There was this strange glint in his eyes. Almost an epiphany. He disclosed his grand plans to us. He had everything carefully written down and sketched out in his notebooks. He would turn his two-storey house into a big centre. A centre for the people. That's what he called it. People would come flocking there. Including people from faraway countries. Not just to swim in the lakes as in the old days. He was going to build an aquapark at the back of the garden and there would be a playground instead of the greenhouse. He had already purchased the slides and some climbing frames; they were piled up under the walnut tree. There would be shops in the big house. And, most importantly, there would be a nudist beach on the roof, on the house's flat roof. His eyes gleamed.

I will never forget the hospital attendants chasing him around the garden.

\* \* \*

And then, eventually, death; what else. I rarely revisit those months in my mind, so my recollections might not be entirely accurate. I was eighteen, in my first and, as it turned out, also my last year at university, studying French. Dad was living with us. The house and the garden by the lakes were running to seed, nobody ever went there anymore. Dad spent all the time in the bedroom, sprawled on the bed, profoundly depressed. He would get up only when he needed a drink of water. I suppose he must have been eating too, at least a little. But I don't remember ever seeing him eat anything, only drink water. His trembling hands fishing out a glass from the sink, filling it with tap water and drinking it. While I sat at the kitchen table learning vocab, he would sometimes turn around in the doorway and stand there staring at me. I found it annoying. He would stare for a long time. And then he'd start saying these things. He would take me to task, 'Svetlana, you must never smoke or drink or take drugs. Do you hear me? It's important. I wasn't able to tell your sister, and now she's turned out like me. I mean, not quite. Because I'm going to die. I will die very soon, I'm sure of that'. I sat there looking at him, with all the cliché responses running through my head – what are you talking about, stop scaring me like that, come on, you'll live to be a hundred – but I couldn't bring myself to say any of those things because I knew he was right. He was going to die. You just had to take one look at him. He would die quite soon. He was dying already. He repeated this countless times. For about a month he kept drumming it into my head, with slight variations, night after night, that I mustn't stray from the path of righteousness, nor give in to temptation, as if it hadn't been obvious that even without cigarettes, alcohol and drugs I was already crippled for life. Eventually he couldn't handle it anymore and had himself admitted voluntarily, asking for the hospital to send someone to get him. This time they didn't need to chase him around the garden. The last time I saw him was as he was loaded into an ambulance in a wheelchair. He died a week later. From a heart attack. He had the heart attack in the evening but instead of doing something about it they let him die slowly in the loony bin. It wasn't until the early hours that they decided to take him to the university hospital in Mickiewiczova Street, but he died in the ambulance. The way they informed us was quite peculiar. We received a letter telling us to come and collect his clothes. What do you mean, will he no longer be needing his clothes? Is he going to walk around naked from now on? Only the clothes, not a word about Dad. It took exactly six months for me to have a breakdown. I managed to get through the winter in a kind of hibernation, or rather, by force of inertia. I didn't break down until spring. Until the end of the semester. One day I was supposed to go to university for an exam, but I never went. I just stayed in bed.

# IVANA

At the time I was born, Ivanas were ten a penny and you couldn't move without bumping into an Ivana. In primary school there were three of us in my form alone, in secondary school there were four. Once at a PTA meeting my mum swelled with pride when she heard the teacher sing Ivana's praises, what a bright and clever girl she was, how well she was doing, until she realised that the Ivana in question was the girl who sat next to me in class, so yeah, I got used to being Ivana number two or three to most people. But when it came to horses, well, with horses I was Ivana number one, so it made total sense when another Ivana, who joined the club after me, was renamed Nina after her sister, and I gradually forgot that this wasn't her real name, that our names were the same. Anyway, long story short, she was my great pal Nina. But when it came to horses, I was Ivana number one, Ivana the Great, the one and only Ivana, because horses were my life, I would have given my life for horses, and actually, in a way, I did.

This is the first time in eighteen years that I've been able to think about horses, to recall that period in my life without getting the shakes, without having to rush to the medicine cabinet for a Xanax to calm my nerves. Memories flood into my head like blood, one after the other, I can recall everything in the minutest detail, such as Tristan's brown leather saddle, Mr Ble's wrinkles, the way his whole face creased up when he screamed at me at the riding school to keep my hands down, 'keep them down!', Žofia's blonde hair as she cantered past on Vrana's back. It's all suddenly coming back to me, but it doesn't bother me now, the memories don't rip my insides apart the way they used to over the past eighteen years, when the slightest hint, a single ill-chosen word, an image on TV, would be enough to shatter me into pieces, now I just register it all and set it to one side in my head, in a neat pile next to all the other memories. And it's all thanks to him. Thanks to R.

Mum is in the kitchen, she takes out the cutlery, spends a little longer fussing around the stove, gives the spoon one last lick, tastes the Szekler goulash she's just made. She's convinced that I love it, she makes it for me at least once every two weeks, cooking up the stuff in industrial quantities, it keeps me going for three or four days. I sit at the table browsing through the newspapers and journals Zuzka brought over yesterday, all that matters is making sure Mum doesn't notice any change in me. 'Three dumplings with your goulash, or four?' 'Three will do', I shout in the direction of the kitchen because I know that if I say four, she'll plonk at least five onto my plate. So now the Szekler goulash with four dumplings is served, Mum joins me at the table, placing the heaped plate before me, next to the pill dispenser. 'Are these the magazines from Zuzka? Just make sure you don't get food all over them again, you're such a pig, always making everything greasy'. I keep my mouth shut and push the papers and journals towards her, she opens *Plus sedem dní*, all she's having is a slice of bread and butter anyway. My mum doesn't eat freshly cooked food on principle, she cooks just for me, and eats the leftovers only after I've refused to eat the same dish for the fifth time in a row, I'm allowed to do that, to say no the fifth time. I stare at the pill dispenser and suddenly I wonder, is this still the old one? I can't remember ever having any other, this one is looking rather worn, the Tuesday and Saturday compartments have lost their lid. I take out my evening dose and make it go down with a dumpling.

My psychiatrist in Tehelná Street told Mum, 'never on an empty stomach, don't let her take her medication on an empty stomach, make sure she always has a bite first, a wee bit of bread, some cheese, a radish'. My mum looms over me every morning before I leave for the daycare centre, checking that I've had a bite to eat with my pills, a wee bit of bread, some cheese, a radish. She's taken it literally, never a pepper, tomato or cucumber, it's always a radish, it made me hate radishes at the age of thirteen. And the expression 'a wee bit of bread'. This revolting 'wee bit', why always call it a 'wee bit'? Plus, I never used to eat breakfast, I only had a cup of tea, so every day on my way to the daycare centre I felt I was going to be sick from the wee bit of bread, the cheese and the radish.

After dinner Mum settles down in her armchair to watch TV, there's a discussion, something about politics, but she doesn't stop browsing the journals, while I lock myself in my room. Here, behind the closed door, I can think about it, now that I'm relatively safe. What was it R said to me? 'That sounds interesting,' he said, 'you must tell me more next time.' I try to recall his exact words, his tone of voice, and especially the way he looked at me as he spoke. It lasted just a moment, then the others changed the subject, started talking about the need to separate church from state, or was it the impossibility of separating church from state? who knows, anyway something to do with church property and taxes. R said that as long as the church didn't have to pay taxes, or something or other to do with the Vatican, with property, half of Rome belongs to the church, that sort of thing, I couldn't follow it all, I was really thrown off kilter by the fact that he had spoken to me. Zuzka brought up the topic of paedophile priests, that's her beef, I know, something she cares about, she's not impressed by Francis's apologies, 'a fat lot of use they are now to the victims', she says. No one was paying attention to me anymore, but this moment, the moment when R looked at me and said that it sounded interesting and I had to tell him more about it, that moment did happen, it really did! And that's something no one can take away from me.

Time to water my plants, to spray their leaves, I usually do it every evening although it's quite pointless – it's not like they've been out on a balcony in the scorching sun all day – they're not on a balcony and besides, outside it's seven below. I take a look around my room, I do have tons of plants, the walls are practically covered in them. I got most of them at Ikea because they're cheap there, and while Zuzka claims that whenever she buys plants at Ikea they're dead within a year, mine are thriving. I have green fingers. I have palm trees, the enormous date palm I inherited from my dad most prominent among them, but there's also an areca, a rubber plant whose leaves I wipe down every night, a rhododendron, some asparagus plants, an aloe vera, a kalanchoe that has yellow blooms just now, I love watching as they close up at night. The window sills are mainly reserved for cacti, will I get married? won't I get married? do I believe in superstitions? does it bother me? And orchids, of course, at least one is always in bloom all year round. My bamboo plants are also doing quite well, they have pride of place in the middle of the room, although they don't have as much soil as they should but they get plenty of water, I make sure of that. Then there's my beloved dieffenbachia, like the date palm I've had it since I was little, I no longer remember where I got it; there's even a carnivorous plant Zuzka got me a few years ago at the Flora exhibition, so tiny that it only manages to catch fruit flies but it does look after itself, I nearly broke it once when I tried to toss it a bluebottle. Then there is the dracaena with its gorgeous leaves of yellow and green, a cyclamen that is also in bloom. My room is generally filled with the scent of flowers but I'm not even aware of it most of the time, oh and I nearly forgot the croton with its beautiful, variegated leaves, I wonder why I'm so keen on poisonous plants but since there are no children or pets living with us it's not a problem, and I'm not crazy enough to chew poisonous leaves or blossoms. If I had a balcony, I would most definitely get an oleander as well.

I told Zuzka it was a stupid idea, I wasn't going with her, what would I do there, but she insisted, 'come on, do come along, it'll do you good, you'll see, don't worry about anything, you're a friend of mine, a writer, and that's that', but I said, 'me?, a writer?, I didn't even finish secondary school', but Zuzka said, 'come off it, everyone is a writer these days, so what if you haven't finished secondary school? even better, you can say in your bio that you've graduated from the school of life, you've tried your hand at a gazillion menial jobs, that's all the rage nowadays, people love that', said Zuzka with a chuckle, then she continued, 'all the others just go on and on about writing, the creative agonies they suffer morning till night, but they never publish anything, a slim half-baked pamphlet at most, so you're a writer who's been writing for the drawer, you're waiting until you're sure that you're ready to launch your great novel about the state of the world', and when I objected feebly, clutching at straws, 'I've never seen a writer who looked anything like me, what will they make of me', Zuzka said, 'there's no such thing as a writer's look, it's just something you've seen in those lifestyle magazines I give your mum.' And that is why, when R asked me straight out what the book I'm writing was about, I gave a straight answer, 'it's a novel about horses'.

But Zuzka was dumbfounded to hear that, even though she and I used to go horse riding together, which is how we met. Zuzka is my only friend, she's been with me through thick and thin, through everything that happened there, our early days as helpers, both of the Jurajs, Mr Ble with his basset hounds after we progressed to being regular stable hands, Tristan's death, the three days I went AWOL wandering around Žitný ostrov, and everything that happened afterwards. And despite all that she's remained my friend. Through all those years. Once she realized that I didn't want to talk about it, she never brought it up again, accepting my silence, it was something that turned into a minefield for us. Which doesn't mean she has no life of her own at the same time, unlike Mum, everything stopped for Mum when I had my breakdown, the world turned upside down. Zuzka went on to study journalism, now she's with a major newspaper, of course I know that 'major' sounds a bit grand for our part of the world, but I don't know how else to put it – she's working for one of the top newspapers? Zuzka has always stood up for the weak and disadvantaged, helped the homeless, she writes for that magazine of theirs, cooks traditional cabbage soup for them at Christmas and so on and so forth, so sometimes the awful thought flashes through my mind that I might be just one of her charity projects, but I usually manage to chase it away. Obviously, I have great admiration for what she writes and how she writes, the interviews she conducts, I envy her for going out with men, in fact, it all goes back to our riding days, when she pulled Little Juraj, who almost all of us girls fancied. And I admire her for her courage in inviting me to one of the regular get-togethers with her journalist friends, me who never goes out or socializes, turning up with me definitely took some courage.

But if it hadn't been for her invitation I would never have met R, she was the one who introduced us. Although I recognized him of course, I knew who he was, Zuzka had told me a lot about him, I often saw his picture in the papers, I'd seen him on television too, actually, my mother has the telly on all the time, she says it keeps her company, as if my company wasn't worth mentioning, as if it didn't really matter, wasn't sufficient. Whereas TV, that's something else altogether.

R! I feel like writing his name over and over again, R, R, R. He said I had to tell him more about the novel I'm writing, but at that moment my mind went totally blank and the only thing I could think of was that time Zuzka and I were trudging from God knows where to God knows where, the only thing I remember is that we were walking along a highway, somewhere out of town, we must have been on our way home from riding, or on our way there, how old could we have been, twelve, thirteen? what the hell were we doing all alone on the highway at that age, but I'll set that aside for now. Anyway, we were trudging along and Zuzka was telling me about a film she'd just seen, it was called *The Horse Whisperer* and there was this girl in it who'd had an accident while riding, one of the animals died and the other was left traumatized, to say nothing of her friend, who didn't survive, and then the horse was taken away someplace where there was this chap who knew how to talk to horses and so on and so forth. This is what went through my head, the dark path alongside the highway, me and Zuzka, the headlights of passing cars and the horse whisperer, and as R was looking at me I thought that if I started to tell him the plot of this rather well-known film starring Scarlett Johansson, he would look at me as if I was mad, 'that sounds rather familiar, reminds me of something I've seen before', and when this occurred to me I just grinned to myself and mumbled as I hung my head, 'I will, some other time'. So now I have to come up with something to tell R next time, seeing as Zuzka introduced me as a writer.

Come to think of it, does that really mean there will be a next time? That I'll see R again? The thought makes my head spin, I open the window, lean out into Vajnorská Street, there's a nip in the air, it's January, the spell of record-breaking temperatures is over but minus seven is quite respectable too. I look at the candle burning near the pedestrian crossing where someone was run over, the candle has been burning day and night, devoted relatives. I will see R again, the awareness hits me like a thunderbolt, and for the first time in ages I feel something I don't quite dare call happiness.

But before the riding school in Petržalka, the proper one where it all happened, there was another place, on Castle Hill, the Ekoiuventa club, a stone's throw from my primary school, so close that from the stairway leading into the imposing building I had a view of my classroom windows, and sometimes, when I was skiving off school to go riding, I took care not to be spotted, goodness, I really thought that the teacher might recognize me from that far. But I kept it up on my way to Ekoiuventa as well, when the trolleybus passed my school, I'd duck under the seat, just to be on the safe side. And there, near Horský Park, where Braňo was our instructor, the three of us – me, Nina and Edita – were inseparable. We were all crazy about horses, we came every day and fought over who should ride Máša, who would get Šumienka, and which of us would be lucky enough to ride the fierce Dakota, we tried to outdo each other grooming our horses, to see who got their horse's coat shinier and hooves cleaner, which one of us could load more dung onto a wheelbarrow and empty it more quickly onto the muck heap, we'd often stay all day and I clearly remember standing in the corridor of the rear building, the one by the forest, after someone had daubed the word Zoo above the door, standing there confronting two boys who'd been pestering us for a while, throwing stones and frightening our horses, and I remember us goading them, 'come on, what do you want from us', and the taller one whispered to the shorter one, 'I'll take the one in the middle, you take the one on the side'. It bothered me for years, because, of course, Nina was the one in the middle, the prettiest, the tallest, the bombshell, while the two of us, me and Edita, flanked her on either side, and though Nina had always secretly assured me that by 'the one on the side' they must have meant me because Edita had crooked teeth, a pug nose and generally wasn't much to look at, I wasn't so sure because the two boys never showed up again to 'take us'.

Anyway, who knows how Edita's life has turned out, I haven't heard from her for ages, she must has a family by now, a husband, kids, a job, a home, a normal life, so whoever was meant to be the third one back then, at the end of the day it's me, I'm the one that nobody wants.

It's taken my psychiatrist in Tehelná Street years to fine-tune my medication, to find the right level between my mood swings and make sure I was neither too subdued and slowed down, or too hyper and upbeat, that I was under control, hers, Mum's, my own, that I didn't get so high that I would have to be dragged down to earth, or get so low that I would need to be helped back onto my enfeebled legs, in a word, so that I would be myself again, albeit within some sensible, clearly defined limits, myself, but not too much myself. But before we got there, before she found a way of keeping me safely enclosed in my little sandpit and playing with my bucket and spade, the medication tended to push me into a depression that kept coming back without anyone understanding why, no one apart from me that is, but I never stayed in bed all day as often happens, I always managed to make it to the daycare centre, I didn't have suicidal thoughts, even though they didn't always believe me. Whereas in the manic phases I was convinced the whole world was there just for my benefit, waiting for me laid out on a platter and instead of the daycare centre and art-music-drama therapy, I would spend all day wandering aimlessly around Bratislava, convinced that something major or life-shattering was about to happen, convinced that everything I saw, everyone I met, was there not by accident, that everything around was a sign meant for me alone. It took a huge amount of effort, many years, I had to drop out of secondary school, but not permanently, there's nothing stopping me from going back anytime, even past thirty – right? – but what difference does it make now, who cares about education, it was a matter of life and death. I know I have only my psychiatrist to thank for the fact that now, at the age of thirty-one, I can see myself and my situation with such clarity, that I'm able to take a step back from myself – yes, always from a distance, that's the way!

But best not overdo it. I believe in medication, in psychotherapy not so much. Or rather, it's not something I'm interested in. Apart from the obligatory sessions at the daycare centre, in which I never took a very active part, I've refused to submit myself to further dissection. I've endured a few sessions with a psychologist but they had to be cut short because when she tried to jog my memory – 'remember going AWOL on the bank of the Danube?', or 'do you recall the day the horse died?' – her questions made me want to scream, I couldn't stand anyone talking about Tristan and his death in that way, let alone a total stranger, someone who knew nothing about it, like this nice psychologist lady, I would scream and throw myself on the floor in a frenzy and refuse to calm down. That's why we've stuck with the meds. Pills are something tangible, they deal with the problem, take care of your present as well as your long-term state of mind, of your soul, spirit, call it what you like, pills don't ask difficult questions, they try to put you back together again, rather than take you apart. And perhaps today I might even say, meds can glue you back together, even if quite a few fragments have got lost along the way, in the grass perhaps, or in the reeds on the riverbank, some in Mr Ble and his posh, shiny cars, but the most important fragments, the crucial ones, in the riding school, with those innards just lying there behind the stables.

Yet thinking back, it all appears bathed in light, I recall the joy I felt, that first informal riding club at Ekoiuventa, I recall Braňo, our instructor, who was anti-establishment before it became fashionable, there was this sense of bliss and fulfilment the like of which I'd never known before, here at last I had found a meaningful way of spending my time. Braňo was fond of me, his number one Ivana he used to call me, he even let me get away without paying my membership and riding fees, he charged only those who came to ride irregularly or rarely, while I practically lived there, came every day straight from school, and somehow I managed to clock up more points than there were days in the month because working weekends counted double and I worked really hard.

One day we were having a riding lesson in the lower school, me on Šumienka, Nina on Máša. Braňo was shouting the orders, and then suddenly he stood against a tree to have a pee, Nina and I looked at each other and as we went closer, he gradually came into full view, we giggled in a girly way into the palms of our hands, Braňo was quite something, he couldn't be bothered to walk as far as the Zoo building where the toilets were and relieved himself right there on the course. I also liked him, he had long curly hair, a wavy beard and the pals he used to hang out with looked as if they'd escaped from some medieval guild, I took his side when he fell out with the management and left, taking his horses with him, I remember shouting at his boss in Horský Park and calling him a stupid twat while I rode the chestnut Dakota and wondered what would become of us when Braňo was gone. He went to Lamač, which was too far away for me to go every day after school.

The next morning I wake up feeling better than I have for ages, I slop around the flat in my nightie, Mum has just returned from the supermarket, she's unloading the bags in the kitchen, 'don't walk around barefoot, go and find your slippers this minute', I do as she says and don't let her rattle me, then I sit down to breakfast and force down a wee bit of bread, some cheese and a radish to help the medicine go down, mustn't take it on an empty stomach. I'd seen R on the TV many times before, he often takes part in the talk shows Mum watches, including the political ones, but yesterday was the first time I really saw him, until yesterday I'd never taken proper notice of him, even though he's so nice and so good-looking. Actually, I was aware that he was good-looking. In fact, that's something that should put me off, I've never gone for your standard good-looking guys. Zuzka laughed her head off when I confessed at the riding school that I fancied Big Juraj. Because Little Juraj was the one all the girls at the stables drooled over. Big Juraj may have been the better rider, won more rosettes and more medals, but he was dreadfully skinny and had a pockmarked face. I suppose he wasn't as handsome as Little Juraj, but I fancied him anyway. Whenever I found a photo of him from a riding competition in a magazine, I would cut it out and stick it into my diary and scribble something about how I loved him, how he looked at me – which made me happy – or didn't look at me – which plunged me into despair – how I longed for him, I would rave about how wonderful he was and what a brilliant rider, and especially about the time he let me walk his horse after he'd been jumping. Until one day Mum found my diary, hidden under a rug in my room. She read it all and knew everything, everything about me. And she read me the riot act. I brought shame on her, she said. I was twelve years old. I haven't kept a diary since.

So, obviously, I have to be more careful when it comes to R. Before lunch, when Mum asks me how Zuzka is, I don't tell her that I met some of her journalist friends, I just say, 'Zuzka's fine, she's working on a series of interviews with actors, she might bring it out as a book, a publisher has shown interest.' Mum nods and grumbles that Zuzka needn't have included Pauhofová, who cares about that stuck-up actress anyway. I give a shrug, although, in fact, I remember that the interview with Pauhofová got the greatest number of clicks online, but I keep that to myself. When Mum settles down in front of the TV for her cookery show, I reach furtively for the papers and journals Zuzka brought yesterday. I start browsing, there's bound to be something in there. And then my heart skips a beat. R. Not just an article by him, but a photo as well! Good God, those eyes of his. Should I cut it out? But how do I do that without Mum noticing? I'll have to wait until she's finished with the paper and left it in the milk crate with the other papers to be thrown out. Only then can I cut out R. I'll have to hide him somewhere she won't find him, she *mustn't* find him. I'm not twelve anymore but I know that she would have the same reaction. Or even worse maybe. I start to read the article, it's on philosophical anthropology, the notion of good and evil, instrumentalization, the categorical imperative, I don't understand what half of the words mean but I read on with growing interest and growing dread. Interest because so much energy is invested in this article that it startles me, and with sheer dread because… here's someone who can write like this, and I – I! – am supposed to produce a novel about horses for him?? I fold the newspaper, walk over to my room, sit down by the window, snowflakes float in the air and melt the moment they reach the ground, there's another plant I've been growing on my windowsill, it's only tiny, I put it there because it needs light, it's my little act of defiance, my little domestic rebellion. Zuzka brought it a while ago and I revel in the fact that Mum has seen it a thousand times and yet it would never occur to her that right here, hidden in plain sight amongst my palms, bamboo shoots and orchids, I'm also growing weed.

But then again, am I not being ridiculous? The way I fret that Mum might find out about my crush on R? It's been so long since I fancied anyone. It's strange to be feeling this way after all these years. In fact, Big Juraj wasn't the only one back then. I also fancied the Bear, who was doing civilian service at Ekoiuventa, instead of being conscripted into the army. We called him the Bear, but his real name was Martin, and his job was to look after the horses that were left behind after Braňo had gone: the black Upa, my chestnut Virbius and Mišo the white pony. The Bear was actually supposed to look after all the animals in the zoo. The rabbits, guinea pigs, snakes and the mice. He certainly had his own way of looking after them. One day he and another young man doing his civilian service got hold of a rabbit and carried it, squealing and thrashing, to the back of the stables. I climbed onto the roof quietly and lay down there to see what they were up to. The other guy kept whacking the rabbit against the wall until its neck broke, while the Bear looked away in disgust. 'Don't be such a sissy', the other one chided him while skinning the little cadaver, 'you don't mind a hymen in bed and now suddenly you're freaking out?' The Bear gave a laugh, I didn't quite understand what they were talking about. Fortunately, they didn't see me spying on them. I suppose they cooked the rabbit and had it for lunch.

Years later, after I told the story to Zuzka, she brought me Válek's poem Killing Rabbits. I loved it. I cut it out and put it under the glass of my desktop. Mum had no objection to that.

But another reason I found the Bear irresistible was that he had a motorbike, I could hear him coming from afar, he always arrived long after me. I dreamt that one day he would take me away on his motorbike. I pictured myself climbing onto the seat behind him, putting my arms around his waist and him lifting the front wheels as he started the engine. But he didn't take me anywhere, he took another girl, another Ivana, of course. She was fifteen, wore ripped jeans and had long blonde tresses. I couldn't hold a candle to her with my leggings, glasses and ponytail. I was almost four years younger and didn't even have proper breasts yet.

Mišo the pony understood my depression. After the Bear completed his civilian service and Upa and Virbius were taken to Kladruby – and presumably sent on to Italy to be made into salami – the pony was driven mad by loneliness. He would get aroused by his own reflection in the glass door of the main building at Ekoiuventa. I couldn't drag him away and he nearly smashed the glass by jumping at it. So Mišo was the only horse left and I knew it was high time I found somewhere with more horses.

All of a sudden I'm running a fever. I was fine at lunchtime, had my portion of Szekler goulash, took my pill, just one, but in the afternoon as Mum and I are getting ready for our afternoon walk at Kuchajda, I suddenly feel dizzy and almost faint in the hallway. Out comes the thermometer – 'let's see, 38.6. You must be doing it on purpose', Mum mutters, 'to stop me getting out of the house again'. Even though she's been at the shops this morning and I'm the one who's not getting out, again. I'm lying in bed, feeling woozy, I get worse and worse, my whole body feels hollow, its entire surface seems to be pulsating, the plants get blurry and merge into one big green splodge that I see through closed eyelids, it's snowing outside, Mum's hand on my forehead, it's gone up to 39, swallow this, drink that, I do as she says, but I'm not taking anything in, her voice is coming from afar, 'if it goes on like this, I'll have to apply wet packs'. Wet packs, what packs? the meaning of the word escapes me. For some reason, I imagine stacks, haystacks at Ekoiuventa, I once stayed there overnight and slept on a haystack, I told Mum I was going for a sleepover at Edita's, Edita told her parents she was sleeping over at Nina's and Nina said she'd be at my place, so there we were, lying on a haystack gazing at the stars. We were able to sleep out in the open so it must have been summer, my last summer there, and now I finally click, Mum means wet packs, the sort she used to give me when I was little. I stagger out of bed even though everything is spinning, it's gone dark outside and Mum has dozed off in front of the TV, her mouth slightly open, it's all clear, but to be on the safe side I tread gingerly as I walk to the bathroom, climb into the bathtub and allow myself to sink into the lukewarm water. I'm not having that, no wet packs for me, no thank you. The water is doing me good, I almost fall asleep lying there, suddenly I'm startled as Mum starts banging on the door and shouting, 'open up, open up, why have you locked the door, you know this lock gets stuck, what if you can't unlock it, open up this minute'.

I stay in bed for a few more days but my temperature doesn't rise above 38, it's no longer as dramatic as on the first day, I have a runny nose, a cough, I talk to Zuzka on the phone, Zuzka tries to make me laugh, tells me that she was sent on an assignment with an older colleague, to report on escort agencies, and the colleague's wife took it upon herself to come into the office to try and stop him and when she failed, she kept phoning him throughout the day, presumably to make sure that he kept a professional distance, that his breathing wasn't getting ragged, 'it was awful', laughs Zuzka, 'I hope I don't end up like that, a jealous hysterical wife', then she adds, 'I'd never have this kind of problem at home, even if I went to report on male strippers or gigolos, I doubt it would distract my Maťo from his raw food lunch and power yoga'. I laugh too, I let her do the talking and don't ask about R, don't ask whether they're going to have another of their get-togethers, she raises the subject herself, says she'll take me out to meet some people when I get better, what else could she mean by that. I don't get a chance to respond, Mum shouts from the living room to give Zuzka her regards, I pass on the message, Zuzka sends her regards back, then we change the subject. Actually, I'm rather enjoying these quiet days, Mum goes shopping in the morning, instead of Szekler goulash there's suddenly baked rice pudding, but only twice, it is replaced at breakneck speed by fish with boiled potatoes, a full tray of it, I eat that too, perhaps I will get better. My snotty handkerchiefs are strewn all over the place, Mum picks them up and throws them out without a word, they don't disgust her, only once does she mock me for the way I blow my nose, 'why on earth do you have to block one nostril, why can't you blow your nose like a normal human being, both nostrils together, who taught you to do it like that, not me, surely'. Was it really not Mum who taught me how to blow my nose? I forget, but from now on I blow my nose in secret, in my room or, if I'm somewhere else in the flat, I wait until she's not looking, what's wrong with blocking one nostril while blowing my nose, I've seen loads of people do it that way, it's just as normal! Hers is not the only right way!

These days, as I spend my time just pottering around the flat – not that I do anything exciting or absorbing at any other time – I go through all the newspapers I can lay my hands on, I even dig out old ones from the crate in the hallway, there might be something in these too, I carefully pull out the pages with anything written by R and fold them away in books in my room. In the morning, while Mum is out shopping, I even risk watching some footage of him on the internet, I make sure to do it in incognito mode, I don't think Mum checks my browsing history, but you never know, I'd rather it didn't show up there, just to be on the safe side. Meanwhile I wonder what I will tell R if he asks about my proposed novel about horses, Jesus, what am I going to say? And another, even worse question keeps haunting me, what if he's forgotten all about it in the meantime, what if he's forgotten about me as well, forgotten that I even exist?

Fresh scraps of memory float to the surface, including some of the most disagreeable ones that I've long forgotten, that I may have tried to suppress because, let's face it, Mišo the pony wasn't the only one turned on by his own image, there was always a powerful erotic element to horse-riding, it hung in the air, between the people, between the horses. One of my first gross memories relates to a stallion, he was in his box and I went in and gave him a sugar cube, he gobbled it up gratefully, licked my hand just as gratefully and went on and on licking it gratefully, it tickled my hand but I let him, it was quite nice in a way, I had to admit, his warm, prickly tongue, but then I was horrified to see the stallion's penis come stretching out, it was nearly a metre long, black at the root then turning pink, a terrifying sight. And another time I saw the same stallion in the riding ring on his hind legs, with his shaft erect, in pursuit of a mare in heat, and what made it even more terrifying was that Simona was sitting on the mare and Roman was riding the stallion, everyone knew that Simona and Roman were sleeping together, so at that moment it was as if Roman was pursuing Simona in full view of all and sundry and had borrowed his horse's metre-long shaft to do so, oh God, out, get out of my head, and even that first time I ran out of the box as soon as I could, terrified that the horse might jump me.

Yuck, these animals, they resemble people too much, only it's all unfiltered, undisguised by good manners, they get straight down to business, many times I've seen a dog mounting a bitch in heat in the park, first a sniff of her arse and then it's straight down to business, no silly small talk, no messing about, give me plants any day, at least they don't stick anything out at you when you water them.

I won't say a word to Mum about R or the others, I mention only Zuzka, Zuzka is the only friend Mum has allowed me to keep, the only one she puts up with, but this time even going out with her was a close shave, goodness, what an apt turn of phrase, because after six days in bed, when I felt better and Zuzka asked me to go out with her on Friday, Mum announced that she was going to make an appointment at the hairdresser's for both of us, this Friday of all days, because we hadn't been able to go earlier, I had been ill and she was looking after me, as she couldn't resist pointing out as she ran her hand through her hair, 'see, my roots are showing, I need to have them coloured, and you're coming too, I'm fed up of looking at your split ends'. I nearly flipped out, 'but Mum, I haven't been out for a whole week, can't we go to the hairdresser some other day?' 'Of course we can, but you can go out with Zuzka some other day too', she snapped, but gave in eventually, it turned out that the hairdresser was too busy this week anyway, that's what's saved my bacon, and I thought, of course I can see Zuzka whenever I like, but R, I can only see R this Friday.

I feel terribly on edge on my way to the get-together, I won't say anything to Zuzka, but in my mind I keep going over all of R's articles that I've read, all his ideas and opinions. I want to identify with them, I also try to embrace his interest in the whole wide world, something I've always lacked. I even try to think of the right words to describe my planned book about horses, yes, I've prepared that as well, to some extent. But once we're there and I spot R, my heart starts thumping, and although I end up sitting next to him, I can't make myself bring up everything I've prepared because of this gorgeous young woman with short brown hair, lots of bling, I have no idea who she is, Zuzka hasn't introduced us. So this woman keeps talking about someone called Marie Kondo, how she's rearranged her home in line with Marie's advice, and everyone starts talking about it, everyone seems to have read the book, everyone has been tidying up their home like her, even though they all try to look very blasé about it and make snide remarks. There's this stocky chap who goes as far as to claim that since reading Kondo's book he's had an epiphany and now he no longer torments his socks, he has stopped scrunching them up into a ball, instead he now lets them breathe, 'yes, friends', he shouts, 'it's because the threads in the socks have to breathe, they have to relax after working hard all day, squeezed into that tiny space between our smelly feet and shoes!' Zuzka joins in, too, saying she's tried storing her jumpers vertically next to each other instead of stacking them on top of one another and she's been bowled over by how much space she's gained in her wardrobe, the perfect overview of her clothes she now has. I take a sideways glance at R to see if he's going to join in as well, if the magic way of tidying up has changed his life too, but he just smiles, sips his spritzer and lets the others talk.

As I sit there listening to them I'm slowly beginning to wilt, I have nothing to add, I feel very unsociable, I'm aware that I don't really belong and to cap it all it seems that this time I won't get a chance to exchange a single word with R, even though he's sitting right next to me, and that depresses me. I'm sure Zuzka won't dare to bring me along again, what am I doing here anyway. Now a middle-aged journalist is talking about an article she's writing about the Japanese phenomenon known as hikikomori, meaning confined, it concerns young people in Japan who spend years barricaded into their rooms, communicating only via the internet and only occasionally opening their door at night for the tray of food their caring parents have left for them. 'But if you think that this sort of behaviour is limited to Japan, you'd be wrong', the journalist insists, 'similar cases have been reported worldwide', and I totally believe her, I can vividly imagine a case like that in Vajnorská Street in Bratislava and I think to myself, R is bound to chip in now mentioning some typical aspect of Japanese society, I'm sure he knows everything about it, he's researched it, knows all there is to know and can offer an explanation. And R does indeed speak up, but not about the Japanese way of tidying up or social withdrawal, he leans towards me as if in passing and asks quietly if I feel like popping out with him for a smoke, I leap up, surprised, my adrenaline level instantly shoots up.

We fight our way out through the chairs and other journalists, Zuzka gives me a wink, or maybe I just imagine it, but now R and I are standing outside the café and although this is exactly what I've been longing for, I have no idea what to say to him, I can't just let it all come tumbling out, out of the blue, 'my novel is about' – but R is not bothered, he helps me put on my jacket as it's cold outside, close to freezing, he's wearing his coat, he wraps a scarf around his neck, lights a cigarette and gives me a smile, 'we seem to be the only two people not yet sleeping on futons'. And even though I'm not quite sure what futons are, I smile back and start telling him that I was ill for a week, locked up in the flat and unable to go out, how I nearly went bananas and how happy I am to be breathing fresh air at last. I then hastily add that I've read his article in the paper – I only dare to mention his latest, most recent one, so as not to arouse suspicion – and how fascinating I find what he said about the notion of good and evil and then, when he actually asks me – he hasn't forgotten! – if I've made any headway with my novel, I say I have, but I've been a bit slowed down by my illness, so finally here's an opportunity to let rip. 'My protagonist is a girl who loves horse-riding, she's in a riding school run by Mr Ble, who also manages a car plant, it's set in the darkest days of Mečiar, the era of turbocapitalism. She meets some nouveau riche kids who feel so entitled they think they can do whatever they like,' I'm almost shouting, 'they're arrogant, rude, revolting, it's about injustice, about abuse'. At this point I stop, maybe I've said too much, maybe I sounded childish, but R is still smiling, 'you'll have to let me read it later', he remarks, and I'm on cloud nine because at that moment I forget that I don't have anything to show him.

And as we elbow our way back to our seats in the café, I continue in my head, and then, one day, the girl goes AWOL, spends three days wandering around Žitný ostrov drinking from puddles on the road, she doesn't eat or maybe just a few berries, some plants, or wild roots maybe?, or perhaps she grazes like a horse, and by the time she's found she's deranged, gone wild, feral, 'what's that bird's nest, my dear – your hair?' And ever since that time she's been on disability benefit, looked after by her mother.

As a matter of fact, plants are the same, they all flaunt their reproductive organs more ostentatiously than anyone else, all those blossoms, stamens, pistils, they reproduce in plain sight, there's no escape, it's everywhere, it's the same all over. I don't hold it against the plants though, I like plants, not because of their beautiful blossoms like most people, or because of their scent, it's probably just because of their apparent immobility as their unchanging nature has a calming effect on me, and also because of their resilience to everything, including abuse. It's not easy to hurt a plant, if I break off a stalk, it won't even yield a sigh, the wound doesn't start bleeding, almost as if the plant hasn't noticed, it will grow another stalk, it's no big deal, I can even raze it to the ground, but as long as its roots remain it will sprout again, and if I pull it out by the roots, it won't hold that against me either, it won't fix me with a reproachful gaze in its dying moments, it won't defend itself, fighting for survival, and the most I might feel is a pang of regret. Just a tiny pang that I forget instantly, before I shove the plant into a plastic bag, toss it into a container in the courtyard, and next day I go and buy another, prettier, better one.

Once I turned seventeen and stopped going to the daycare centre, my psychiatrist asked what I would like to do, what I felt up to doing now that I'd dropped out of school. I said I would enjoy looking after the city's greenery, its parks, hedges and flower beds. The psychiatrist smiled and said, 'yes, I have quite a few people with Down's looking after the city's greenery, it's a perfect fit for them'. So I created some greenery in my own room instead, I've been making a little money by painting the tiny toy figures that come with Kinder eggs, my mum's friend found me the gig, hand-painting, working from home, you see, it only takes up a few hours and the main benefit is that it's very calming, like the grown-ups' colouring books you see in bookshops nowadays, Zuzka gave me one of those for Christmas, but I didn't find it very inspiring, I'd rather paint a Smurf hoping it will make some child happy. When I was little, I had a whole shelf in my room reserved for my Kinder egg toys, I still have them, Mum hasn't let me throw them out, 'if it were up to you, you would throw everything out! as if money grew on trees!' She packed them into a Tupperware box and took it up to the attic, they'll come in handy one day.

We also used to go and mow the grass, for the horses, back in the old days when Braňo was still there, he'd mow the whole meadow and leave the raking to us – me, Nina and Edita, the three most loyal members of his ad hoc fan club. We would rake all the grass cuttings into a pile, load it all onto a van and leave it to dry in the hay sheds, we'd cut all the grass in Ekoiuventa and when that wasn't enough, we'd climb into the van with Braňo and drive around town. Once he took us to a spot under Bôrik Hill, close to the waterworks, a huge expanse, it took us nearly three days to cut the grass, and one day we spent a whole afternoon at the tennis courts by the tram line near the railway station. I still recall getting all covered in sweat, slaving away like a navvy, but the thing is, I actually enjoyed it and wanted to do it, I'd pour all my energy and enthusiasm into the raking, we always had lots of laughs and teased one another. That time Pišta came along with us, the only lad who was worth anything, Edita made a point of letting us know they were an item, claiming that while Nina and I were working behind the station, the two of them were snogging away. We listened to her gobsmacked, it never occurred to us to ask Pišta if she was telling the truth, to give us his side of the story. I was jealous that Edita had a boyfriend, in those days it never occurred to me to doubt what others said, as I myself never made things up, never told fibs, in fact, even now I rarely make things up, I only do so if needs must, never just to make myself look better, to show off in front of someone. So you have to take my word for it when I say that by the time we finished raking the grass, our calves and thighs were really sore, scratched, stung, burnt by the sun and covered in bruises.

But obviously, lying and covering up is what I have to do with Mum, so on Monday, as I walk across the living room and spot R on the box, towards the end of the evening news, I try to act as natural as possible. I plonk myself down in an armchair, grab a handful of nuts from the coffee table, quite casually, like there's nothing strange about me suddenly being interested in the evening news. Fortunately, Mum pays me no attention, R is at some event or other, there's a band playing in the background, a woman reporter asks him what does it deal with, who are the intended readers, oh my God, what? what is she on about? I can't… I get a hot flush as it dawns on me what this is all about, R has a new book out, today, just three days after we met, R is launching his new novel published by a major – oh no, not major again! let's say prestigious – publishing house. When the culture segment is finished Mum switches to a Czech channel, I stay there, how embarrassing, I can't move, I can't get up from the armchair, only this Friday I blathered on to him about my 'horse novel', a work of, hah, total fiction, while around the same time he is publishing a real – a *real* – book! And what's worse – he didn't even mention it. Not a word. My God. I must mean nothing to him. But then again, why should I? Some Ivana with writing ambitions. I bet he knows hordes of Ivanas like that. Ivanas like that are a ten a penny. There's a shedload of Ivanas like that.

The mere fact that R has written a book throws me off balance. I go to bed but can't sleep. As I lie there, my own room transforms into a night-time jungle. With shadows of my plants everywhere. Especially the largest palm, whose branches reach down almost to my feet. Mum claims my dad planted it years ago. He grew it out of a date stone, just like that. He was too lazy to go to the bin and instead spat it into a flowerpot. And it's grown into a palm tree. It kept growing and growing, he barely managed to keep pace with repotting it, in the summer he'd take it out into the garden to give it some sun, he'd water it with a hose, and when he died and the house was sold, Mum couldn't bear to throw the palm tree out, even though by then it was really huge, she had the removals men haul it up to our first flat on Castle Hill and then to our current flat, on Vajnorská, along with the rest of the furniture. I don't remember any of this, I was only four when my dad died. I wonder if R also loves plants, if he keeps any in his room, actually, it occurs to me, R may also be in bed right now. Perhaps not so far away from me, probably somewhere in the centre of town. Or – I resist the thought, but it forces itself upon me and I'm unable to chase it away – he's still out, it's only midnight, not that late really, he's out and about in the city celebrating the publication of his book, having a drink in a bar, or … maybe he is with someone.

And this triggers the fantasies, I see R with some woman, gorgeous, no doubt, they're in a bar, in bed, I feel my entire body instantly stiffen with stress, it's all generated by my head, that's the source of all the evil, that's where it always springs from, I'm on the verge of tears, I go completely rigid, unable to move, my eyes are wide open and staring into the dark. Someone like him is bound to be with somebody, I've never asked Zuzka about that, no need, it's quite self-evident, why should he wait for some crazy Ivana, I'm nothing, neither to him nor to anyone else, I'm just a burden to my mum, R can have any woman he chooses, he has his pick of actresses, models, journalists, like the brunette with bangles on her wrists at the get-together who talked about the Japanese writer and her revolutionary method of tidying up. I can't bear it, I know I have no ownership rights, I have no right to anything, not even to say sorry, or to be thinking this thought, and yet I can't bear it. It's midnight, Mum will have dozed off in the living room in front of the TV, I'm slowly getting my breathing under control, now I have to get my blood circulating again. I try moving my foot slowly, it does move even though it's gone a bit numb. I don't feel tired at all, I'm more awake than I was all day and I know that that's a bad sign. I know I won't fall asleep now. My usual night-time dose of meds is just not enough to obliterate the image of R with another woman. I'll have to take something stronger.

I sit up and get out of bed. The flat is still but as I open the door, I hear some rustling, some faint voices and see the blue glow of the TV, I guessed right. Gingerly, I walk into the kitchen. Just keep it down, Mum is a light sleeper. I take out the box with the meds and rummage in it for a while, Xanax is useless, Neurol I'm not sure about, Mum takes it, I haven't tried it, better not to take any risks, ah, here it is. Rivotril. That always works, Rivotril I can rely on. It's an anti-epileptic, it relaxes the muscles, but it also helps to relax my brain and my thoughts. I put five drops onto a spoon, its overpowering taste fills my mouth. I go back to bed and some five minutes later I feel myself slowly drifting off, now totally calm, R can screw all of Bratislava for all I care right now. The last thing that pops into my head is the word

Rohypnol. Rohypnol, Rohypnol, sounds terribly familiar, what was that again… but it's too late, I'm swallowed up by the jungle.

The next day I'm in a bookshop, there's a pyramid of R right by the entrance, I carefully pick up a copy and stare at the photo on the cover. Oh my God, I get a lump in my throat like I do whenever I see him, yes it's him, and I've actually met him, only four days ago I was standing next to him outside a café, talking to him! I stay there for a moment, browsing through the book, I read a sentence here, another there, what is it actually about, I skim the table of contents but it doesn't tell me much, never mind, it's him, his ideas, a product of his mind, I really want to have this book, in truth, I need it desperately! but when I snap it shut and check the price I get dizzy, 16 euros, no way can I justify to Mum spending 16 euros.

Hang on, I suddenly realize, would I be able to justify to her why I bought the book in the first place?

Initially I suspect there might be a flaw in my diabolical plan and that I might have to come clean to Zuzka, but Zuzka is my Zuzka after all, even if she goes on to interview every famous actor on the planet, she will still be my Zuzka, and it turns out that I don't really need to go into a lengthy explanation, it's enough for me to hint on the phone that I've seen R launching his book on TV and Zuzka immediately gets my drift and offers to bring me a copy this very afternoon when we meet in a café – despite Mum grumbling, 'we'll never get to the hairdresser if you're out all the time' – Zuzka also brings me the book by the crazy Japanese woman, as she calls her, adding with a chuckle, 'to inspire you to finally start clearing out that attic of yours when your mum is out shopping!' I give a hesitant smile, whenever she talks like that, I'm a bit embarrassed for having badmouthed

Mum. And then she reaches across the table, here's our darling R, here you are, complete with a dedication. Thrilled, I glance at the few scribbled words, yes, there it is, To Ivana, I wonder if he remembered my name or if Zuzka had to prompt him, but no, I'm sure he remembered, it would really be outrageous if he didn't even know my name. He asked me to go out for a drag with him, that's got to mean something, maybe not a lot, but surely it does mean something. He gave me his undivided attention, and now I also have a copy of his book. I barely hear Zuzka for the rest of our meeting as she tells me how hard it is living with her boyfriend, how he obsessively works out for hours on end in front of the TV, I just sit back and relish what I have, what is mine and what no one can take away from me, actually, my face darkens suddenly, maybe not take it away, but there is someone who might make nasty comments if they see it.

As I head home from the café I decide to hide the book somewhere, read it in secret, maybe at night, I can't sleep anyway and I don't want to get addicted to Rivotril, not another pill, that's the last thing I need. My heart is thumping because I nearly, very nearly asked Zuzka if R has a girlfriend but the question stuck in my throat, I don't really want to know, it's quite obvious that he must, so why torment myself even more, with the certainty, with the fantasies, my head produces enough fantasies as it is, without outside stimulation. I hide R, give Mum her magazines and newspapers and ostentatiously place the crazy Japanese woman's book on the table. Reading R is an adrenaline sport, every time I hear something stir in the flat or Mum's footsteps in the hallway, I fling the book behind the bed and study the revolutionary technique of tidying up, but Mum isn't interested in what I'm reading, she's happy with her magazines, but what troubles me more is that soon I have to admit to myself that I actually find the book about tidying up more enjoyable, I mean, to set the record straight, R's book is wonderful, wise, profound, I just don't understand much of it, whereas the advice to throw out everything you don't need is much easier to take in, oh well, let's face it, I'm unimaginative, uneducated, I spend more time wondering if there's some way of sorting out the stuff in the attic without being noticed, it's impossible to move around up there, I spend more time thinking about that than R's story of Abel roaming around some biblical space where all the world's languages merge into one, even though I know perfectly well that I'll never pluck up the courage to tackle the attic.

But soon after we come home from the hairdresser's and Mum starts putting my clean underwear into the wardrobe, something does happen, and it's horrible. I just mention in passing that I would rather she didn't roll up the socks into a ball, it would be enough to just fold them to give the threads a break, Mum fixes me with an incredulous look so I launch into a frantic explanation, 'I've read it's better that way,' but when she hears me say that, she suddenly loses it, not even letting me finish, 'so here I am, slaving away over a hot stove for you every day, I do all your shopping, I tidy up after you, I wash and iron all your clothes and I even put your things away in the wardrobe so you can find everything, you'd never manage on your own, and all you can do is go on at me about rolled-up socks?! Who do you think you are, treating me like your chambermaid, it's unbearable, you never lift a finger, you spend all day and every day lounging about, flouncing around town, and to cap it all you're stupid enough to believe every kind of drivel! if it said in some book that it's good for your circulation to stand on your head and bounce around on your ears, I'm sure you'd make me do a headstand straight off, I mean, really, you fall for any nonsense you happen to read, I just can't believe it! I've been rolling socks into a ball all my life and no sock has ever complained about having its threads stretched!' Mum is now yelling at the top of her voice, her face has turned beetroot red, I can't remember when I last saw her blow up like this, I'm sitting on my bed in a state of shock and don't dare to say a word as she rolls up all the socks ostentatiously right in front of me, slamming them down – if they could make a sound, that is – on the wardrobe shelf, and then she slams the door of my room shut, this time for real.

I sit on the bed biting my fingernails, knowing I should have kept my mouth shut, I know Mum is right, she's been doing everything for me, she's looked after me, sacrificed her whole life for me, but I've never asked her to put my things away, I've offered several times to do it myself, but she's always fobbed me off saying I couldn't do it right. I look around, this is something she won't forgive me so easily, now I feel that it really was an outrageous thing to say, of course what I meant was that I could put the socks away myself, that was all I was suggesting, but there's no way I can explain that to her now, my eyes wander over to the dieffenbachia on the desk and its beautiful green leaves with their white splodges, and all of a sudden I tear one off, some liquid comes oozing out, I start to crush the leaf, ripping it up bit by bit, like picking petals from a flower, he-loves-me, he-loves-me-not, but no such luck, finally I scrunch it up in my hands, which makes them go sticky, I bring one hand to my face, sniff it and gently touch it with my tongue.

I lie down, the poison is starting to work, my hands are turning red, it stings, they were a bit scratched, the poison has entered my bloodstream, or am I just imagining it, exaggerating as usual, maybe nothing will happen, no one will notice anything. My eyes alight on the bamboo shoots, goodness, I ought to water them, there's no water left at the bottom of their pots, but I don't get up, I do nothing, I feel kind of detached from myself, empty inside, a bit dizzy, I'm slowly starting to feel queasy, my thoughts are wandering, they're somewhere out there with Little Juraj and Big Juraj, our childhood crushes. It doesn't really count but that's all there was until now, after all I could hardly fall in love with the drooling, sedated or medically overstimulated patients at the daycare centre in Petržalka, ah Petržalka, the backdrop to everything, to every important event in my life, the longing to get my horse to gallop, every time there was a show jumping competition and our horses were sent for a few days to the racetrack in Petržalka, the longing to get onto the track on Tristan and try to forget that he's an old hack fit only for kids, try to make myself believe that I can get him to gallop because galloping is when a horse's legs lift off the ground for a moment, Tristan is clearly not up to it but I want to experience that feeling, what it feels like to fly, so I dig my heels into his belly and follow Zuzka, she's riding the livelier Penelope, who sometimes kicks out with her hind legs, I stand upright in the stirrups, grip the saddle between my knees and lean forward holding on to his mane while trying to achieve the impossible, the fastest possible speed, the only real freedom there is.

During that show jumping competition – perhaps I ought to go and wash my hands after all? it's now quite obvious that I'm not imagining it, they're swelling up, I focus on the stinging and my queasiness – both Jurajs were also there, I was in the riding ring putting back the jumps that the horses had knocked down,

Big Juraj sailed through flawlessly, that made me happy, then he asked me to walk off his horse, which was really quite something, he helped me into the saddle, clasped his hands together to support my knee as I mounted his mare, he touched me, the thirteen-year-old girl I'm sure he hadn't noticed before, but that was all I needed, just loving him was enough for me, that feeling of being in love. Later that evening, after the races, Zuzka and I surreptitiously watched the two Jurajs set up the jumps in the indoor school after everyone else had gone home, and jump over them without the horses, they managed to leap over jumps as tall as themselves, Zuzka and I crouched under the grandstand and kept peering out, giggling and goggling, we couldn't understand how they did it, how they managed to leap over jumps that high, what was their secret, they weren't just the top young show jumping riders in Slovakia, they also had the best horses! Zuzka insisted that we should make our presence known, just come out, take a seat on the grandstand and cheer them from there, even if it made them freak out, but I held her back, I lacked the courage, whereas she did find the courage eventually, a day later I caught her in Quebec's box snogging Little Juraj.

Back then Zuzka already had what it takes, and she would leave me further and further behind, changing boyfriends while I was changing my meds, she went to discos while I went to the daycare centre. That moment, as we sat there watching the two Jurajs, that was the crunch, me in love with one Juraj and she with the other, both of us crouching, giggling and crazy for boys, for our first romance, like every thirteen-year-old, but I screwed up right there, because I couldn't pluck up the courage, and I screwed up again just now, this time by having the courage to do this stupid thing. The stinging in my hands is unbearable,

I feel really dizzy, my vision is blurred, I cross the hallway to the bathroom as fast as I can and let the cold water run over my hands. My eyes dart around the bathroom in desperation, where's the plastic bowl, I think I'm going to be sick.

The day after the incident with the dieffenbachia there's another disaster, Mum has discovered R's book. She came into my room to tidy up, normally I do the hoovering, it's one of the few chores assigned to me, one I am considered capable of, but today my hands are all mangled, I haven't fully recovered, I'm not up to it, and as she pushed the bed away, Mum discovered the book together with its dedication, she opened it of course, read the dedication of course, I know because I found the book on my desk, I know because over dinner – my favourite, deep-fried cheese, on the menu for one night only – as Mum browses the newspapers from Zuzka and comes across an article by R, she comments, 'incredible the kind of stuff he churns out, a typical right-wing moron'. The cheese sticks in my throat, I look at her. I have read R's column of course and not just once, it's nothing to do with politics, it's about the useless town-planners in Bratislava, clearly something else is the problem, Mum is trying to provoke me. I almost choke on the fried cheese, but then I can no longer control myself, I have to speak up for him, she can't badmouth him just like that for no reason, 'Mum,' I tell her, 'in my opinion, R is, if anything, on the left.' 'OK, a left-wing moron then, it comes down to the same thing, so you have met him? it's just that you've never mentioned that.' I keep my mouth shut. What can I say? 'Aaww, To Ivana, with love, fancy that, how touching,' Mum keeps needling me, 'so you've been meeting people without telling me? You've kept things secret from me? And about an idiot like that to boot.' I'm gobsmacked. 'Did something happen between the two of you to make you damage your hands like that?' I jump up and though I know it will only make things worse, that I should rise above it, and there's nothing she can do to me, but I can't take it anymore, I feel the rage mounting inside me, that good old rage that I can usually keep under control, that I've become so skilled at suppressing, but not this time, I start yelling at Mum, 'R isn't an idiot, he's actually a smart and well-read journalist, a writer, why do you have to badmouth people I have respect for, people you've never even met?'

Just as I'm about to march out of the kitchen in protest before my rage boils over and I say something I'll come to regret, Mum orders me to sit down, and goes on, calmer now, 'let's have a talk, without all this'. Eventually I sit down and Mum says, 'you're right, I don't really have anything against him, I've never even met him, for all I know he may be a wonderful person, I was just surprised that you've met him and never mentioned it. I know you: there must be something behind it, you know how it ended the last time you kept something secret from me. I just want to make sure you don't end up in casualty again. I don't want anything to happen to you. I don't want some, erm, well-read journalist to turn your head and then you won't be able to cope when he starts stringing another girl along. I'm your mother, who'll look after you if you have another breakdown? You think R will?' 'But Mum', I interrupt, 'I don't know what you're talking about, we just shared a table in a café, there were loads of other people there, and he gave me his book, what's wrong with that?' And then I can't help myself and start explaining that it's really good, she ought to read it as well, R is very knowledgeable and smart, but also a really decent person, he's never tried anything on, and anyway, I get desperate as I hear myself jabbering, goodness, this is so embarrassing, what am I apologizing for, I've done nothing wrong, has R done anything wrong? In the end Mum calms down, at least I hope I've managed to soothe her, set her mind at rest, so that she will now leave me alone, but the next day – a Friday – I discover that the opposite is the case.

'I'm going out with Zuzka,' I announce, but now Mum knows Zuzka stands for a whole bunch of other people, especially R, 'no need,' Mum says, 'you've seen her once already this week.' I give her an unbelieving look, she's never said anything like that before. 'So what if I've seen her already this week, I want to see her again.' Mum shakes her head, 'oh no, you're not going anywhere.' 'Mum, I'm thirty-one years old, I'm a grown-up, I can go wherever I like.' 'Oh, can you now, you don't say, in that case, why don't you have a husband, children, a job, why are you living with me, if you're so *grown-up*? As long as you are living under my roof, you do as I say.' I can't believe it. She can't be serious! 'Mum, I'm just going out and that's that.' Mum, 'go on, try.' I shuffle my feet, I feel like jumping at her, but try a conciliatory tone, 'I thought we'd worked things out.' And then, 'no need to worry about me.' Mum, 'oh no, I'm not worried.' 'So what then?' 'I just don't want you to see him.' Oh my God. This goes on for half an hour, until Mum yells, 'go on then, off you go, you're obviously not interested in doing anything else anyway.' I am tempted to shoot back, 'what do you mean I'm not interested in anything, what are you trying to say,' but as she's actually throwing me out, I have to grab my chance, I quickly slip on my coat in the hallway and I'm off, almost without saying goodbye.

Zuzka and I are a bit late getting to the café, R isn't there yet, which alarms me a little, he's never been late before, has something prevented him from coming? Everyone else is there,

I know all these people by sight now, most of them are journalists, colleagues of Zuzka's. They're chatting away, we join them, again I sit there without saying a word, I try at least to listen, I won't have anything to add anyway, I'm only interested in R, Mum was right, of course. Out of the blue this very young journalist – Zuzka said she has a degree from Cambridge – announces that she's heard that our dear R has four girlfriends on the go, X has reliably told her, apparently. The fellow who held forth about Marie Kondo and socks the last time tut-tuts her, 'your informants are not reliable, my dear, it's not like that'. 'So what is it like?' 'Well', the stocky fellow goes on, 'there may be four of them this minute, but yesterday there were two and the day before maybe one.' 'Oh, I see, and tomorrow there'll be five of them!' Zuzka cuts in, laughing, and the fellow goes on, 'exactly, it's a changing situation, it's fluid, the current state of affairs can't be regarded as permanent, just because R has four lovers now you can't expect it to stay like that for ever and ever. Don't make me laugh.' Everyone is laughing except me, I'm paralysed and there's nothing I can do about it, I don't want anyone to notice but I'm convinced they have, Zuzka keeps casting furtive glances at me even though the conversation has moved on, I realise I've been biting my fingernails furiously, I lower my hand at once, reach for my ginger tea, but the movement seems to take an age, I'm suddenly conscious of my every movement, I can't even pick up my cup in the normal way, I'm all one great big cramp, it seems to me that everyone can see what's happening to me as I take a sip of my ginger tea, but just then I see R pushing his way towards us, in his long scarf and coat, he's apologetic, he's been held up, the ginger stings my mouth, one of his lovers, maybe? And I'm not even sure I'm glad that he's again found a seat by my side.

This time it happens right there at the table, we don't even have to go out for a smoke, R beckons to the waiter, orders an espresso with milk, mineral water, and within five minutes he leans towards me and asks how I've been. Since this is a question I can never answer out of the blue, not even with the standard *fine*, this time, too, I launch instead into a sincere and exhaustive analysis of my state, musing out loud about how I've been, while in my mind I wonder what R would say if he knew that I'm at daggers drawn with my Mum because of him, that we had a row about him, if he knew the names Mum called him, oh my God, that would be too embarrassing. He must never find out how I live, what I really am, so I tell him that I was trimming my house plants without realizing that some of them are toxic and this is the result. I wave my hand in front of his face but it's too fast for him to see, I don't want him to see, it's not a pretty sight, he might find my hand repulsive, but he shows interest and concern, asks if I've been to see a dermatologist, they could prescribe some ointment for it, 'nothing beats aloe vera' I say, 'I've got some at home', and so we drift further and further away from the others, we're just talking and he's incredibly nice and considerate, and oh so handsome, so slim and tall, and that three-day stubble, everything I heard about his four lovers gradually evaporates until it's completely gone, it can't be true, R isn't someone who would do that to women. It's only at that point, silly old me!, that I remember to thank him for his book and the dedication. With somewhat forced enthusiasm I start talking about his book and the characters in it, Abel as he gradually stops understanding the words coming out of his own mouth, as well as the present-day storyline that features Cain, the bit on drugs, on him and his psychiatrist friend experimenting with LSD, carefully monitored hallucinations and similar experiments dating back to the 1960s, altered states of consciousness. R smiles at me, R brushes off my praise, 'you're exaggerating, I haven't written anything earth-shattering, there are others, Hunter S. Thompson and his gonzo journalism, who partly inspired this section of the book', and so we keep chatting. I feel really happy, and when he asks about my own progress, I say I feel a bit silly with my childish stories about horse-riding, 'and to tell the truth, I've had a bit of a writer's block these past few days, there's this character that I can't quite get a handle on. He's the owner of the riding school, and is supposed to be the villain but how do I write about him without it being too black-and-white and obvious.' Just then – no idea where I get the courage – I ask for his email address, no, I'm not on Facebook, but could I write to him, I could do with a bit of advice on certain passages and who else should I turn to if not a great writer like himself, and he gives me his address, he actually does!

I don't realize what I've done until after I get home, just before going to bed, because first I have to deal with Mum's resentment. 'What took you so long? I rang you twice, why didn't you pick up? Make sure you have the mobile on you next time, don't keep it in your bag, I nearly called the police to report you missing again', so only after all that, as I'm lying in my bed, the same bed I've had since I was little, does it dawn on me that I'll actually have to produce some writing now, or at least think it through a bit more, come up with some scenes from my life, I can't bother R for no reason and send him pointless emails, but I do want to write to him. I'm so happy that I have his email address, that he is now accessible not just on Friday evenings in the café but anytime on the internet, I'm so excited that I can't sleep, I lie there thinking about the things I told R about his book and wondering if I made a fool of myself, said something stupid as usual but nothing comes to mind, maybe I didn't, my palm tree is reaching out to me again in the dark, the bamboo plants have also started to bend down, I've been neglecting them lately. I gaze out of the window, the building across the street is dark, it has offices of some kind, the streetlamps are lower than our windows, one floor below, but my room gets some light anyway, and just then something occurs to me. I switch on the little desk lamp and go over to the windowsill, yes it's here, I've almost forgotten about it, my weed, why am I growing it anyway, just for decoration? I'm sure R would have made use of it a long time ago, but I don't even know how to do it, should I get a pipe from an ethnic shop or ask Zuzka or what.

I wake up with a headache, that's all, I potter around the flat, a parcel is delivered, fresh work for me, it will keep my hands busy for a few days, great, at least something, since I'm not sleeping well, hallucinations are the last thing I need, dreaming of Mr Ble as an evil spirit haunting me, but was he really as bad as I remember him? He loved animals after all, didn't he? everyone who loves animals gets a few brownie points, it's so heartwarming, surely a person who loves animals can't be all bad, ha!, but then again, I love animals too, horses especially, don't I, Hitler was very fond of his dog too, I read somewhere, so why do so many people think that a person who loves animals can't be totally evil? Of course he was a villain, I will depict him the way I see him, even if it's only in my imagination…

In my second riding school I was also the principal Ivana, I was Ivana, Mr Ble's main stable hand, he was the top boss, above all the other bosses, Mr Ble, a short fellow with a stern face but very resolute, very firm, a riding crop always at the ready by his side, polished boots, no, he didn't hit us, God forbid, just the horses if they bucked, if they disobeyed, he was always nice to us kids, he was kindly and I was his favourite because – it always comes down to the same thing – I was the one who gave it my all, every afternoon at the yard, not giving a damn about school or homework, it's so much more satisfying to spend time sprinkling the ground and then sweeping the stables, brushing the horses and picking out their hooves – oh, that feeling when you lean against the horse's side, lift one of his legs and start picking out muck from it, with the hind legs there's always the danger that the horse will suddenly object and kick you, send you flying to the far end of the box. I was Ivana, the one who helped with all of Mr Ble's horses, which included some top-class jumpers, champions! I would get them ready for riding, I'd hack them out and afterwards as a reward, I was allowed to ride one of the horses that no longer competed in races, because me and the other regular stable hands like Zuzka, we were not just ordinary helpers, we had our pick of the horses, we didn't have to follow each other round in single file like idiots, we had the school to ourselves in the evenings, sometimes with an instructor, sometimes left to our own devices. But I was singled out for special treatment by Mr Ble, being his devoted Ivana, always at his disposal, I didn't give a toss about a D in German, when Mr Ble came down to the stables, sometimes with his bassets in tow, sometimes not, he would stop by the tack room and call out, his voice ringing across the yard, 'Ivana, where are my spurs?' but it wasn't a question and I knew it, it was an order, an order that I always obeyed, without a word, whatever I was doing, I'd drop everything and run to the tack room and once there I'd bend down to Mr Ble's feet, kneel before him as if he were some deity, take out his spurs from the lower shelf where they sat next to the brushes, and – still on my knees – clip them on to his boots.

So, yes, I really would like to have something nice to say about Mr Ble, but nothing comes to mind, and with hindsight what I hold against him most is the competitions, the times when the horses had to be driven somewhere in a box for a couple of days. He'd ask me to come along and of course I'd say yes, I'd ask to be let off school – *for family reasons!* – and sit in the box squeezed in by the horses as we drove to Mosonmagyaróvár, Ostrava, or wherever the competitions were held, although, to be fair, I was always very well looked after once we got there, I was fed and given a place to sleep. Except that afterwards, when we got back to Bratislava, which was often late at night, Mr Ble, after a moving reunion with his bassets, would get into his posh car and zoom off to his villa on the Slavín Hill, leaving me to traipse home alone at one in the morning, through the grove on the bank of the Danube, stepping over drug addicts and the homeless, across all of the Ovsište and Petržalka estates. Because buses were few and far between at that hour, my Mum was waiting up for me, of course, sitting in the window and praying I'd make it home unharmed.

And then there was that incident with Logan. Logan was sired by the finest stallion in the stables, great hopes were pinned on him, that he would follow in his father's footsteps, but then again, maybe not. It wasn't a clear-cut case, Logan seemed a bit dopey, when walking he swayed from side to side, he had no grace, he was all legs, though not exactly steady on them either. The only way to make him trot was to kick him in the belly, and as for a canter, give me a break, anyone ever seen this placid thing canter, actually, yes, on one occasion almost everyone saw him canter and I was the one riding him when it happened. It was a spring day, we were outdoors and I was walking him, warming him up for Mr Ble who was to ride him later, after he finished his cup of coffee at the bar. I was supervised by the riding instructor when Logan suddenly bolted, God knows what did it, maybe a rollerskater or a cyclist passing on the embankment, or perhaps a dog barking, that's what usually makes horses bolt, but be that as it may, Logan suddenly started to canter and I couldn't stop him, the instructor kept yelling, 'tighten the reins! go on, tighten the reins! stop him!' but there was nothing I could do, I was past listening to her well-meant advice, I was happy I managed to stay in the saddle, because then, all of a sudden, I was no longer sitting, Logan was charging a fence head on and just before reaching it, stopped abruptly, and I sailed over his neck and over the fence, like in a silent slapstick film, and I landed on the concrete path head first. All I remember is blacking out for a moment and once the colours and the world around me returned as I came to, I saw everyone, including the instructor, running towards me from the stables, from the riding track. I struggled to my feet, my head was throbbing, but it was nothing serious, everyone congratulated me, helped me to walk, everyone was amazed, 'you're alive? you all right? thank God!' Even I couldn't believe I could survive such a fall and – as I later discovered – without even getting concussion, and just then I see Mr Ble calmly striding towards the scene of the incident, polished boots, crop, helmet and all, a smile on his face, I assume he's smiling because I survived the fall, but no, Mr Ble is walking towards Logan, caught somewhere on the far side of the embankment and being led back, Mr Ble walks right past me, takes Logan by the bridle and says with a smile and loud enough for everyone to hear, 'our little sleepyhead has woken up!'

I don't think anyone will hold it against me that I didn't shed a tear when, six months later, Mr Ble fractured his collarbone.

This, I think, was the first time I really noticed Žofia. Žofia, who wasn't a stable hand or even a helper, because Žofia actually owned a horse, this being the highest, unattainable goal for us ordinary mortals. I took notice of Žofia because a few days later she gave me a photo, she had snapped me riding the runaway Logan, with my hands somewhere on my chest and certain death in my eyes.

At first I hesitate, tormented by doubt – won't it be too forward? won't he be annoyed? is it appropriate even? what if he turns me down? but then I dive into it headlong and discover that it's a lot easier than I'd ever have thought. I find that writing emails to R makes all my inhibitions fall away, even making things up comes naturally, I don't have to think about it in advance, I just churn out all sorts of guff about working on my novel, about Mr Ble and the key passages, my relationship with individual horses and how the yard resembled a page in a catalogue for garden furniture with its perfectly manicured lawn and all the dirt swept under the carpet, like in the lobby, where I would regularly brush all the dust while sweeping the floor. And that's even before I get around to writing about myself, then it's no holds barred, I long to tell him as much as possible about myself, tell him almost everything, so that he knows me and accepts me despite it all, I long to lay myself bare to R, and oddly enough, he doesn't try to brush me off, he replies to every email, admittedly his replies are not very long – he must have countless obligations, a journalist and writer of his stature! – but he does take note of what I write, honours me with his attention, and that, to me, is the greatest miracle of all. Although it does worry me a little how easily I succumb to flights of sudden inspiration, the urge to overshare, all it takes is not being face-to-face with the other person, all it takes is channelling it into writing, through virtual space, it dawns on me that I might be capable of giving away everything about myself.

Sometimes I get a fright afterwards – have I gone too far? did I bring up something too intimate, something that might make him angry with me, make him stop talking to me? But at the same time, it's like a high-adrenaline sport, at least as I imagine a high-adrenaline sport to be, testing his limits, seeing how far he lets me go, how close he lets me get to him. There are other kinds of anxiety as well, of course. I still talk and behave in quite a childlike way, I live with my mum like a child, I fear that he'll get annoyed, exasperated by how infantile I am, that he'll realize how far I am from being grown-up, I'm just an overgrown spoilt kid, I fear that he'll see through my superficiality and lack of education and will stop wasting his time on me and devote it instead to his four, or who knows how many, lovers, that'll surely be a better way for him to spend his time.

And now, on top of everything else, Mum has begun to suspect something, she keeps snooping around behind my back, I quickly click on other tabs that I keep open in the top bar of my screen, so that as she passes me I read gardening tips on propagating house plants, but it doesn't stop her grumbling. 'All you do all day is sit at your computer, I wonder what's so interesting there,' then she tells me off, 'your plants are dying, haven't you noticed? Look at the bamboo plants, you used to be so fond of them, but now you hardly ever water them', she goes to fill the can, 'I can't bear it anymore, they're all drying out.' When she says that I briefly search my soul and admit she's right, I ought to look after them better, but all I can think of is R, in my head

I've started writing another email to him, trying to articulate some aspect of my life. Every now and then my eyes stray to the palm trees, the cyclamen and dieffenbachia, but I don't get up to water them, quite the opposite. Sometimes I wonder why I've let my room run to seed, all those branches and twigs everywhere, rubbing against me, sometimes they slap me on the back of the legs, I have to force my way through this thicket to get anywhere. Increasingly I feel that I'm suffocating in my own room, I'm more and more aware of the overpowering scent of the orchids, this is not meant to be a jungle, this should be my space, just for me, I need to be able to breathe here too.

And when Mum says she's going to have a word with my psychiatrist because lately I seem to have taken a turn for the worse, I haven't been behaving sensibly and seem to be lost in thought, not care about anything and making no effort to get better, it would be a good idea to talk about this with my psychiatrist the next time I see her, to check if perhaps my medication needs adjusting, if the dosage needs to be increased or lowered, or if I need some additional meds or to stop taking some. She is driving me up the wall and when she says I ought to see a gynaecologist for a check-up, because she's noticed something, some kind of a discharge, that's the last straw – is she inspecting my knickers now, or what?! I feel like screaming that from now on I'll wash my own things! also that there's no need to do anything about my meds, I feel like yelling out, Mum, I'm in love, just leave me alone! but I don't, because I know that this is the one thing Mum would never forgive me.

I know it's true, and I also know that if I ever write something, it will be only for R's sake, to make him like me, but there's the rub, how should I write to make R like me? The advice he gives in his emails makes it sound too complicated, overthought, it's not enough to sit down and write whatever happens to be going around my head. He might be right, I don't know, but anyway, how can I write anything if I haven't even finished secondary school, all I ever read is tips on tidying up and propagating house plants and that is why – I reach this decision in the middle of another Szekler goulash period, with the obligatory four dumplings – I will have to get R's attention some other way.

But how? I stare at myself in the mirror in desperation, I see nothing I could be proud of, nothing that impresses me, I've never paid much attention to my looks, I couldn't afford to anyway. I can hardly go on a spending spree on my disability benefit and my meagre extra earnings on the side, but the basics are there, the basics aren't that bad, my nose is not too large, my ears don't stick out and my skin is unblemished. But everything seems to be hidden beneath the sediment of all those years, my episodes of mania and depression, the meds that have given my complexion a slightly yellowish tinge and made me fill out a bit. I wouldn't say I'm fat, just sort of chubbier. I used to be an angular child, with bones sticking out left, right and centre, but that's all in the past, my shape is no longer clearly defined, everything is less defined, though my weight might be about right. I could never afford expensive clothes, I've never worked out, and to be honest, it has never bothered me. Not that I ever thought that what mattered was what's inside, it's just that there was never any reason to make the effort.

But there is now. I wonder what his lovers look like, no doubt they are very pretty, stylish, charming, I'm sure I couldn't hold a candle to them. But in that case, why is he stringing me along and showing interest in me, why does he write back, talk to me during the get-togethers, ask me to come out for a drag. He must have figured out by now that my interest is not purely *literary*, so why is he doing all this if he's not serious about me, good grief, what kind of language is this, I'm channelling my mum. All right, let's say there is some interest on his part. However absurd it may seem, and hard to fathom from the outside, R does fancy me. So, what then? I've never had a relationship, I don't know how to behave. Zuzka would probably say, 'get into shape, the rest will just fall into place'. So that could be a start. Working out is not on the cards, Mum would immediately clock what's behind it, maybe I could take up running, for example, after going to the post office I could run around Kuchajda twice. I could eat less – but that will be harder to pull off, how do I hide the food I don't want to eat, or ask for smaller servings, that would mean – just the thought makes me instantly break into a sweat – taking longer to get through each particular thing she's cooked, instead of four days, the goulash would last me five or six, oh no, perish the thought. But perhaps I could give it a try, gradually, we'll see.

A few days later Zuzka and I are in a second-hand clothes shop and she wants me to buy something totally hideous, a gold-coloured pleated skirt, I'm not sure if she's being serious or pulling my leg, does she think I'm a total moron, a cripple with no taste, or does she really think that this stuff is actually right for me, and afterwards, when I go into a changing booth at her insistence and come out to look in the mirror, I'm really annoyed. I look dreadful, or is it just the harsh lighting? how come I've not lost any weight, even though I've gone for a run twice this week and have been eating less, yet there's no visible result whatsoever, and in all honesty – I look exactly the same with make-up on as without, no detectable improvement, blue eyeliner makes little difference. Everything is bugging me, especially Zuzka, I find her super annoying, she's not helping at all, she seems to be laughing at me, maybe she's guessed why I'm punishing myself like this, maybe I shouldn't have asked her how R was, what was the point of asking her. I'm an idiot, only this morning he replied to my latest email, I know more about how he is than she does, but I couldn't help it anyway, I just wanted to say his name, wanted to talk about him, so this is my reward, a pleated skirt in gold, I take it off, I'm not buying it. Furious, I return it to the assistant, Zuzka seems disappointed, I feel like telling her off and shouting – go find yourself some other peabrain!, as we used to say at the riding school, but she's already dragged me to the nearest café. 'Wait a sec, I'll be right back', I walk past the tables to the toilet and discover my period has started, of course, why didn't I think of that earlier, the bloated stomach, the weight, the irritable state, it explains everything, a cycle that in my case is completely pointless.

Actually, it's not that I'm still a virgin. It happened at the riding school, where else, though not with the Bear, or Pišta, or either of the two Jurajs, it's an embarrassing thing to admit, but there it is, I lost my virginity at the riding school or, to be more precise, while riding. I think it was Oskar, a big, bony horse, riding him always meant being tossed to and fro, and one day in the changing room, after riding practice, I noticed some blood in my panties, I'd been having periods for two years by then, but it wasn't due that day. I wasn't scared by the thought of what might have happened, when I got home, I just stuffed the panties into a plastic bag and threw it into a rubbish bin outside the house so Mum wouldn't notice. I completely forgot this entire episode, I had more serious problems to deal with. I didn't recall it until some five years later, when I went for my first gynaecological check-up and the doctor said that I was no longer a virgin, my hymen was gone. This time, too, I said nothing, I didn't dispute it, even though I'd never had sex, and only later did it occur to me that it might have had something to do with this incident.

This was about the time that Janka took a liking to me, Janka was a lawyer who kept her horse, Apollo, at our stables. Apollo was a calm brown gelding, and as Janka was too busy to ride him every day, she asked me to take him for the occasional ride and to look after him a bit. I was game of course, happy as a lark to have a proper jumper entrusted to my care instead of another old jade, happy to have it all to myself on certain days, proud of my new responsibility. It turned out, however, that management wasn't all that keen, especially Mr Ble and Roman the instructor, who started to make my life hell in all sorts of ways. They kept me busy around the stables, made me sweep the office and the corridors and the yard. When Roman saw me on Apollo, he asked in his patronising way, 'I see, so you're no longer one of us, you're a law unto yourself?', he was much more critical of me during lessons, 'keep your hands lower down, stop flapping them about, how is he supposed to relax, can't you see you're making him nervous, hands lower, do you hear me? and straighten your back, you're always bent double like a hundred-year-old, heels down, Jesus, how many times do I have to tell you?' And Mr Ble suddenly had all these tasks for me, suddenly I was indispensable even though he had other helpers to choose from but, as he kept saying, I was the only one he could truly rely on, so I had to spend four hours walking Quebec around the compound when he had colic, stay late every day to groom the horses and train the other helpers, while my school results became more and more alarming, and to cap it all, that was when Zuzka left the riding school. She could no longer take the constant bullying, whereas I couldn't imagine a life without horses. And then I suffered two further humiliations.

The first one had to do with money. One day Roman took me aside and informed me that he'd been going through the accounts and found that I hadn't paid my riding fees for two years. I knew he was right, I hadn't been paying, but I had a gentlemen's agreement with Mr Ble, I was looking after his racehorses for free after all, and thought that settled it, and so it did, I suppose, until I got up to mischief, that is, started to ride Apollo privately. So suddenly this posed a huge problem for Roman, he explained that I should be paying the same as all the other helpers, even though none of the other kids did anywhere near as much work as I did. They turned up twice a week at most and brushed down their old plod before a ride, while I was the one sweating blood in the stables every day, but I couldn't bring myself to say this to Roman, I just stood there listening as he told me, in his patronising way, that he could let me off those two years' fees but that I would have to pay from now on. I wondered how to break it to Mum, she'd been fed up with my horse-riding since it was the reason for my dismal results at school and I was on course to get a D in chemistry, how was I going to break it to her that from now on I would have to pay for all my activities as well.

The other humiliation had to do with Žofia, of course.

No, no, I mustn't think about that now, I'm meeting R tomorrow, it'll be just the two of us, I can't believe I've found the courage to organise it. I can't sleep, I can't control my racing thoughts, I'm at their mercy at night when the city outside goes quiet and the trams have stopped running, there's only the odd car every now and then, the candle that's always burning at the pedestrian crossing, the plants in my room slowly stretching, reaching out towards me in the dark, as if trying to comfort me. But at the same time there's this awful racket in my head, I can't stand the racket that starts in my head as soon as everything around goes quiet, it's as if my head was about to burst, that's why I took the Rohypnol that time.

Mum thought it was a suicide attempt, my psychiatrist thought so too and treated me accordingly, everyone knew that this was what it was all about, I, for my part, said nothing, as always, even though I wasn't trying to commit suicide, I just hadn't slept for two weeks and couldn't take it any longer, I was willing to go to any lengths to knock myself out for a while. That's why I took some of the out-of-date Rohypnol Mum kept in the medicine cabinet, because Mum never throws anything away, not even medicines past their use-by date, they might come in handy one day, and these certainly did, the Rohypnol left by my father, yes, it had been quite a few years since my father died, but just at that moment I didn't care, I would have taken anything, and since I hadn't slept for a full two weeks, I popped about a dozen pills out of the blister pack, and swallowed them all at once, to catch up on all that sleep, I wanted to sleep for two weeks and not wake up, not emerge from oblivion, until I'd left everything far, far behind.

But this time it's different, the insomnia is mingled with happiness. I can't sleep because my mind and body are so thrilled about seeing R tomorrow. I can't feel happiness when I'm asleep, that's why my body stops me from sleeping, it wants me to be like this, wide awake, psyched up, in love. In his latest email this evening R said that he was looking forward to seeing me, those were his exact words, no beating about the bush, so of course I wrote back to say I too was looking forward to it very much. I wondered if I should expand on that to indicate that there's something more to my looking forward to it, exactly what my mum is worried about, that's why I had to lie to her. I invented a reunion at my primary school, our teacher Miss Obrcianová was sure to be there too, I would really like to see her again, I wanted to avoid another unnecessary row, but never mind that now, I will lie to Mum every time I consider it necessary, so that I can have a life. Never mind Mum, never mind the horses or Rohypnol, all I want to think about is R, I long to touch him, I've been so close to him, and yet the distance seemed insurmountable, there have always been other people around, obviously I couldn't play footsie with him under the table or anything like that, it just wasn't on. But tomorrow I'll have to do something, anything, unintentionally brush him with my fingertips, shall we go out for a smoke? or I'll go out of my mind.

As we are about to meet, it occurs to me that I haven't worked out what I'm going to say if he asks about my novel. But then I decide that it doesn't really matter, we'll talk about his book, that's a better idea, more likely to grab him. When I see him coming towards me, I'm so happy and anxious that I get a lump in my throat, this is about me, he's come just because of me, I can't decide if I should stand up, hold out my hand, or offer my cheek, or say hello, or all three, I'm so nervous that I stay seated, and the moment he sits down, I start raving about his novel, I've started reading it for a second time, because I missed some things the first time around, I keep discovering new associations and connections. R listens to me, not in an indulgent or patronising way as before but with such an earnest face that I get all jumpy and wonder if I'm making any sense, he breaks in, 'you know, not everyone reads it that way'. I ask what he means, he waves it off, 'oh, they've laid into me in the rival newspaper, more attacks are in the works', I'm all ears and full of sympathy, but also dismay – what? someone has dared to criticize my R and his book?! – so to comfort him I say casually, 'if I were you, I'd ignore it. I'm sure they're just jealous of your success as a journalist'. He waves this off again, as if trying to dismiss the whole topic, he's not that sure it's jealousy, I really have started re-reading his book, but in all honesty, I find it rather hard-going, whereas I devoured the sequel to the magic tidying-up book in a single day, but this is not the time and place for honesty, and anyway, why should I be honest, all I want is to make him happy.

But then, without warning, R goes on the offensive, all of a sudden, he starts asking questions about me, about my life, because, he says, our common friend Zuzka, great and brilliant and fantastic as she is, will give nothing away about her friend. So now it's my turn to start sweating, because R really wants to know what it is that I do, apart from writing a novel about horses, surely I must be doing something, he wants to know what I'm interested in, what I enjoy in life – good question, what *do* I enjoy in life? – I try to weasel out of an answer and change the subject, mutter something vague about problems, about having been through some tough times in my life, and if it weren't for my mum, I wouldn't be sitting here in the café with him today. Then I start talking about my childhood, the only period I feel safe discussing, the only time I've been healthy, not a mental cripple, this is not the way I put it, of course, instead I tell him how I used to be a bit of a tomboy, yes, me with that innocent smile of mine, how I used to run around with the boys – 'by the way, you're not going for a smoke today?' he smiles and starts to roll a cigarette – how I carved the words 'Obrcianová is a cunt' on the loo door and the whole class was given detention until the culprit came clean, but of course I didn't come clean, and so on and so forth. Who doesn't have loads of stories from their schooldays, anything to not talk about the damned time when I hit thirteen, because there's only one thing, one event anyone really needs to know about me, yet that's precisely what nobody knows about, the only act I committed aged thirteen is the one thing I can't tell him about, but just then R suggests, 'let's go for a little walk' and he takes my hand, surprised, I tilt my head back to look at him, then glance down at our hands and out of the window, it's gone dark already.

We're walking in the town centre and it's wonderful, I keep talking, I just jabber on and on, I'm cold and imagine what it would be like if he put his arm around me to keep me warm, if he threw his scarf around my neck, instead of putting up with all the nonsense I'm spouting. Just then he offers to walk me to my tram and before I know it we're at my stop in Kamenné námestie, standing slightly apart from the other people and I don't want to look at the illuminated clock that shows me, that reminds me that I should have been back home ages ago, I don't want to take out my mobile to check how many times Mum has called – I muted it before I met him as a precaution, so I have no idea – and there's the damned tram coming now, I look up at him, he's so tall, and I think, right, now I will give him a peck on the cheek even if it's the last thing he ever lets me do, and he looks at me and says out of the blue –' I'm worried that I might hurt you, Ivana, you look so vulnerable', and kisses me on the mouth.

Now, this is something I'm not used to, someone who treats me like a human being, sees in me something more than an unfortunate wretch, a crazy person who has ruined her mother's life, right now it doesn't matter that he's wrong – me vulnerable? me sensitive? – in what way could he hurt me? by bending down towards me, by touching me? In fact, just what he's already done is worth so much more than all the psychotherapy I've had since I was thirteen.

I know that no man has ever loved me and probably never will, well, I suppose they didn't want to hurt me, being so vulnerable, such a fragile little plant, what am I saying, not a plant, a delicate flower. A flower that kicked a five-hundred-kilo horse to death.

There. Now, I've said it at last. In my head. I've put it into words, into a sentence, it's funny actually, how a short sentence says it all.

I'm barely conscious of how I got home, I must have got on the tram, got off at the right stop, walked down Vajnorská Street, entered our block and rung the doorbell on the fifth floor – that bit I do remember. I recall Mum yelling at me, 'where have you been all this time', she had supper waiting for me, how many times she rang me and I didn't answer – the rest of the day is a blur, but later, lying in bed, with his book across my chest, unable as usual to fall asleep, I detect a change of some sort, it's not quite happiness but it's not the wild excitement of the past few days, rather, it's something more like a determination.

In fact, it doesn't even throw me very much when Mum returns from the shops the next day, bringing the tabloid *Nový čas* along with the groceries, and before lunch, as I idly leaf through it, I come across the headline SHOCKING REVELATION!!! IS THIS THE LOVER OF THE WRITER AND JOURNALIST R?!

Complete with photos that show them leaving some bar holding hands, who cares, one of his four lovers, I knew all about that, so it's no big deal. I look at her, a rising starlet of some sort, younger than me although she looks older, very pretty but, most importantly, she looks totally normal, something you can't say about me. She seems to have lived her life the way you're supposed to, school, friends, university, the odd trip abroad maybe, and now an actress. No disability benefit, no meds, no illness, no mental illness to define her, I want to be just like her, I don't want to be constantly recalibrated to normal, to have my meds adjusted, my mood swings levelled out, it's about time, I think, to crack down on this merry-go-round, to put a stop to all this, and simply accept reality, unfiltered, whatever the consequences.

'Hey, you with the broom, get out of the way!'

I remember this sentence word for word, it's exactly what she said, Žofia, as she passed by me walking her chestnut Vrana, the instructor was furious with her and said, 'Žofka, she has a name, she's Ivana, this is our Ivana, not, hey, you with the broom, that's not a nice thing to say!' But Žofia just laughed and I said nothing, I got out of her way, so that Vrana wouldn't crush my foot. I stopped sweeping the yard for a moment and watched Žofia with her long straw-coloured hair, tall riding boots, riding crop in hand, wearing a gilet, the entire outfit straight out of a catalogue, always so neatly turned out, even her Vrana seemed cleaner and better groomed than the other horses, everyone was incredibly nice to her, almost subservient, even Roman and Mr Ble, only many years later did I learn from Zuzka, who just happened to mention it in passing, that Žofia's father was the director of a bank, you know which one, no I didn't know, Zuzka was surprised, she always thought everyone knew about Žofia, but back then

I couldn't connect the dots, to me she was just a girl who was incredibly lucky to have parents who had bought her a horse.

My greatest and most impossible childhood dream – 'Mum, will you buy me this horse please, will you please buy Virbius, he's old, he has a limp, I'm sure he's not that expensive, I promise I will look after him every day, if we don't buy him, he'll be sent to Italy and turned into salami'.

All the horses end up as salami. All except Orlando, who was allowed to live out his days as a pensioner because he had been the best jumper Mr Ble had ever ridden, so Orlando was spared. He was given the freedom to walk around the riding school compound, to graze alone and undisturbed.

'Would you eat horse meat?' Žofia asked me as I was getting Logan ready for Mr Ble, scraping the dirt from his hooves, I turned around, I didn't recognize her voice at first, we didn't usually talk. I let go of Logan's fetlock and looked at her, she stood there smiling as she leant against the box. I shook my head, 'never, it would make me sick', but Žofia kept smiling and, what's more, clearly had no intention of leaving, she just stood there watching me groom Logan, saddle him, place the bridle bit into his mouth and put the bridle on. It occurred to me that I should pay her back for last week's humiliation and say, get out of my way, as I lead Logan out of the box. But instead, all of a sudden Mr Ble turned up, I thought he came to get his horse, but no, he looked at Žofia and asked, 'well, are we ready?' Žofia nodded, walked over to Logan, 'excuse me?', took him by the reins and led him out. They left me standing there, paralysed and I watched in disbelief as she mounted Logan in front of the stables and then went on to jump, supervised by Mr Ble, not an instructor, but Mr Ble himself, outside, on the course! Žofia, who'd joined the riding school only six months ago, was allowed to jump already, and I'd just got her horse ready for her.

That night I had my first fit of hysterics, or whatever you call it, it was an intimation of things to come. Janka rang to ask if I would take her Apollo for a ride the next day, she was busy and couldn't make it, but I refused to take the receiver from Mum, went to my room, flung myself on the floor, and lay there kicking and screaming that I would never ride Apollo again, I didn't care, I might as well ride old jades for the rest of my life, because nothing better would ever happen to me in that bloody riding school no matter how hard I tried, nothing would ever change, even if I killed myself sweeping the stables every day, grooming all the horses and failing all my exams at school!

I don't feel up to getting in touch with R, I just can't right now, I don't think it's because of the photo of his girlfriend in *Nový čas*, well maybe it is, just a little, but I've been avoiding Zuzka too. She rang and wanted to meet but I brushed her off, I said I was too busy, another consignment of Kinder egg toys had arrived, which was true, though it has never stopped me from meeting up for a coffee before. I'm in this weird state, I can't concentrate on anything, my mind keeps wandering, especially around Ovsište, the riding school, Žitný ostrov. Attention deficit, I'm in two places at once, in two different time zones, and R is incredibly far away, I can't connect with him, even our meeting seems terribly remote, even though it was only a few days ago. But the present is increasingly being overlaid by the past, which is becoming more and more tangible, but it's a necessary process, it's something I need to go through, I'm not yet that worried.

Mum, on the other hand, keeps yelling at me, 'anybody home?, why aren't you answering me? I'm talking to you, hello, have you gone deaf?' she gives me a shake and then starts going on at me, 'I do everything for you, I've sacrificed everything for you and you can't even be bothered to answer my questions, you don't think I deserve it, you ungrateful child, you', then she comes out with threats, instantly jolting me back to reality, 'just as well you have an appointment with your psychiatrist in a couple of days, she'll sort you out, she'll get your feet back on the ground, because I'm at my wits' end.' I look at her and know that this time I'm not going anywhere, certainly not to see my psychiatrist, wild horses couldn't drag me there, that's precisely what I mustn't do now, what I must avoid, preferably forever, but I don't say anything to Mum yet, I just shut myself in my room in a huff and wonder if I should stop taking my meds openly or cover it up, disguise it somehow, so that she doesn't notice.

But at the same time, I feel that I have to tell R everything, otherwise there's no point. I must find a way of writing it up that will make it difficult for him to tell if it's a passage from my novel about horses, or a childhood memory, if it really happened or if it is just a figment of my sick mind that's intent on hurting me all the time and won't stop until it makes me sink down to my knees, so that he knows, so that he's aware of the worst thing about me and accepts me warts and all, including the evil inside me. But how could I, how could I confess such a thing, it would be too much for Zuzka as well, and she's known me since I was eleven.

Mum continues to make threats all day long, 'we're going to see your psychiatrist tomorrow, we're going to see your psychiatrist tomorrow', her words reach me, but they sound almost absurd – what psychiatrist? I don't know one, I don't even recognize the word, I don't know what it means. I'm forcing my way through the thickets, the undergrowth, the tall grass, my feet sink into the mud,

I can hear it squelching in my shoes, I feel thistles catching my trousers, rose bushes slashing my body, my face, they get caught in my hair, where on earth am I. I bend down to tie my shoelaces, I've never been so far away, I've gone much further than when we walk the horses, from time to time the blind arm of the Danube comes into view on the left, stagnant, dead, but otherwise it's almost impossible to move in this place, it's so overgrown, my hands and face are covered in scratches, not to mention the nettles that are as tall as me, and the rocks I keep stumbling on. It occurs to me that I could climb a tree, I'm good at climbing trees, I could sit in the branches of a cherry tree and stay there, nothing more, just stay there, but first I have to tackle all these weeds, a scythe would come in handy, the kind Braňo used for haymaking, or rather a machete, to cut a path through, the way they do in the jungle, or a knife, or at least a pair of scissors. I would cut it, chop it, mow it all down until there's nothing left here, not a stone remaining, just me and empty space. Yes, that's better, I'm standing in the middle of my room, the big kitchen scissors in my hand, I'm at last beginning to make out the four walls in the dark, my space, all mine, the branches, the leaves, the flowers, the flowerpots, everything is on the floor, chopped up, broken, slain, a scene of carnage, just the kind of carnage I need right now.

I don't know where I was headed back then, I suppose I just wanted to leave, to disappear after seeing him at the back of the stables, so I would never have to see anything like that again, to get as far as possible from where he was lying, or maybe I was scared I'd be sent to a young offenders' institution for attacking Žofia, I'm sure I hadn't thought it through, I had no plan, like, why not spend three days wandering around Žitný ostrov and take it from there.

I was thirteen when I killed him.

Žofia had finished jumping Logan –' I say, Žofia, I think you could even manage an oxer' – the staff and helpers have all gone home, just a few people remained at the yard so I took Tristan for a ride, although I didn't feel like riding at all, I just wanted to distract myself, or maybe convince myself that there isn't a big difference between jumping Logan and riding Tristan. Except that there is a difference, a world of difference, I'm sitting on Tristan and that dimwit refuses to obey, I want to go at an angle but he thinks I want to do a figure of eight, I have to give him a kick to get him to trot, he's barely able to negotiate a bend on the track, he's all lopsided, almost teetering from side to side, and as for a canter, forget it, he won't do it, does he even remember what a canter is? I'm wondering if I should jump off, fetch a crop from the cabinet and give him a proper thrashing, in fact it's really myself I'm cross with, I still can't hold my hands low enough, I keep raising them and yanking, as long as I ride these old jades that can't even manage a trot I'll never learn how to do it. Tristan is tired and keeps juddering to a halt, I keep kicking his belly with my heels to make him go, canter, move, why does this old jade keep stopping, dammit, they really should send him away to be turned into salami, I grab him by the mane, lean down to him and whisper, 'you should be made into salami, do you hear me, Tristan?! you'll go to Italy to be turned into meat, that's all you deserve, you're not even a horse anymore, you're carrion,' I'm the last person left at the yard, I jump off and lead him to the stables, yanking the reins so furiously as we walk that he starts to resist, my blood is boiling with rage, I feel that my head is about to explode, I must be all red in the face. Once inside the box I totally lose control, I explode in the box, as soon as I take off his saddle I start punching him with my fists and kicking him in the belly with all my might, I hold him by the reins and push the bit hard into his throat as if I wanted to rip his muzzle out, I lash him with the reins, I batter him on his sides, I kick him in the belly, he has nowhere to duck, nowhere to escape, the box is small, he just stands there shuffling his feet and jerking his head up, I see his eyes staring at me in terror, but I still can't stop, I can't control my rage, I just keep thrashing him again and again.

Žofia, sitting on Logan holding her hands nice and low, her heels down, rising gracefully on the trot, 'excellent', shouts Mr Ble, 'excellent, Žofia, you're getting the hang of it', Žofia standing behind the stables with her state-of-the-art camera that also shoots video, Žofia filming Tristan. As soon as I arrive the next day I'm told he's lying behind the stables, I go to have a look, it's a nightmare and the first thing I see is Žofia with her camera, but then I suddenly see Tristan, he's lying on his side, partly covered by a blanket but part of his belly sticks out from under it, his belly is wide open, the bowels and innards protrude, spilling out onto the concrete, his eyes are glassy and his belly is ripped open. My Tristan! And this bitch is filming my dead horse, I kneel down to him but I'm too scared to touch him, this is my work, I realise, and yet I can't believe it at first, he was still alive when I left, I did give him a thrashing but I didn't kill him, surely I didn't kill him by doing that! and that's when I get up and lunge at Žofia, 'how dare you film this, are you mad, can't you see he's dead!' and I snatch the camera out of her hand, or rather, knock it out making it fly off and land on the floor. I give her a shove and have a feeling that I might be capable of grabbing her by the throat, I might be capable of killing her, throttling her, there's that uncontrollable rage again, like yesterday, only this time it's not directed at the horse but at her, Žofia, and that's when Roman comes running, takes me by the hand and says something, tells me off, but I can't hear him, I break free and start running out of the compound, onto the embankment, I run and run and have no idea where I'm headed, all I know is that I've killed Tristan.

But how come his belly was ripped open, I wonder, as I lie in my bed in the dark, that's a question that has never stopped haunting me all these years, no matter how hard I try to banish it, far, far from my mind, anything but think about why Tristan's belly was gaping wide open, was it really me who killed him? do I remember it right?

All those years, I couldn't bear to think about it, I had to suppress the memory with meds, choke it back, mortify myself, camouflage what I really am, mainly from myself, I wasn't able to accept it and now, looking back after so many years, I'm capable of thinking about it at last, I'm able to recall it, I can look back on those days, at what I've done, without shattering into a million tiny splinters. I, who loved horses so much, have killed one. And then, suddenly, it dawns on me, there is no illness. There's just me. With all the evil that is a part of me.

And that's when other memories appear in my mind's eye.

It's a sweltering day in August, I'm sitting on Tristan, Zuzka is on Penelope, we've gone for a trot on the far side of the embankment, and suddenly the instructor says, 'that's not the way to do it, we first have to cool the horses down'. We think she's gone round the bend, but she really is headed for the Danube, 'come on, follow me', we all wade in up to the horses' flanks, Zuzka and I laugh our heads off as we wade into the cold water, yes, our shoes are soaking wet now, the horses snort and dip their nostrils underwater as they walk against the river's flow, a strange new sensation, something between walking, trotting and floating.

And then another walk, in winter, in freshly fallen snow. It might even be New Year's Day, all of Bratislava is covered in snow, huge snowdrifts everywhere, but we've gone to the riding school anyway, of course we have, Zuzka had waited for me at the tram stop for forty-five minutes because my tram was late, but she did wait, and the instructor took us out and now I'm sitting on Quebec, and Zuzka and I are bringing up the rear arguing who's better, Little Juraj or Big Juraj, Zuzka has a crush on Little J, I on Big J, we can't agree who is better, we laugh so much that the instructor has to yell at us from the front. We're laughing because we both think it's obvious that the other one is better, that Little Juraj is not in the same league as Big Juraj, that Big Juraj is nothing compared with Little Juraj, when suddenly Quebec lies down in the snow, throwing me into a snowdrift, he starts rolling to and fro and that makes Zuzka laugh even more, she shouts that even Quebec can't bear to listen to me anymore, that's why he dumped me, and I just sit there dumbfounded, confused and wet, and Zuzka shouts, 'serves you right!'

And finally, the last, most distant memory, from my first riding club, with Braňo. Šumienka was about to give birth to a foal, she was due any day, I was restless at school, worried that it might happen while I was sitting in a useless physics class, so, as soon as school is over, I dash hell for leather over to Ekoiuventa. Braňo is there and doesn't want to let us kids in, he comes out of the stables, fetches buckets of water and towels before going in again, he's covered in dirt, 'nearly there', he says, 'any minute now, hold on,' and then he comes out and signals to me, his favourite girl, his *first Ivana*, 'all right, you can come in now, come and take a look, Ivana'. I follow him into the stables, trembling all over, I stop in front of the box and see Šumienka through the bars, she's lying on the ground and by her belly there's something dark, something I can't even make out at first, then I see, it's a colt, black all over, even though Šumienka is grey. It seems huge considering it has come out of Šumienka's belly, it lies there with its legs folded under its body and Šumienka is licking it all over while Braňo goes in and helps her push out the placenta. I watch the scene and then suddenly the foal tries to stand up on its wobbly little legs, rising first onto its knees, then up onto all fours, a first attempt, then a second, a third, and suddenly it's up on its feet, legs splayed out, next to Šumienka who is watching it from the ground, a genuine miracle, I see that it's standing upright, within minutes of being born, but at the same time I know that its balance is still precarious, it's unsteady on its feet, it's so vulnerable, all it would take is someone to give it a gentle poke or just breathe on it, and it would go weak at the knees and sink down on the ground, just like me.

# OLIVIA

I know when it first occurred to me that I might end up like Gloria Rosboch.

I wave goodbye to the porter and walk out of school, the sky is the colour of steel, it's getting dark, in the wan winter light everything seems so impersonal, detached. Dead. Two days ago we had a bit of snow, it's stayed on the ground up here, on the hill, in Pino Torinese but down in Chieri, where I live, all the snow has long turned to slush. As I walk to the stop of the number 30 bus, I try to remember what I have been planning for tonight. Eventually I give up on my useless head, take out my mobile and check the calendar. 'PPP'. I see, tonight it's the dramatized reading of Pasolini's texts at the Circolo dei Lettori. I sigh, I'm not that keen on Pasolini, but I didn't find anything more tempting in the listings in *Torino sette*. Anyway, it's better than being stuck at home glued to the telly like some people. Like those I didn't manage to talk into coming with me. I put the mobile back in my bag. It starts at nine, I've got plenty of time to go home, grab something to eat and get changed. I'll have to take the car, as the number 30 bus runs only once an hour in the evenings, it might as well not run at all. But that's not an issue, it's usually quite easy to find somewhere to park near the Gran Madre di Dio and from there it's just a short walk. I've now reached the Pino Centro bus stop, I'm the only one here, my feet are sore from standing in front of the blackboard all day long, from walking up and down the school, but there's no way I'm going to sit down on that ice-cold metal bench, a bladder infection is all I need.

The newspaper kiosk next to the bus stop is plastered with magazine covers. A billboard catches my eye: *Gabriele Defilippi in prison: 'I want to die. Gloria, forgive me.'* And underneath, in smaller print: *He lost 10 kilograms in forty days. The doctors are concerned.* I can't stand it. I can't stand myself, the fact that I'm reading it, that I'm following the developments in this case. It's been the talk of the common room for the past two months. But I don't want to be like them, those old fishwives who poke fun at the poor unfortunate Gloria over their coffee breaks. I'm appalled that this woman has become an object of mockery in and around Turin. Even the text messages have been leaked. Her infatuated missives, his revolting lies. How could they have published them, have they no scruples left, is it really 'anything goes' these days? It's outrageous, is there nothing those journalist hyenas will stop at? A human interest story, people want to know, so who cares about some Gloria and her family. All that matters is how to exploit it to the hilt. Provide people with some entertainment. Bread and circuses for the masses, particularly my colleagues, Carla and Franca. This is their favourite topic at the moment; just a few months ago it was the sex life of one of our fifteen-year-old students. I still remember Franca leaning over to me in the corridor and whispering with a giggle, 'have you heard about Elisa, you know the one in form B, the cute one that used to flounce around like a queen, she's got genital herpes, who knows who gave it to her, I bet she'd been at it with the whole class, I got the lowdown from her PE teacher, strictly confidential', and off she went to her classroom with a wink, the bell had already rung. I just stood in the middle of the corridor, stunned.

As I'm checking the timetable to see when then next number 30 is due a few people turn up at the bus stop, two girls and two boys from the form I don't normally teach, except for the past couple of months, when I've sometimes stood in for a colleague who has to go for oncological tests. Fifteen minutes, meaning I've just missed a bus. I note that the girls are quite happy to sit on the freezing bench, even though they're wearing just leggings, the boys are hanging around them. They acknowledge my presence with a half-hearted hello and then proceed to light up as if I wasn't there. They're talking about Belén Rodríguez and her latest Facebook video. The girls' names escape me for the moment. One is grossly overweight, with rolls of fat under her unbuttoned jacket but she doesn't seem to be insecure and self-conscious the way fat girls used to be when I was growing up. On the contrary, it's as if her substantial girth lent her extra authority, gave her the right to be first to speak, to voice her opinions. Now she's guffawing at some remark I didn't catch, something one of the boys muttered, probably to do with Belén's video. I can't take my eyes off her, her body is one enormous wobble, she is practically grunting, her face covered in make-up, her long purple fingernails perfectly groomed, three piercings in one ear, six in the other. Oh well, I suppose that passes for someone's idea of beauty.

Just at that moment one of the boys catches my attention. He's actually one of my students, but I've never before had a chance to take a good look at him, only now at the bus stop, as he keeps making the little group laugh with his wisecracks and witty remarks. Unlike the overweight girl, he is good-looking. Symmetrical features. Longish hair. Face covered with delicate silky down. He looks very similar to Defilippi in one of the photos that keeps cropping up in the media. It occurs to me that I could check the internet on my phone to see if there really is a similarity or if it's just my imagination, but then I feel ashamed that something like that has even crossed my mind. This isn't me, I'm not into this sort of thing, I'm not Carla or Franca. I have followed it only in passing, only to the extent you can't avoid watching the news, meeting people, working with others. If anything, I've tried to ignore it. And to focus more on art, cinema, books, or jogging, instead of tabloid gossip and crime reports. But you can't always keep your mind firmly in check. I can't really tell my mind what to think and what not to think. Not that I wouldn't like to. I'd love to be able to take charge of my thoughts, to dismiss all but the lofty ones. Who wouldn't? But what really matters is the way I deal with the bad thoughts, whether I banish them or get out my mobile and type 'gabriele defilippi' into the browser. I suppress the urge. I look over to the far side of the road, towards the pharmacy, to distract myself. Anything I need from there? Not really, I popped in this morning for some vitamins. My mobile stays in my bag and that's that; seriously, I might as well join the students' conversation about Belén and about her new video, oh I see, it's a porno, it's just gone viral. I glance at the boy again and can't help wondering what he makes of the obese girl. Is he also aware of the Michelin tyres, of how vulgar and crass she is? Is it even remotely possible that he fancies her? Sees her as a charming roly-poly? Is he flattered that she laughs at his jokes? Could he be hitting on her? Could he bear to touch her?

Take Carla and Franca in the common room, showing me photos of Gloria Rosboch, or rather, the single published photo of the plain, forty-nine-year-old French teacher, and a few selfies of her good-looking twenty-two-year-old beau and former student Gabriele Defilippi downloaded from the internet, pointing at the photos with their fingers, chuckling and spluttering, shoving the newspaper under my nose – 'take a look at this, don't they make a lovely couple, a perfect match? A right pair of turtledoves, aren't they? And she fell for it, she really believed that he was head over heels in love with her, oh Gloria, sweetheart, I can't wait for us to be together, please withdraw the 187,000 euros from your bank account so we can buy our lovenest, just for the two of us', Carla wipes the tears from her eyes, 'imagine if one of our students fell in love with you'.

How many times in all those years has it crossed my mind that some student might fall in love with me?

When I started teaching, at the age of twenty-five I was closer in age to my students than to most of my colleagues. But I soon realized that I was digging my own grave by being too friendly with the students. I wanted to be that charismatic English teacher with whom you can do more than just analyse phrasal verbs and conjunctions, with whom you can also discuss the meaning of life and the message conveyed by *Jonathan Livingston Seagull*. My own teacher at secondary school was someone I admired, he taught Italian and sometimes would perch on his desk and talk to us about life, love, the meaning of literature, what inspires people to write, and all sorts of other things. He always addressed us in the formal *voi*, spoke to us as his equals, he saw us as his partners, not as a gang of little shits needing to be tamed and punished. And it worked, we admired him hugely in every way. But when I started teaching, I soon discovered that all that kind of approach achieves is to make my students see me as a soft target. Makes me a laughing stock. Makes me look pathetic. At first I thought that this was because my Italian teacher was a man and I was a woman, but later it dawned on me that I just don't have it in me. I lack charisma. Anyway. Talk about life? What kind of advice could I give them, I who'd been stuck for years in a dysfunctional relationship that ended in failure, I who had been a promising musician and painter as a child, promising in so many ways yet failing to translate any of that into something tangible? And years of teaching pushed me even further. I blame the students of today. They are superficial, stupid, full of themselves, not interested in anything, unable to get excited about anything, with zero stamina and resolve. They have everything they need and don't know what to do with it all, they've never in their lives had to fight for a thing, they get everything handed to them on a plate. And the minute these thoughts cross my mind, as soon as I articulate them to myself as I watch these four perfect specimens at the bus stop – the bus can finally be seen rounding the corner – I know that things are bad, that I've become just like my older colleagues, both in terms of age and opinions.

What kind of teacher might Gloria Rosboch have been? Was she strict or kind? Was she effective as a teacher? In her photo she looked a bit like Franca, a bespectacled barrel, but she would have been more reserved, I'm sure she would not have made fun of her students if they caught genital herpes, I wonder if she'd ever been with a man. Carla and Franca told me in a whisper that Defilippi 'had allegedly hopped into bed with her' but rumour and reality are often two different things. And even if that were the case, had she ever been in a relationship with anyone else apart from this con artist? How profoundly desperate and lonely she must have been to believe that someone that good-looking wanted her, plain and old as she was, with her sticking-out ears, that he desired her physically, that she was the object of his erotic fantasies?

I get on the bus, walk down the aisle and take one of the raised seats at the back, the students are seated some four rows in front of me, they keep giggling at something like idiots. I notice that the woman sitting opposite me has a big cold sore on her upper lip, it's covered with white salve that has caked up and cracked. Herpes again. There are days when I feel there's hardly anyone around who doesn't have it. I glance into my bag to make sure I have my antibacterial wipes for when I get off the bus.

In fact, sometimes I do imagine that the students are eyeing me up, that they fancy me, and I'm absolutely sure that I am more attractive than their classmates, who are already overweight at fifteen. But how can I, an adult, compare myself with fifteen-year-old kids and consider I come out on top, tell myself that I am one up on them?!

Well, actually, it's quite easy. I think I'm still quite a looker. Even though I'm thirty-nine and know that I'm no spring chicken, have crow's feet around my eyes and my body betrays me sometimes and is no longer one hundred per cent reliable in the way it used to be, I don't think I'm past my sell-by date just yet. To my immense regret, I was forced to give up dancing years ago, I'm no longer supple enough and keep dislocating my shoulder, but I go jogging regularly. I work out, unlike some colleagues, who can barely walk up the school stairs without wheezing. I've joined a runners' group in my neighbourhood in Chieri and take part in long-distance runs. Two to three times a week. Depending on the weather and if I feel like it, I'm not a slave or a fanatic. I've been gradually training for a half-marathon, I'm also quite tempted to try the full one in Paris, but that's more in the realm of dreams, maybe-one-day-if. So, I do take care of myself. I think it's fair to say that I look quite fit. I have long hair which I wear down or tied with a headband. And while I go along with the saying that it's what's inside that counts, I do have quite a pretty face, if I say so myself. A bit gaunt, admittedly, and then there are those crow's feet I mentioned earlier, but I have big light-brown eyes, strong cheekbones, my nose is neither too long nor too short, and I don't feel that I'm unpleasant to look at. At the age of thirty-nine I'm grateful to have the looks that I do. So, yes, I'm evidently one up on many a fifteen-year-old who doesn't have a clue about a healthy lifestyle.

And there's something else. I rank well above them in the pecking order.

I take out my mobile, we've left Pino by now, the world outside seems ghostly, I take a picture of the landscape that appears to be aglow in the greyness because of the snow and I make a cropped segment of the photo into my profile picture on WhatsApp. Those who care for me should have a chance to enjoy this lovely view. The bus is still half-empty, but the four students are making quite a racket, I've never understood what it is these young people find so funny all the time. Are more things funny these days than there used to be? I don't recall being in hysterics all the time about something or other when I was an adolescent or a young woman. The overweight student turns her head and as our eyes meet, she pivots back, giggling, whispers something to the handsome boy and both of them burst into even more uproarious laughter. Are they laughing at me? Never mind, some people are obviously beyond help even though they still have their whole lives ahead of them. My mobile chirrups, my heart skips a beat, someone has sent me a message, I open WhatsApp, the students fade out, but it's just my mother. Of course. My mother commenting on my new profile picture. 'A great shot', she says, 'what a shame it's out of the bus window, and when are you coming over?' I sigh. Sometimes it's as if my mother lived her life on WhatsApp, Facebook and Twitter. She is always the first to comment on my every post, every new photo, every new friend, she even comments on my every comment on the posts by friends we share, whichever app I open, the first thing I see is my name followed by hers. And when we meet, she's quite prepared to give me a dressing down: 'how come you didn't check your WhatsApp all day Saturday, I was worried when I didn't see you online all day, I was afraid something might have happened to you and wanted to ring you, but your father talked me out of it'. I know why I don't go to see Mother very often.

Jesus, they're so crass. So young and already so gross. What kind of people will they grow into, what kind of immature monstrous adults will they become – the kind interested in nothing but their own gratification? In my most difficult moments I have always sought solace in *The Little Prince*, the most truthful book I've ever read, whenever I feel sad or loneliness gets the better of me, I read a few pages in the evening and for a while I feel happy in this world again because I know that there are some people out there who feel the way I do, people who are sensitive, authentic, who reflect on this world, and

I know that it hasn't all been for nothing. But this lot? These four little shits? The only book they're likely to read is *Fifty Shades of Grey*, and even that only to discover the best position for sticking it up their arse. They make me sick. They get genital herpes at fifteen and throat cancer by the time they're twenty from all the blowjobs they've given. What I don't understand is whether they were born that way, if all of them are like that, or if they just follow the herd, buy the advertising and the trash that comes pouring out of everywhere. It's the girls I'm most baffled by. From what I gather, or heard Franca and Carla discuss in the common room, oral sex is quite routine for them, like shaking hands or saying ciao or how are you. They're all into it. I could never put it in my mouth, just the thought of it makes me gag.

So actually, there is one way that these obese and plain girls are one up on me. From the boys' perspective, that is.

Shoo, shoo, must find something nice to think of, expunge this filth from my head, but nothing comes to take its place. I take out my mobile and start browsing through my recent pictures, a few hills, the snow-covered pine tree in our courtyard, Gertrude Stein in an encyclopaedia and her quote *A rose is a rose is a rose,* my bracelet on a shelf, light streaming through the blinds into my room. I look up, we're at a bus stop, the students are finally getting off, pushing and shoving, giggling away, and quite openly casting mocking glances in my direction. They know I won't be the one marking their exams. I read the message from my mother again. She may be difficult but at least she's brought me up to be a decent human being. I have to give it to her. Unlike other people's mothers.

Gloria Rosboch, too, seems to have been a decent human being. I see some similarities, some parallels between her life and mine, which I find unsettling, I have to keep reminding myself that there is simply no chance of my becoming that kind of person. I won't end up like her. Everyone has their own fate and although our trajectories may cross every now and then, they never merge, and neither are they two parallels headed for the same infinity. Gloria was forty-nine – that is, exactly ten years older than me – she lived in Castellamonte, a small town near Turin, I live in Chieri, a small town near Turin, she taught French at a comprehensive while I teach English at a grammar school, she wasn't married, I'm not married, though I used to be, I was married for a long time and, this is the crunch, I don't live with my parents, and apart from my mother stalking me on social media I've been quite successful in managing to avoid them. That's the crucial difference. And last but not least – Gloria had 187,000 euros in her bank account, which I certainly don't, and at the same time, I have judgment, which she evidently lacked. 'Oh, my sweet Glo, I can't wait to hold you in my arms, a blissful life in Antibes awaits, all we need is money.' Judging by the testimonies of her friends, colleagues and neighbours I read in the papers she can't have been very bright.

And most importantly – Gloria looked dreadful, Gloria was exactly the type that has been of no interest to any male for a long time, in fact, Gloria didn't even look like a woman. There was something vague and indefinable about her. She was a kind of sexless being. Whereas I still look like a woman, and a rather attractive one at that. Nobody can take that away from me, try as they might.

My God, what rubbish I'm thinking, that won't do. Pathetic. This is not me. I shake my head and look out of the window, we're just entering Chieri.

Recently I read this interesting book, about free and strong women, an assistant at the Luxemburg Bookshop recommended it. I read it in English as it's not out in Italian yet, its title was *Spinster* and I couldn't put it down. As I read it, I kept telling myself, yes, this is what I could be like, a confident woman who doesn't need a man just for the sake of it, just to prove something to those around and to herself, as if a woman without a man was incomplete, pathetic, pitiable. But in fact it's not true, a woman can be on her own and still live life to the full, all her life long if she so chooses, so why does the idea fill me with increasing dread, the idea that I will never find someone and will always be alone, even though I know full well that I'm by no means the only one in this situation, so why am I obsessed with poor, duped Gloria Rosboch's sad story, even though I'm sure I can't possibly end up like her?

The bus has arrived at my stop, Piazza Cavour, I get up and walk down the aisle, still a bit stunned by the spectacle those four rude cocky students made of themselves. I step out into the frost and reach for an antibacterial wipe straight away, I haven't forgotten, that's something I never forget, no matter how far my thoughts may wander. I wipe my hands thoroughly, especially my fingertips, I throw the used wipe into the nearest bin and start walking homewards up the hill, past the church of Santi Bernardino e Rocco. It's almost completely dark, the slush beneath my feet is beginning to crunch, it's started to freeze over, I take care not to slip on the pavement, I wonder if it's a good idea to drive tonight, but it seems that the roads have been gritted. As I walk, I am painfully aware of my lower back, I woke up with a sore back this morning, it's been like this for several days now, maybe I should put some gel on or a plaster when I get home.

A lot can happen over the years, ten years are enough to lose one's sense of judgement or even to go completely crazy, ten years is quite a long time, especially if you go through it on your own. A lonely schoolteacher can delude herself into thinking that her students fancy her, that they are interested in her, not just in the subject she teaches, but in her as a person. As was the case with Gloria. How often do I think that a cheeky student is eyeing me up. The way one does a female with eyes, hair, tits, thighs, a bum. Whenever I become aware of this kind of male gaze, it makes me uneasy, yet I always, subconsciously, sit up straight. As if I craved their approval. But what effect can a woman pushing forty have on a secondary school kid? A kid who draws distinctions even between their peers and those just a year older or younger? Would a brat of this kind even see me as a female, given that the way Gloria allowed herself to be duped is regarded as both tragedy and farce, turning her into a laughing stock before all of Turin, if not the entire country?!

But I'm definitely not lonely. I don't spend my time pondering the pathetic life of a divorcée, I can't abide self-pity, I don't give in to it, I keep busy, I'm interested in a thousand and one things, I go to a different event every night and generally not on my own. I go with a girlfriend, or a male acquaintance, though that happens less often, men are too predictable, they always want to walk you home after a concert and I don't care for that, I don't want that. It's just that tonight it hasn't worked out, I couldn't find anyone prepared to go and see PPP. The seriousness of the subject must have scared them off. Although this will be some kind of a theatre production, if I understood the leaflet right, who knows, I may be in for a pleasant surprise. And maybe I'll meet someone there.

I have nothing against a new relationship, but all in good time. I certainly don't want to bring men home, casual relationships are not my kind of thing. And gratifying my own needs even less so. What kind of needs are we talking about anyway? There's nothing I'm missing in that department. I'm doing just fine, thank you very much. I'm not like some, and here I'm thinking of the girls at my school, who feel they have missed the boat if they haven't lost their virginity by fifteen and then they immediately have to try out every position in the Kama Sutra, or —

Goodness, there I go again. If it goes on like this, a few years from now I'll be tut-tutting the students on the bus for not giving up their seat to me and yelling at them in the corridors: 'off you go to the classroom, you cheeky bugger, you!'

Must stay calm.

Seriously though. I may be old-fashioned but a relationship between a man and a woman should be about more than satisfying animal urges. About exchanging bodily fluids. But these little shits haven't realized that yet. And who knows if they ever will. I, on the other hand was not in a hurry, I lost my virginity with my husband. It happened before marriage but only after I was quite certain that I wasn't making a mistake, that he wasn't going to leave me high and dry, and when I could imagine spending the rest of my life with him.

And he never put pressure on me, all in my good time, he waited until I was ready for the big milestone. And, most importantly, he didn't demand any of that filthy stuff from me, never, he never even hinted, neither in words nor gestures, that he might want more than I wanted myself. We would kiss, hug, embrace, I let him penetrate me, we'd make love. The normal stuff. Sometimes, when I was tired in the evening, I did it for him with my hand. On one occasion, we were married by then, he came sooner than I expected and some of it landed on my face. He apologized. He said he didn't do it on purpose. Back then I thought it only right and proper for him to apologize. I just wiped my face and assured him that nothing had happened. And nothing did happen. I thought we understood each other in this respect, that we were on the same wavelength. Later, however, I kept replaying this moment in my head, particularly when our relationship cooled off and we seemed headed for a divorce. What if all that time he'd actually wanted something more, something different? What if he'd actually been longing to do that filthy stuff that makes my stomach turn – just the thought of it, just the words for it? What if that had been the actual stumbling block?

Throughout our seventeen years I'd never caught him watching porn and only after we divorced did it occur to me that he might have done. He could have watched porn, and I could have caught him in the act. Yet it never crossed my mind while we were married, not once. Admittedly, sex was slowly disappearing from our life, but I thought that was natural. I didn't really miss the sex all that much, in fact, I'd never given it much thought at all. What mattered to me above all was that we still got on well. But what if he was suffering all those years because he had to make do with what there was, because he couldn't grab my head and thrust himself upon me, squeezing my face with his hands and ramming his prick into my mouth with such force that I would nearly choke and gag, that my eyes would pop out and make my mascara run?

But what gives me pause is that he found a replacement so quickly. I'm not saying he left me for her, but she did appear on the scene within the month. As if you could swap one person for another just like that, like goods you buy in a shop and when you're not happy with it, you return it the next day. Take it back after seventeen years. And demand a different, new, better model. And get it.

All right, I had never let him come in my mouth or arse, but I'd given him so much. Of myself. Of my energy, my time, my life. It wasn't until our marriage was on its last legs that I became apathetic, letting days go by, showing no interest – yeah, you're right, whatever you say – I stopped giving him the total support I'd offered for the previous seventeen years, I just waited for him to tell me it was over. It wasn't me who left him, I left it up to him, made him do it by behaving the way I did. I allowed the relationship to die, although not in any joyous or callous way – it's up to you to complete the work of destruction! – nor with a sense of satisfaction – I told you so! – nor with sarcasm – come on, you bastard, just say it's over! I was sorry but I just couldn't carry the burden any longer. It was thanks to me that my husband evolved continuously throughout those seventeen years, he grew, forged his career, transformed from a timid little boy into a confident man. Except that in the meantime, while *he* did his growing, I was somehow forgotten, there was no room left for me, actually, that's a good question – where *had* I been all those years?

Why was every evening devoted to discussing his work, his problems with his colleagues? We worked together on all his reports, I was always expected to check them for him, to read them carefully and, even more importantly, to come up with something, be it a comment, a suggestion for improvement, a change in the order of the words, and if I didn't, he would accuse me of not giving a damn, of not caring how it would go down with his boss. Why did we always go on holiday in the mountains, always trekking up to mountain chalets, how wonderful, yet another stamp on a postcard, whereas all I wanted was a few days, a week or so by the sea, and then one year, when he gave in and we spent ten days at a camping site near Savona, he never stopped moaning. About the grumpy chefs and the Ligurians in general, about the dirty water and the rubbish floating in it, about getting sunburned on his back. And not only did I tolerate this kind of behaviour, I very nearly apologized, mea culpa! mea culpa! and after that I never again insisted that we go to the seaside. Why did I agree to stay in Chieri even though ever since I went to university I knew that I wanted to get out of this provincial backwater and move to Turin, a place that is vibrant, where you can go out every day and always find something new to see.

Talking about something to see. I, who have always adored art, particularly dance and music, that is, concerts, as well as literature, cinema, exhibitions, theatre, how could I have settled for a life that consisted of eating dinner, watching the evening news, then doing some work or maybe reading a bit, watching a DVD in the evening or listening to a CD as our cultural highlight, the cherry on the cake being an outing to Lingotto on a Saturday afternoon to see *Avatar* in 3D, putting on glasses like little children, because he was interested in sci-fi, because he enjoyed films about extra-terrestrials, and since he enjoyed films about extra-terrestrials, obviously I had to put on the tinted specs and sit there for three hours watching tall blue UFOs with yellow eyes clambering around trees with Sigourney Weaver.

Actually, I know why it happened. I know exactly why. I thought that if we did everything together, if we had shared interests, which in practice meant me adapting to his interests, we would grow to be an ideal couple, pure bliss and harmony, all the way to our coffins. Which we would also share, of course, and lie there side by side.

But lately I've been seeing him in town, arm in arm with the other woman, Chieri is a small place, it's a provincial dump, forgive me for badmouthing my hometown, but it's a fact. It's been a year since our divorce – well, I call it a divorce, although technically it's only a separation, divorce isn't yet possible – and the other woman has lost no time, that's right, she's expecting. It shows already, even under the oriental print winter coat she wears as she parades alongside the former man in my life. And there you have it. Bingo. The second sticking point. Children.

Children – why did things turn out the way they did? Now everyone takes me to task for it, asking that question, overtly or covertly, but I'm actually not so sure, I keep wondering about it myself. Was it me who didn't want children, or was he the one who didn't want them, did we both want children and they just didn't materialize, had we planned to have children later on but it ended up being forgotten somehow, in the hustle and bustle of everyday life, that's it, that's probably it, however implausible it may sound that we forgot that we wanted children, but I suspect that's exactly what happened, and it's more or less the answer I give to the question my friends and relatives bang on about, or are dying to ask – married for seventeen years and no children?!

I don't remember this ever being an issue for us, I don't recall discussing it, perhaps we did at the beginning of our relationship – what name should we give her if it's a girl? It's got to be Chiara! no, Bianca! Perhaps after we moved in together, when we discussed contraception, but that was a long time ago, I forget the details, and the thing nobody, but nobody, can understand is that I have never missed having children. And I still don't. The battery in my biological clock must be slowly running down but have I ever heard it tick, have I ever felt, in those seventeen years, that I was going to miss the boat, that it was now or never, that I was letting something slip that I could never catch up with, that I could never put right? Not really.

And when he found the other woman, when she got pregnant and people started to draw attention to this and do everything possible to hurt me, or at least insult me when we met in the streets of this shithole called Chieri, where I'm walking now, in total darkness, there's no street lighting on this stretch of the road, whenever they did that, all I felt was anger, a kind of rage directed at no one in particular. All right, I didn't produce children, I will never have kids, but why should that mean having to admit that I've failed as a woman, that I am not adequate as a female, somehow incomplete. That there is a void inside me that troubles me, that my sex organs have been created for no purpose and that you should all feel sorry for me because I've been deprived of the most wonderful thing a woman can experience, and clearly that poor fellow was right to leave me for another woman, one who was willing to give him children?

You little shit, so now it turns out that what you've always wanted was children? Is that what you've just realized? How fascinating. Who would have thought.

I can't help it, I may be a seething mass of emotions but the desire to have children is not one of them.

I believe that a person, I mean a woman of course, can be just as happy without having children, except that lately I've had the strong impression that I'm the only one who thinks that way. It's as if all these people, especially strangers, although it's none of their business, had a problem taking me seriously just because I'm childless, because I don't wear a wedding ring. As if a person, there I go again, not a person, a woman, as if she wouldn't be a fully-fledged adult unless she's given birth, as if only that would help her understand what life is all about and allowed her to join the ranks of seasoned or worthy birthgivers. Until you've given birth, you're just a girl, a *signorina, signorinella, ragazzuola*, no matter the crow's feet around your eyes, even if you're thirty-nine and have endured everything that life can throw at you. This is how I'm often treated, especially by embittered *signoras*, women in their fifties or sixties. Just the other day, when I was introduced to one, she glanced at my bare ring finger and corrected herself straight away, 'excuse me, my dear, I've been addressing you as *signora* but you're still a *signorina*', she said sarcastically and with a spiteful grin. I gave her a forced smile, 'oh no, that's fine, you may call me *signora*, we're all ladies here after all, a real class act'. That made the smile freeze on her lips, the bitch.

And to think that I would devour manuals on how to be a supportive wife, how to maintain and nurture a relationship, how to assert your influence over your husband – he'll be a new man by Friday! – that I internalized the key points, every trick in the book. And applied them religiously. Never criticise him come what may, on the contrary, make sure you motivate him, wax lyrical about his strengths, always have a word of praise ready for every little trifle, show appreciation when he deigns to open the lid on a jam jar for you, wow, what a strong man you are, thank you ever so much, what would I do without you. And if he can't manage it – never mind, let me try, your hands must be greasy.

And if he won't do the decorating, slip on a pair of tracksuit pants and an old T-shirt, fetch the ladder from the cellar and paint the walls yourself. If he can't screw something in, get hold of a professional set of screwdrivers and take on all the small repairs, it's no big deal, not worth mentioning, it's as straightforward as assembling Ikea furniture. Study articles on LED lights and halogen lamps in technical magazines to design the most economical lighting for your flat; get on first-name terms with the electrician, the plumber and the assistant at the hardware store. Know everything there is to know about silicone guns, have one at home and seal the cracks on the dilapidated balcony to stop the rain from leaking down and flooding the flat below. Remove mould using a vinegar solution instead of those carcinogenic products they sell in the shops. I could go on and on listing men's jobs that landed on me, but these are just platitudes, I would have happily done all those things if he'd ever shown any appreciation for me.

But how can you expect appreciation from an only son who's always had it his way, from the perfect *figliolo*, whose mother never tired of subtly hinting that I was the one who wasn't good enough for him —

Enough, I must stop! I'm just tormenting myself.

I'm home at last, I enter the building but don't take the main staircase on the left, the flat my family has helped me buy is at the back, in a two-storey house with courtyard balconies, hidden from the outside world. I walk down a stone path, past a pine tree, past the windows of my neighbour the electrician– here's hoping he doesn't spot me, luckily, it's now dark and he his lights are on, I'm safe. Then it's up the stairs to the second floor, along the courtyard balcony, past my neighbours' flats, they are students and they're being noisy again, probably a party, there's always something to celebrate, I walk all the way to the end, to the final iron grille, take out my keys and let myself in.

The place isn't big, just two rooms, a tiny kitchen and a bathroom, I've lived here for six months but it looks worse now than when I moved in, there are piles of books, CDs, DVDs everywhere, stacks of paper, cards, clothes and leaflets from various cultural institutes and libraries and clothes all over the place, sometimes I picture the mothers of my students telling their kids off for being messy and imagine what they would say if they saw this, the mess in their teacher's home. The place is clean though, don't get me wrong. It makes me laugh when I remember how I used to obsess about cleanliness in the flat I shared with him, our cosy love-nest. A scented candle and decorative posters on the walls were a must of course. I've always been very tidy, I still am, in fact. I tell myself that this is only temporary, a kind of delayed reaction which has been dragging on. But every time I tell myself, right, I'm going to get this place sorted properly, I'm overcome by a sudden weakness – what's the point anyway, who's ever going to visit, who do I need to tidy up for? myself? Plus, this whole thing reminds me of something I'd often heard of but never experienced – a creative mess. And I'm pleased that I have now managed to create one. I step over my French textbook – *oui, mesdames et messieurs*, I've taken up French in my spare time, that was before the Gloria case, now I would probably go for Spanish instead, but never mind. I gently touch the framed poster that shows Exupéry leaning against a plane and walk over to the kitchen but just then my mobile chirrups again. I tap it to wake it up, take a look, it's my friend Silvana, one of those who didn't want to come with me tonight, she said she'd seen the first twenty minutes of *Salò* and that was enough, not even wild horses would drag her to PPP. I haven't seen even twenty minutes of *Salò*, but that's beside the point now. She has created a WhatsApp group to which she's added me, now she says, *mega event on Saturday at the Settimo Cielo shopping centre, Burger King, birthday party for Junior, let me know if you can join us. With partners and your brood.*

Junior. Brood. What sort of language is this? Just the other day Silvana took me to task, saying that I was unhinged because I changed my profile picture three times a day, literally unhinged, and now she's started a whole WhatsApp group just for a damned birthday party. And my mobile will never stop chirruping all day. I'm not having that; I'm going to mute it. But I'll read it anyway, the gazillion comments and questions, what doesn't he have, what toy, what would make him happy, what size T-shirt he wears. And hints I don't understand. And sentences that aren't addressed to me. Maybe I should decline the invitation and leave the group, problem solved. No, I can't do that. She would be offended. All Silvana does all day long is post photos of her *brood* in every kind of position taken from every kind of angle, whereas I, at least, post charming photos, a landscape or a picture that might be of interest to someone else, not to show off about being perfect, about all the things I manage to fit into my life.

The thing is, Silvana is a friend I'm not so keen on. We were in the same class at secondary school, the three of us – she, Gabriela and I – used to be inseparable. Then each of us went to a different university, I stayed in Turin, Silvana went to the Statale in Milan and Gabriela all the way to Basle, and we stopped seeing each other, although we all came back to Chieri for the holidays. Later, when I started teaching in Pino and would no longer run into them in the street in Chieri, I completely forgot about them. It wasn't until a few months ago, when I joined Facebook – I hadn't been tempted for a long time, I didn't think I could get anything out of Facebook until someone explained that the one thing it's great for is cultural events, you receive invitations, all kinds of newsletters, first-hand info – that I suddenly wondered what Gabriela and Silvana might be up to and decided to look them up. Gabriela had married in Switzerland and stayed there. Silvana had also got married and returned from Milan, she now lives in Turin in the Borgo Po neighbourhood. But the thing that threw me most, or hurt me I might almost say, was seeing that the two of them had never lost touch. When I first worked it out from our online chats, I felt as if I'd been hit over the head with a baseball bat, but then I came to terms with it. I didn't feel like raking over who'd been better friends with whom, who'd gone behind whose back and so on, what good would that do, plus I soon realized that I wasn't necessarily the one to blame. The thing is, Gabriela and Silvana are still on the same mental level as they were in secondary school. It was like being thrown back to the old days, the same little jokes, snarky remarks, opinions, gossip, only encrusted with an unbearable number of emoticons, to sum up, aged thirty-nine, Gabriela and Silvana talk like two adolescents, even though they both have families and children! It's quite pathetic. As for myself, I believe I have moved on since secondary school. Silvana and I meet every now and then – it seems like the thing to do, seeing as we live so close to one another, but our meetings so far have only confirmed the impression from the internet. I've been wondering for the past few weeks if I should just defriend them on Facebook, even if they take offence, they can do what they like and slag me off me to their hearts' content for all I care but I feel no inclination to participate in adolescent chats about *boys*, I'm a grown woman and I know what I want from life and from Facebook.

I go to the bathroom and give my hands a thorough wash. I stare into the mirror. The newspaper reported that Gloria didn't have any close friends, hardly left her parents' house, and before Defilippi came on the scene she always went straight home from school, had dinner with her parents and then the three of them sat in the living room, most likely watching films or soap operas. Then she said goodnight and went to her room, the same room she'd had since she was a child, for crying out loud. I shake my head to chase that thought away, but why did she never go out? had she given up completely? meeting interesting people is not all that difficult. I have a new friend now; her name is Marie and she's from Senegal. Black, of course. We first met the other day as I sat on a park bench reading, next to a playground at the foot of the Superga, close to the Po. She was there with her son and although all he did was run up and down the gravel paths and swing around the climbing frames the way kids do, the other mums reacted as if her little boy was afflicted with AIDS, if not something worse, and had arrived from Africa for the sole purpose of infecting their pure-blooded Italian babies. One mother shouted at her daughter anxiously when she saw her talking to the little black boy and when the girl didn't stop, she went over and dragged her away by force. At that moment I felt a sudden surge of shame, for this woman and the way she behaved. Admittedly, we all have our share of fears, paranoias and anxieties, I for one, am scared of herpes and syphilis and avoid touching strangers in general, but this really went too far. Even for me. The black woman, Marie I mean, actually looked perfectly normal. Decent clothes. Subtle make-up. She was not your average beggar or Gypsy woman in a garish skirt with dirt under her fingernails rattling a plastic cup under other people's noses, or making a grubby child, dressed in a tracksuit with holes at the knees, swipe other children's toys. I couldn't help it, I got up from my bench, walked over to her and apologized. I said I was ashamed for that woman. Marie gave me a doleful smile and muttered that I had nothing to apologize for. So that's how we met.

I open the fridge, but I don't feel like eating anything, lately I haven't been feeling hungry, I've even lost some weight, as if that was what I needed. I should eat something though, it will be too late by the time I get back from the Circolo. In the end I cut off a slice of dark bread and spread some *stracchino* on top. I add a few slices of cucumber. Me, who used to consider myself a gourmet, loved grilled prawns and would go all the way to Pasticceria Ghigo to buy the best meringues in all of Turin, who used to look forward to every trip to Genoa to shop for fresh pesto or stuffed pansotti with walnut sauce. And now? I don't enjoy food, nothing inspires me. I eat only to fill the hole in my belly.

Marie and I went for some salad and couscous at Exki the other day and she told me the story of how she came to Italy five years ago on a student scholarship and stayed, met Karim and had a son, Christophe, with him, how Karim abandoned them and went to France because he couldn't find any work here and she hadn't heard from him since, all he left behind was the son as a souvenir. She told me about the time she was on a tram full of people and got screamed at by some madman, maybe he was a racist, or a racist madman, just because she happened to glance at his bag and that wasn't the done thing. He wasn't having that, his bag and its contents were none of her business, that's what he shouted, sounding very aggressive, the other passengers just watched in horror but no one came to her defence, they inched further away instead, pretending it had nothing to do with them, no one interfered. 'In a word, there wasn't anyone on that tram like you,' Marie said to me and it felt good to hear that. Luckily, that was the end of it, the racist madman got off at the next stop, but she had a little cry at home in the evening. I listened to her with fascination and thought to myself, now isn't this something, how different from Gabriela and Silvana and their adolescent drivel. This is a real woman who's been through a thing or two in her life, someone you can learn from, and I couldn't help myself and had to tell her, I said, 'you are one strong and admirable woman, I like you very much,' I said, 'I'm so glad I've met you, I don't want to be like those Italian people who've made your life hell in this country.' But Marie didn't seem particularly cheered up by that and kept looking at me with those sad, resigned eyes. I was rather taken aback. So I left it at that.

Not for the first time it occurs to me that I might have offended her somehow. After all, she comes from a culture I know nothing about. But even on reflection, I can't see anything objectionable about what I said. I think it's good to be open with people, to tell them how you feel about them, to spell it out – I think you're nice, I like you. I used to find that difficult, I was shy, but it's something I can do now. People rarely say these things and I think it's a shame. And the only reason it makes people uneasy is because they are not used to it.

As I eat, I glance at the calendar on my mobile to check what else is on this week. I am going for a run tomorrow, on Wednesday I'm going to an exhibition at the GAM with Giselle, on Thursday I'm seeing my mother, I promised I would finally drop in on her, on Friday I'm meeting a colleague from school for a coffee, and I might go to the Langhe at the weekend, a bit of *agriturismo*. I can't complain, my schedule is always full, I have some good friends, people I can rely on. My situation is totally different from Gloria's. Although admittedly, it's usually me who takes the initiative, but that's only natural, my girlfriends are around forty, most have a family, a job, obligations, they don't have the time to keep up with what's happening in and around Turin, to keep track of all the exhibitions, films and shows, of every *sagra del tartufo*, Artissima and so on. I have slightly more time to spare. And if I can't find anyone who is game, if no one is available on a particular day, I don't mind going to the cinema on my own. Lately I've been into children's films. Not silly stuff like *Alvin and the Chipmunks*, I don't stoop so low, but family movies such as *Ice Age* – really witty, I've seen all three parts several times, or Tim Burton's *Alice in Wonderland* – the cinematography, the imagery! or *Kung-Fu Panda* – I could do without the action scenes but the general message appeals to me. It seems to me that, on the whole, children's films are often better than those for grown-ups. They have a message. Such a shame that the children don't always get it and that they are just interested in the action scenes. And then they grow into the kind of people who turn up in my classroom and sit there without understanding anything and responding to nothing.

I've never been like that. And I'm still not. Ever since I broke up with that twerp whose appreciation of art was limited to blue UFOs in 3D, I've enjoyed life to the hilt. I have to catch up on all those years I wasted in front of the telly with the likes of Luciana Littizzetto in *Che tempo che fa* as my only form of entertainment. Trying to fool myself that this was what genuine marital bliss was all about.

Like this exhibition of contemporary Chinese art I've been to recently. Some of the paintings were just breathtaking. For example, a large canvas looking like a misty bathroom mirror, and in the only tiny bit of surface that's not fogged up you a see a woman wrapped in a bath towel who's just come out of the shower. Or a painting showing a scene as if viewed through the windscreen of a car, a lawn at night or rather some clumps of grass illuminated by the headlights at the front and disappearing into complete darkness at the back. Simply beautiful. Taking pictures was allowed there. I took photos of everything. I would have preferred to buy a catalogue with reproductions of all the paintings, but I'd have to be earning rather more to afford the catalogue of every exhibition.

Maybe I could make the painting of the woman wrapped in the towel my profile picture. Or maybe not, my mother might get the wrong end of the stick and start bombarding me with messages, taking me to task for posting such immodest bathroom pictures of myself, thinking it's me. Mother has to have everything explained. Mother needs to be in on everything. Or rather, she would like to be in on everything. She'd like to keep an eye on me constantly as if I were fifteen, but I saw through her a long time ago. I share with her only the bare minimum of information about what I'm doing. I'm sorry, but at a certain age you have to cut yourself loose and stop expecting your parents' approval for everything. I mean, your mother's approval.

As for my father, he might as well not be there. Not now, nor when I was growing up. Greyness is his essence. He blends in with his surroundings. Doesn't push himself forward. Has no profile. I've never seen him excited or angry about anything. He just is, although he might as well not be there, it wouldn't make the slightest bit of difference. My father is fixed in my memory sitting in an armchair and reading *Tuttosport*. Although I wish he could really be into football, like a proper fan. Not quite an English hooligan, but at least something. But he isn't. He will watch the news, throwing in the odd comment if Mother happens to be in the room. Or not, if she's not around. He doesn't even go to a bar to watch the games with other men. He watches at home. And if Mother wants to watch something else at the same time he doesn't protest. He just goes to bed early. I've never heard him shout: 'YESSSS!' Actually, have I ever heard him shout at all? Be upset? Tell me off, or my sister or my mother? In short, as I say, he might as well not be here.

Actually, hang on, he did get angry once. It was the Christmas before last, probably the last Christmas we all spent together at my parents' place. Father had been a civil servant, working at the town hall. Retired at forty-eight, that used to be quite common in the civil service, but he has this bad habit, or maybe even an urge: when other people are around, he will sometimes say that he's tired, he's worked enough in his lifetime and everyone should just leave him alone. I don't think he really means it. Or that he means anything by it. He just says it. He could just as well say something else, in that dull voice of his. But this is what he says. And at that Christmas Eve dinner it really pissed my sister off. My sister is fifty-one, so when he was her age, he'd been retired for three years. Whereas she is a doctor at the Molinette Hospital and works really hard, I have to give it to her. No slacking like in my job at school, which leaves me enough energy to go out in the evenings to cultural events and have coffee with my girlfriends in the afternoon. My sister works proper shifts, plus she has a family, two children. So, my father started singing his old tune about how he'd done enough work in his lifetime and wanted everyone to leave him alone. And my sister said, sarcastically, 'of course Father, absolutely'. And he said, 'what are you trying to say?' And my sister, 'oh come on, nothing, just go and read your newspaper, FC Turin is bound to lose without your watchful eye'. And she went on like that until Father exploded, stood up, banged his fist on the table and yelled, who did she think she was, the little brat. My sister got up as well, she didn't bang her fist on the table, she just said, 'I've had enough, how dare you, I'm not a five-year-old anymore', and then, turning to her children and husband, 'we're going'. And that was the end of our traditional family Christmas.

But other than that, unless my memory fails, my father is a smooth surface undisturbed by any waves, not exactly your emotional type. In fact, I envy my sister for managing to provoke him like that, to yank him out of his lethargy. I've never been so lucky. The height of my father's get-up-and-go is mowing the lawn from time to time. Sometimes I think he will die of boredom. That will be his end. The same as his life. My father will stay faithful to himself to his last breath.

I've finished my dinner, I clear the table and put the remaining *stracchino* back in the fridge. I get changed, obviously I am careful to avoid that particular movement as I pull the T-shirt over my head, my right shoulder has a tendency to dislocate, it just pops out of its socket, glenohumeral subluxation is the medical term, it's as painful as hell. I can pop it back in but it can take a while, sometimes I really have to struggle with my body and I've learned now that the longer it takes me to fix my shoulder, the longer the pain will last. That is why I take great care to avoid any hasty movements, I make sure to use my left arm when I need to reach for something that's fallen under the couch, or I take the liquid soap off the shelf in the shower with my left hand, I do the dusting with my left hand too. For all intents and purposes, I've been retraining myself to become left-handed as a grown-up, weight-lifting is out of the question, oh well, you have to give up certain things as you age. And suddenly I see my mother before my mind's eye, who knows what she has had to give up late in life, and the thing she must find hardest to accept was that her daughters are trying to keep out of her way.

Because my mother, by contrast, is present. Far too present, in fact. The usual story. She compensates. My mother spreads like mildew around the window. She devours everything that happens to find itself in her way. Overpowers it, suppresses it. She's everywhere. When I'm with her, it's as if she was twice my size, with me being just a kind of external appendage to her body that has never managed to cut itself off. How could an appendage cut itself off? It has withered, atrophied, become defunct. She drags it behind her. It no longer tries to respond. It refuses to carry out the functions it is expected to. It may no longer be able to. While, at the same time, it has never learned to be independent.

How can I enjoy being in her presence if that's how she makes me feel?

When I'm alone, when I have only myself to rely on, I feel like a normal grown-up woman. Which I am. A fully-fledged member of society. Maybe not a highly respected one, but even so. But when I'm with her, I'm nothing, just a defective rotten egg that has given her nothing but disappointment.

Of course, I love her more than anyone else in this world. But I can't stand being with her. I can't be myself when I'm with her.

All I can be is that rotten egg that is dependent on her. That's why it's so difficult. And what is even more difficult is that she is not aware of it and would be very hurt if I ever suggested such a thing. She means well, I know she wants to help me, I really do. She keeps ringing me, sending WhatsApp messages, comments on my Facebook posts and my likes. In a word, she asserts her presence in my life more than is healthy. Even though we don't meet face to face very much at all. She would like to, but I resist. And I curse modern technologies that enable her to insert herself into my life. Without asking. Whenever she chooses to. And she makes ample use of these opportunities, she has done so especially over the past year, since I broke up with that twerp. It's no use telling her that I'm doing fine, that I'm quite content, that there is no need to worry if she doesn't hear from me for a few days. She is convinced that I'm unhappy, lonely, in distress. She wouldn't dare do that to my sister, bombarding her with messages, phone calls, demanding a reply. My sister has her family and, what's more important, she has managed to set some boundaries. Enough is enough. Whereas I have only just started to learn – unsuccessfully so far – how to build fences.

I decide to wear my favourite pleated skirt and blouse but before putting on a jumper, I go to the bathroom and struggle to apply some pain relief cream to my lower back, I know it's useless but at least I'll know I've tried. Then the jumper, boots, coat and scarf, grab the keys off the hook in the hallway, and I'm out. The music from the students' flat next door seems to have got louder, heigh-ho, *movida* is everywhere, *movida* has reached even this remote part of Chieri, nothing can stop *movida* and it gets louder and louder as the evening goes on, until it penetrates the walls of my bedroom, but I don't care, I'm going out now. I run down the stairs to the ground floor, my electrician neighbour is still watching TV of course. Through the curtain I catch a glimpse of Maurizio Crozza in a wig – he must be doing an impression of Renzi, that's right, he's showing off his goofy false teeth, these comedy shows, political satire, I don't know, I've always regarded it as entertainment for boring people who have to kill time at night before going to bed and then to work the next morning. People like my sister.

My sister could hardly be more different from me. OK, boring sounds rather arrogant, so I'll try again: normal? settled? not-sticking-out? Grown-up, maybe. That would appeal to her. My sister is twelve years older than me, when she turned forty, I was tempted to wish her happy birthday by saying: 'don't worry, it's all right, you've always seemed awfully old to me', but I stopped myself, of course. However strained our relationship may be, I wouldn't want to be mean to her, even though she is mean to me all the time. But the fact is, my sister turned forty eleven years ago. Now that I am getting inexorably closer to old age myself, how old does that make my sister? I might as well say that we have no relationship whatsoever. I would find it difficult to describe the kind of relationship we had when we still had one. By the time I started primary school, my sister was eighteen and had her first boyfriend. By the time I was in my first year at secondary school, she had given birth to a boy, by the time I went to university, she was on the verge of a divorce and although it didn't happen in the end, I remember her screaming at me that I had no idea what life was about, out of sheer frustration that her husband was cheating on her.

This is actually a kind of refrain that I've been hearing for as long as I can remember. I don't know anything about life.

Real life, that is. About working in a hospital, about family – real family, mind, with children, not that provisional bond of marriage with the twerp. My sister's favourite saying is: 'you can't call it a family if you don't have children'. I don't know anything about real problems, seeing as I'd never had any, had I. Basically, my sister had never felt that my life deserved the label 'real.' Hers was the real life, while mine was just 'as if'. Every time someone mentions a strong sisterly bond, I have trouble imagining what that might be like. One sister confiding in the other? One sister asking the other for advice? Two sisters whispering under the duvet?

I stop outside the front door and try to think where I've parked the car. Yes, I know, *mannaggia*, quite far away, by the post office. My sister thinks I'm a hypochondriac and I don't deny it, I am a hypochondriac and I do realize that it's not quite normal to clean my hands with a wet wipe after every trip on a bus. I accept that I'm not likely to catch syphilis just by sitting on a public toilet or that people with herpes have only herpes and are not lepers to be avoided like the plague, I accept that in certain respects I'm over the top. But do I really deserve to be treated with such open contempt? If I ring my sister in a moment of weakness – she is a doctor after all, who else should I turn to if I have a health problem or a panic attack? – do I deserve to be screamed at and told that I ought to take a homeopathic pill for my nerves instead of bothering her with my pseudo-problems? Because I have no idea – there we go again – what it's like to look after a family and children, 'you have no idea, Olivia dear, what such grown kids get up to, what kind of places they hang out in at night and what shady characters they hang out with, what state they are in when they come home in the small hours, and when they collapse onto their bed you can never be sure if it's just alcohol or if drugs were involved, and you ring me to ask how likely you are to get herpes if your cappuccino was made by a waiter with a cold sore?! Come to your senses, for crying out loud'.

Admittedly, the herpes problem is slightly ridiculous although when I feel anxious, it doesn't seem ridiculous at all, on the contrary, I dash over to the sink and frenziedly run hot water over everything touched by the cashier with herpes, but I do have some genuine health issues. I feel that my body is increasingly failing me, almost like I'm falling apart. My joints, it's the joints in particular, they are slackening, loosening their grip, they no longer hold the bones as tightly as they should. The worst thing is the subluxation of the shoulder I mentioned earlier. The first time I dislocated it, years ago, it happened while I was hanging from a bar on a climbing frame in a playground. My sister's children were still very young and I wanted to show them how to move hand over hand. I used to be good at it at secondary school. I gave a groan, let go and fell to the ground, writhing in agony, not knowing what had happened or how to fix it, it felt as if my shoulder had ended up somewhere else, in the wrong place. My sister's children stared at me flabbergasted. And for around twenty years now I've lived with this dislocating shoulder. I tried rehab but it was no use. I was advised against surgery. They say the result is rarely worth it. I've learned what kind of moves to avoid and sometimes I manage to go for six months at a time before it happens again, I'm quite a pro now. I know I should stop running, but my legs are still functional. Although there are moments when I feel I might end up with a dislocated knee too, or perhaps a thigh, I mean, how should I put it… sometimes as I run there is this strange clicking noise in my legs, as if my entire thigh was about to disconnect, yank itself out of joint. If I'm not careful. But how can I be careful while I'm running? Nevertheless, I keep running like mad, as if my life depended on it. Sometimes I imagine that I will fall apart completely inside, my joints slackening for good and refusing to do their job, that I will turn into a pile of bones floating loosely around my body and eventually beginning to force their way out through my skin, gouging holes in it.

I dismiss the thought. All right, so what is the point of having siblings? I know that people produce two children to make sure the first one is not left alone, that they support each other later in life. When their parents are no longer here. But how many siblings do I know in real life with this kind of strong bond? Siblings who support each other? Two? Three? Sure, I imagine that when you're little, it's nice to have a brother or a sister to play with at home, in your nursery. But later in life? Once they grow up, the siblings go their own way, start families of their own and forget their original family, and they go on to produce two children apiece so that their children don't end up alone even though they themselves, incorrigible as they are, see their own brothers and sisters only at weddings, christenings and wakes, when wills are read, or in court, as the case may be.

As I get into my car and start the engine, I suddenly see Lucrezia in my mind's eye, that wide grin I captured in a photo one day when we were messing about with a camera. Lucrezia was like a sister to me, or as I imagined a sister should be, the sister I longed to have. 'Lucrezia! Lucrezia!' I used to call across the courtyard from our balcony, 'Lucrezia, will you come out and play? Lucrezia, I've got new plastic animals! Come and have a look! Lucrezia, you can't come today? Again?'

Why does it seem that with all my friends I have always drawn the short end of the stick? That all my relationships have been unequal and that it was my friends who have always had the upper hand? Actually, I know why. It wasn't until much later that I understood why my mother resented Lucrezia so much. Lucrezia was always the one who came to my house, never the other way around, she would come and the two of us, shrieking and running around, would turn our flat upside down, only for Lucrezia to go back home afterwards, leaving Mother and me to clear up the mess. But Lucrezia couldn't come very often, because they had visitors, or other plans. Sometimes she didn't show up when she was supposed to and I would stand on the balcony shouting 'Lucrezia! Lucrezia!' at their closed windows, I would stand there shouting for half an hour until a neighbour came out on the balcony and yelled at me to shut up already. My mother never said anything about it. I think she suffered. But later she would always get her own back on Lucrezia. She made her help me put the toys away – 'I don't care if you have to go home' –, or she would pretend for an entire month that we were terribly busy so Lucrezia couldn't come, 'not today, you have homework to do, and certainly not tomorrow, we're going shopping for boots. At the weekend? You must be joking, have you forgotten you have a swimming lesson in the morning?' She used this sarcastic tone when speaking to her, sometimes told her off and eventually Lucrezia said she'd rather we played in the courtyard. Why did we never go to her place? I didn't understand it back then but now I think I know why. Lucrezia had two younger brothers, her mother must have been glad to see the back of her for a few hours and having yet another child under her feet would surely have been the last thing she wanted.

Later, after we moved house, I was broken-hearted to have lost Lucrezia. I was in tears night after night. To console me, my mother said I could keep meeting Lucrezia, we hadn't moved to the other end of the world after all, not even to another city, we were just a few streets away, but she must have known how it would end. Once we moved, Lucrezia vanished from my life for good. But she seemed to stage a comeback again and again, in the guise of other girls: Silvana, Gabriela, Yone, Nadia... And in all these friendships the same pattern would be repeated – I would get extremely attached to them, but vice versa not so much. My mother always held this neediness against me, she must have suffered because of it, I don't remember her being nice to any of my friends, not one. She kept finding fault with them. None of them was good enough for her. One had fat thighs and a hysterical, squeaky laugh, another had ears that stuck out like fans and tried in vain to cover them with her long hair, yet another was pimply and stupid. Not to mention the one who blew it in the first few seconds by addressing my mother as 'auntie' the first time they met. My mother spared no one, it was total character assassination every time. With Lucrezia she constantly pointed out that she was ruining my toys or stealing them, that she was nasty and deceitful, but because that had no effect and I loved Lucrezia just the way she was, my mother would bring out bigger guns and call her a Catholic hypocrite, 'even if she doesn't steal one of your toys, she'll certainly hide your favourite teddy bear in the cubby-hole'. I refused to listen to her, resented her for being so scornful and patronizing, and for making sarcastic comments, and the same thing happened later, whenever I was stood up by a friend or couldn't find anyone to go to the cinema with. I hated the way she kept insisting that

I shouldn't be so needy, that I should stop calling them all the time and beg for their favour and attention, that I should live my life without getting attached to someone else, as if I needed their validation to exist.

Funny she should have been the one to say that. Because, as a matter of fact, she has always been the most irritating and pushy presence in my life. A girlfriend I can always get rid of, but my own mother? How can I ever break free of my mother? I expect that when she dies one day, I'll be left with a great big void in my belly, shooting pains like bullets making my bowels fall out, and I will have to spend the rest of my life with this unhealable wound and suffering the worst anxiety and emptiness imaginable.

The roads are quite empty too, fortunately they've been gritted. I drive through the forest near Pino, then a tunnel, it's really foggy, snow is all I need, as I reach the top of the hill I can't see anything at all, never mind, I can never see the lights on the Superga through the thick undergrowth, but I know it's there somewhere. The girlfriends were just the beginning, of course, my mother always had to have her say about the men in my life as well. Not so much about the twerp, she didn't have a problem with him, he was my long-term partner, the man who had chosen me, it was more my earlier relationships she commented on – over and over again – the sudden crushes that I plunged into headlong. Whenever she sensed that I fancied someone who didn't reciprocate my feelings. When I was younger. I suppose she hated the idea that someone dared to disrespect me, her daughter. Now, seventeen years on and after the twerp, my mother has done a complete about-turn. Now she thinks it's ridiculous that the ageing spinster that I am should be so deluded – as she sees it – as to imagine that someone might want her. And she mocks me especially about my neighbour, the electrician.

His name is Pino, as in Pino Daniele and, like the singer, he is originally from Naples. Recently widowed, mid-forties, receding hairline, a wart on his left nostril. When I moved into my new flat a year ago, I was delighted to have such helpful neighbour who was so good with his hands. I can deal with many tasks thought of as a man's job but there are a few things I'm not up to. And Pino turned out to be very useful indeed. Electrician. Emergency plumber. 'If you ever need anything, Olivia, just call me', he kept saying, 'just tap on my window and I'll be there, I'll be happy to give you a hand.' And when I asked, 'how much do I owe you, Pino', after he fixed my light switch or fitted my sink trap, he just smiled and said, 'oh, forget it, a peck on the cheek will do, *va*'. So I'd give him a peck on the cheek, even though it felt awkward, but there was also something sweet about it, genuinely Neapolitan, I told myself, that's what I call character, that's what I call warmth, that's what I call openness, you don't see that in Piemont every day. But then, one day, he tried to embrace me in the courtyard outside the house, he had a bouquet of flowers, which he said he was taking to his wife's grave, he was a bit squiffy and suddenly gave me a hug, I was so shocked that I froze, and he whispered, 'are you alone tonight, Olivia?' He really was tipsy, I could smell the alcohol on his breath, it was revolting, and I was frightened that he might hurt me. I pulled myself free and spent the rest of the evening at home in the dark. Feeling anxious. Ready for – what? for him to break down the door, to *take me by force*? But he didn't knock, didn't climb the stairs to my flat, I guess he stayed at home and slept off his hangover in front of the TV. It has never come up since but now I know that I can no longer count on him for those small jobs. The awkwardness hasn't gone away, I'm petrified whenever we bump into each other in the corridor or in the courtyard, even if he tries to be as warm and friendly as before. The bastard.

I wish it was just him. My mother mocks me, says I'm paranoid, she laughs that every conversation with a neighbour makes me think they are after me. But I am a woman, and a woman can tell, of course, she can see the difference between a neighbour who gives her a courteous smile and says *buonasera*, and the one who asks in a hoarse, tipsy whisper if she's going to be home alone tonight. Actually, I don't need such extreme examples, it needn't be that transparent. A woman can tell when a man is looking at her with lust, when he might be 'interested', and when he is taking no notice of her. And it seems to me that ever since I've become single, a spinster, since I broke up with the twerp, more and more men have been coming on to me, especially older men, the kind I had never taken into account, as if they believed that I have no choice but to settle for anyone and be grateful, as if they believed that I was missing something basic, something they can provide, the penis between their legs, something every ageing spinster longs for, a casual little dalliance, because obviously a woman my age must have realized by now that no one would contemplate a long-term relationship with her, there are younger women for that, a woman my age has to be happy if a man – any man – condescends to satisfy her, entertain her for a while, plug her hole, patch up the void she feels without a family, without children, without a purpose in life.

Like the chap who runs the newspaper kiosk, every time he sees me, he says 'hello, signora' – with a stress on *signora* and staring me straight in the eye. Or another neighbour, a pensioner – I find these old men particularly repulsive, especially the really ancient ones, those over seventy – my first thought was, he can't be serious, I must be dreaming, he stopped me in the entrance hall the other day and said, 'hello pretty lady, where are we off to, school again, is it? Those kids, they don't appreciate how lucky they are to have such a pretty, charming teacher.' I was almost sick. To be honest, until then it had never occurred to me that a pensioner could look at a woman ... as a woman! Who does he think he is? He should be playing cards, reading his newspaper in a rocking chair, walking along tree-lined avenues admiring the autumn colours, and stocking up on adult nappies to make sure he can move freely, instead of pretending to be a man and paying compliments to a woman thirty-five years his junior. And above all, he should be singing the praises of his careworn wife for making tasty meals, wiping his piss off the toilet, instead of complaining that his wife never wants to go out, so annoying, he's not yet old enough to take to his coffin, ha-ha-ha, he feels like doing something quite different, hee-hee, wink-wink. Spare me, enough of this over-sprightly pensioner!

But if I talk about this to my mother, she just laughs and says, 'yes, Olivia darling, do be careful, they're all out to rape you in that brutal male world'. As if it really was unthinkable that someone might be interested in me. As if that was the most amusing notion in the world. But no, I'm not adequate, not good enough, not even to be raped. My mother gives a laugh and continues: 'the chap with the pasta stall at the market said hello to me the other day, you think he's flirting with me?' And if she doesn't feel like humiliating me quite so badly, she tries to belittle my experience and says, 'come on, you know what men are like, they'll try it on with every woman, it's got nothing to do with you, it's more to do with them, you mustn't take it so personally. Just ignore it.'

On the one hand, I know there's something to what she says, I've discussed this with my girlfriends a few times and they've all had similar experiences with strangers or neighbours, but on the other, I can't not take it personally. I'm sure that it's me they have in mind at that moment, it's me, specifically me, Olivia, they're hitting on. I'm the one who has caught their attention, I'm the one they're lusting after. But then sometimes I shudder and wonder whether I've lost the last shred of common sense and judgement, maybe I'm just deluding myself that every man wants to shag me, whereas in reality they would find the idea laughable at best and all this is just some kind of joke or contemptuous trick, what if I'm just imagining it, reading it all wrong?

Actually, that's exactly what happened to Gloria.

I park behind the Gran Madre di Dio, resigned to the fact that if I don't want to find my car key-scratched when I come back from the Circolo, I'll have to fork out at least one euro to the parking attendant, an Arab, to guide me to a parking space. I walk past the lit-up church and the view of Piazza Vittorio Veneto opens up before me, so beautiful, the beauty of that square never fails to take my breath away. What a shame the Christmas decorations have already been taken down. I cross Corso Casale on red, even though the *serata* doesn't start for another forty-five minutes, I'm in good time, jumping the lights is just a bad habit of mine, one I may have picked up from my students. To ease my conscience, I stop at the end of the bridge and wait for the green light there.

Next to me is a woman with a dog, a funny flat-faced thing, I have no idea what these breeds are called, some kind of a French or English bulldog, a pug, Pekinese, Bichon, I'm never quite sure. I don't know what's come over me but suddenly I bend down to pet it although I never do that sort of thing, the dog looks up at me and wags its tail, rather phlegmatically. Only then does the woman turn to me, I smile and notice that she's quite old. I wouldn't have guessed from behind, probably because she's so slim. She returns my smile. I catch a strange accent, something foreign, I ought to be able to place it, being a linguist, but I can't tell. 'I'm only looking after him for a few days. His owner is away on a business trip in Brussels or somewhere. She'll be back the day after tomorrow'. I nod. 'His name is Max', the woman says. The light changes at last but I'm too embarrassed to quicken my pace and overtake her while she's actually talking to me. We cross the street together and the woman keeps talking. 'I used to have my own dog, her name was Judit. A little mongrel. I got her from a dog shelter, I always took my dogs from the shelter. But it's not your fault that you come from a shop, is it, Maxi,' she says affectionately and bends down to pet the dog. Then she straightens up again. 'I loved her more than any other creature in this world'. I don't know what to say, so I ask, a little inappropriately: 'so what happened to Judit?'

We're now in Piazza Vittorio, the woman says nothing for a while, then she looks at me, shrugs her shoulders, I notice that her lower lip is quivering as she says, 'she died. Of cancer. She was already sixteen'. Then she shouts out, and it dawns on me, Polish, she could be Polish or some other kind of Slav, her consonants are soft as she wails, 'she detected that I had cancer and then she died of it herself.' I am concerned, as I notice that the woman is now weeping. She continues her story in a halting voice, between sobs, 'she was sniffing all the time, she kept sniffing around my left breast so much that I grew suspicious, went for a check-up and they found I had cancer. She found my cancer, do you understand? She saved my life. But I couldn't save hers.' She pauses. She is still weeping.

Alarmed, I wonder where the woman is headed with the dog, is she sticking to her route or has she, perhaps, changed direction just to talk to me? 'I'm so sorry', I try to sound compassionate but in reality, all I want to do is run a mile. Not to have to listen to her anymore. But the woman doesn't let go. 'I've been incredibly lonely ever since she died. She was the only one I had, no husband – no children, needless to say' – sob, 'just me and my Judit. And do you know what that bastard of a vet suggested?!' Suddenly she raises her voice again and it occurs to me that she might have had a drink too many, 'he suggested that I have her killed! I mean, he said put down, but I prefer to call a spade a spade. Can you believe that? He wanted me to kill Judit! They are all bastards, arseholes, these vets are, and they charge fifty euros, that's what they do it for. They're ready to kill a living creature for fifty euros. What gives them the right?! I would never let them do it, never.' I interject timidly – 'wasn't she in pain, from the cancer I mean ....?' The Polish woman, by now I'm sure she's Polish, it's not so much the softness of her speech but rather a kind of lisp, the Polish woman shakes her head but doesn't seem to hear me. Suddenly she grabs my shoulder, 'she died in my arms, we were looking into each other's eyes when she passed away. I've been alone ever since. I have no one.'

In something of a frenzy, I try to think how to get out of this situation. It's getting more and more uncomfortable. The woman is still crying, and I pipe up, quietly, 'couldn't you get another dog? If you miss her so much'. She laughs and says through her tears, 'can you see who I am? Just take a look at me. Can you tell how old I am? Come on, how old am I? What do you think? I bet you wouldn't guess that I'm seventy-nine, I can't possibly get a dog. Who would look after him when I die? It's not far off, I know that'.

I feel myself breaking out in a sweat despite the cold, especially under my armpits, what am I supposed to do? what should I say? I manage to stutter something to the effect, oh, don't say that, you can't know that, I'm sure you still... The woman gives me a sad look, almost as if I disappointed her. 'I should have died with her, every day when I get up, I ask myself, what are you still doing here? You should have gone with Judit. Do you have a dog?' I shake my head. 'Oh well, then you wouldn't understand. You can't understand if you haven't experienced the kind of relationship that I had with Judit. She was a dog in a million. I've had many dogs in my life, but there was only one Judit.' 'I see, I see', I mumble weakly.

We've reached Via Po, and in front of Pasticceria Ghigo the woman comes to a sudden halt. I stop too, ill at ease. I wonder what she's going to say now. But out of the blue, I see her falling onto me, collapsing on top of me, her weight almost knocking me over. I struggle to keep my balance, total panic, this is just what I needed, I prop her up and shout, 'what's the matter? what's happening to you? should I call an ambulance?' Jesus Christ, what am I supposed to do? She leans on me for a moment, not showing any signs of having a will or strength, but eventually, with great difficulty, I manage to get her back on her feet. She runs her hand through her hair, gives a wobble, but doesn't fall this time. She just mutters, 'sorry, I won't bother you anymore'. She touches my shoulder lightly and pulls on the dog's leash, 'come on, Max, we're going home', she walks to the pedestrian crossing and starts to cross. I follow her with my eyes for a long time before moving on.

In Via Bogino I punch in the code at the entrance, climb up the monumental staircase, push the glass door into the Circolo, the girl at the counter hands me a programme, Pasolini is right there on the cover, I catch a glimpse of a large glossy book on the counter bearing the same portrait. *Bestemmia*. Blasphemy. The girl informs me that the presentation starts in a few minutes, there is still time to pop over to the bar for a coffee, to take a look at the book, 'whatever you like', she says with a smile. I smile back, thank her and stare at Pasolini's bespectacled face on the cover, I open the book gingerly and look inside, documents, photos, some private, some from film shoots, sketches, notebooks, notes typed and handwritten, I come across a photo of a serious-looking PPP snapped through a window, wearing a winter coat, and a brief quote from his 'Wealth': *Oh, to withdraw into oneself and think! To say to oneself: there, now I'm thinking.*

When the doors open, I go into the auditorium and take a seat in the back row, near the end. The seat next to me is free, I place my handbag there. Just before the performance starts, a tawny-haired young man with a thick curly beard takes the seat on my left. There's a piano on the stage and a piano player. A huge screen. The lights go out, a young woman enters to the accompaniment of music, and starts to read from a book, she sounds very dramatic, I listen attentively at first, born on 5 March 1922, grew up in Friuli, one brother, Guido, the family kept moving from place to place, his father in prison, the relationship with his mother, summers spent in Casarsa, first poems at the age of seven, but gradually I lose the thread, my mind starts drifting in a completely different direction, only every now and then do some words give me a start – Catholicism, Marxist, petit bourgeois, consumerism, filth, *Idroscalo, Ragazzi di vita* – only to go out of my head again immediately.

All right, I might as well admit it, I was concerned about hygiene from the very beginning, I do like cleanliness, what's wrong with that. I always made the twerp take a shower before lovemaking, a bidet just doesn't do the job, luckily he wasn't very hairy but still, I was bothered by the smell of sweat that tends to stick in certain places and is almost impossible to get rid of, like under the armpits or in the groin. As far as possible I avoided sleeping with him in the summer months, because I couldn't bear it when he worked up a sweat during sex, personally I sweat only when running, I was grossed out by him getting... how should I put it, moist, basically, but as time went on it was no longer enough for me that he took a shower before sex, I felt that even in winter, at nineteen degrees indoors, too much of him would stick to me, so after lovemaking I ended up spending longer and longer in the shower scrubbing myself clean. I suppose he noticed, he must have done, that I spent an hour disinfecting myself after him, yes, that's exactly how I started thinking of it after a while, complete disinfection, there were times when I thought this was terrible but then I felt it was justified, be it as it may, I couldn't help myself, twenty minutes rinsing my vagina with the shower head. I was concerned that I couldn't give my vagina a deep clean, it's impossible, so I ran baths with *lavanda vaginale*, bought soaps with the right pH, tubes of antimycotic gel with applicators, but still it wasn't enough, and when I emerged from the bathroom an hour later I'd find the twerp sitting in front of the telly saying nothing, he didn't say a word, although he must have known what this was about, especially once I started to say no to him whenever I thought there was something wrong with him, like a spot that erupted on his face, or on his nose, spots on the nose are the most horrible, they are more prominent than the others, or maybe not, those on the lips are the worst because you can't be sure if it isn't herpes by some chance. I would often put him through a grilling before we had sex – what's that above your upper lip? are you sure it isn't herpes? why don't we leave it till another time, it isn't worth the risk, what's that red blotch, go and take a look in the mirror, you'll see I'm not making it up, you know what, I'd better not kiss you today, erm, sorry, but have you washed your hands properly? because if you want to touch and caress me down there, then really…

My gaze remains fixed on the screen onto which pages from the book *Bestemmia* are continuously projected, excerpts from poems, scenes from films including *Salò*, which I haven't seen before, not even the first twenty minutes, as I've mentioned already. OK, maybe I went slightly over the top. Living with me can't have been easy and sometimes I can understand why he left me. For that slut who, I'm sure, doesn't disinfect herself and swallows his sperm at the drop of a hat, and lets him stick it up her arse. Actually, I've come to the right place, an evening dedicated to Pasolini, what kind of people can admire Pasolini, it's all crap, poetry, art, highbrow and lowbrow. How could someone crow about art while picking up young male prostitutes and having it off with them in the park, someone who made films full of filth, it's obvious from the clips they're showing here, everyone naked, depravity in every film, not just the odd one, it's depravity upon depravity, yet everyone here looks so uplifted, listening reverently. Beware these intellectuals, the nation's *crème de la crème*, who knows what they get up to at home when no one is watching, when the front door is locked, what kind of dirty stuff. Some smear themselves with shit, others eat it, some enjoy pissing on each other, some shove thirty-centimetre long dildos into themselves, cucumbers, courgettes, maybe a long aubergine, the fags risk rupturing their bowels just to enjoy fist fucking. Men parading in suspenders and high heels, oh, let me be your little girl, a prick rears up under the suspender belt, hairy legs in net stockings. Women who enjoy smearing men with their menstrual blood. Men who enjoy drinking it. And switching partners, organising orgies and screwing cripples and screwing old men and screwing obese people and having two pricks shoved in at once, with a third one in the arse, while licking two more and whipping each other and strangling each other with dog chokers and... enough, enough, I can't take any more.

I raise my eyes and there's Pasolini looking straight at me, *it's impossible to tell what my scream is like,* that stern, ascetic, haggard face of his, *it is true that it is – so terrible as to disfigure my lineaments making them the jaws of a beast,* a stark naked Pasolini photographed through a window, *but it is also somehow joyous – so joyous as to reduce me to almost a child.* Pasolini with his limp but large genitalia, *it is a scream made to attract the attention of someone, or his help*; in an austere room with bare stone walls, *but perhaps also to curse him*; Pasolini sitting on a bed and looking at a book, *it is a scream that wants to let it be known in this uninhabited spot that* I exist *or else,* so relaxed in his nakedness, book in hand, propping himself up on the other, *that not only I exist but* that I know.

*It is a scream*, now he's lying in bed, *in which behind the fear one hears a certain craven accent of hope*, he's looking at me again, *or else a scream of certainty, absolutely absurd, in which there is the pure sound of despair*, he gets out of bed, *in any case this is certain: that*, he's walking towards me, *whatever this scream of mine tries to say, it is fated to last beyond any possible end*. Lights out.

By the time I've pulled myself together the lights in the auditorium have come on and everyone is slowly shuffling over to the lobby. The young man with the curly beard has left, I rush out, push my way through the crowd, 'excuse me, sorry', through the glass door, down the monumental staircase, a few steps along Via Bogino and now, at last, I'm walking down the good old Via Po. A homeless person on the ground here and there, I barely take notice, all I can see before me is Pasolini's emaciated face and inside me there's something akin to rage, this mind of mine that grinds on and on, like some tabloid paper, about Defilippi, and Gloria, about the twerp who has screwed up my life and if not that, it churns out something even more dreadful. I have to chase it away, replace it with something nice, the first thing that pops into my head is that we can see good things only with our hearts, what really matters is hidden from the eye, but if you tame me, we shall need each other, draw me a sheep, shit, why does it sound so silly now?

As I cross Via Montebello, I happen to look to the left and see the Mole, lit up like all of Vanchiglia, I wonder where the *movida* is at now, what they're up to in the bars and the toilets of those bars. All those young people, the hipsters, who I definitely don't belong to anymore, what am I saying, I've never belonged, but then again, do I belong in the Circolo, among the literati and the fans of Pasolini? The only place I belong is probably the school, with all the little shits like the ones on the bus this afternoon. One day I might end up in Via Po, being paid to walk a pug, and weeping about being too old to have a dog of my own because the dog, poor thing, might end up alone when I die, the problems some people have.

I reach the Po, stop in the middle of the bridge and look down into its depths, but there are no depths, the Po is as shallow now as a mountain brook, we've had no rain all autumn. That would make them happy, oh yes, wouldn't it make them happy if I hurled myself down head first, if I let this stupid head of mine that won't allow me to catch my breath hit the rocks down below, hit the rubbish, the bits of flotsam that have washed up there, the bottles and cans those idiots in Murazzi keep tossing into the river night after night, if my head burst like… like an overripe melon, I feel like adding, as it says in one of the exercises I make my students do. And then, I don't know what comes over me, I spit into the river, a thick gob of spittle, what am saying, it's not thick, I just spit like a Gypsy woman, I spit at the idea that I could be tempted, that I should end up like this, either right now or like that lonely Polish woman, or rather, like Gloria. Poor Gloria, strangled and thrown into a pond by Defilippi, wouldn't you like that, but Pasolini got what he deserved anyway, the poofter, the faggot, you may turn your nose up Exupéry but at least he had a positive message, at least he's given this world something *good*, which can't be said of everyone, certainly not of Pasolini. And what about me? what have I given this world? Enough of this kind of thinking, *wealth*, come off it, I tear my eyes away from the river and look towards the Gran Madre and suddenly my legs start running, as if they wanted to escape from me, even my legs can no longer stand the company of my own head, I run and at the end of the bridge instead of heading towards my car, I turn left and race up the Corso Casale, run across the park, my legs carry me along, yes, my legs have realized it, even before I have, that what I need now is to run, and the running is lifting my spirits, as it always does. I'm conscious of having two functioning legs that take me from A to a B, but that is beside the point now, I feel the concrete under my feet, the dark plane trees rustling above me, actually, there's no bloody rustling but who cares, I've fallen into a rhythm and breathe shallowly in the night, I know that this is going to cleanse me through and through, this is going to chase away all those stupid thoughts, all the muck and filth that has accumulated there, if I keep running long enough, if I break a sweat, the running will wash it all out of my body, all the toxins that have been accummulating under my skin for such a long time.

# LARA

As I dodge honking cars in the traffic jam on Corso San Maurizio, I'm aware that I'm not setting my younger son a good example, as I know that in the nursery they tell him, 'don't cross the road on a red light, first look left, then right', but I hold on to his hand and dive headlong into the flow anyway, praying that we don't get run over, that there is no dickhead at the wheel, only mild-mannered and careful drivers, with no desire to end up in prison for manslaughter, who will step on the brakes in time. I know I'm not supposed to do this, that it's not worth risking my life to avoid being five minutes late but actually, I'm running more than five minutes late, it's nearly quarter of an hour and Matteo will be the last child left in the after-school club again, his teacher will make faces again and cast pointed glances at the clock on the wall and Matteo will remain doggedly silent all the way home and when I ask him how school was today, he'll just look away.

Today, of all days, I mustn't be late, I've got plans for tonight, I grin, Luca and I have now reached the Assisi Primary School, because tonight's the night I'm going to the Pasolini at the

Circolo. I can't possibly miss the Pasolini, I've been planning this for a week now, my husband is due back from a business trip later today but I reminded him over the phone, I pleaded with him, 'you will be back on time on Monday, won't you, you aren't going to arrange any of those last-minute meetings or dinners, are you, you haven't forgotten that I'm going to see the Pasolini with Chiara on Monday'. My husband was getting fed up with me, 'all right, all right, go and watch that pretentious crap', like there's nothing more important, and I had to control myself not to explode and remind him how twelve years ago he made such a show of being a culture vulture, how he didn't mind going to see art movies at the Cinema Massimo with me and how eager he was to discuss them afterwards, before he showed his true colours. As soon as we tied the knot, he would park himself in an armchair in front of the TV and he has spent the best part of the last twelve years there providing a running commentary on my artistic endeavours. And my culinary skills. And reminding me that the creases on his trousers are not sharp enough. And that my cats stink, shed hairs all over the place, and sharpen their claws on the curtains. And going on about Jackie the dog I have schlepped in. Which also stinks. And barks. I could go on.

It's been ages since it last occurred to him that he could give me a hand and I stopped asking him to help out long ago. I've stopped counting on him. I've stopped feeling that I'm married. A friend put his finger on it when he referred to him as my flatmate. That's what he is, my flatmate. All we ever talk about is organisational stuff. With me ending up doing most of the organising, of course. I'm the one who makes sure everything is sorted, the bills are paid, no deadlines have been missed, and food is on the table. He's working. Shush, the husband is working. Earning money. Providing for us. So I have to grin and bear it. I can't demand too much. Or complain – come on, he's working, isn't he? What more do you want? What else do you expect a husband to do? That's what really matters, that's what it's all about. That's what my mother used to say before she died. But I also clearly remember the day she sat in my kitchen watching me iron his shirts. Cigarette in hand, she said she'd rather die than iron those dreadful shirts. Those were her very words. Mind you, there was no need for her to get a divorce, her husband died in good time.

I do miss her, I've missed her terribly ever since she died seven years ago. My mum came from Slovakia and even though she spent more than thirty-five years in this country, she never felt at home in Italy. She never had a circle of friends and acquaintances like she used to back home in Bratislava. She could never relax completely, and spent thirty-five years all tense, in a kind of cramp. Only when she went to visit her sister in Bratislava did she relax, as if she'd finally managed to flee from a hostile environment, a minefield. She'd breathe a sigh of relief, 'home sweet home. I'm among my own at last'. Even her Italian was getting worse in her final years. I kept having to correct her – 'Mum, stop mixing up *del* and *dal*, Mum, pay attention to what you're saying. I know you can do it.' She became defensive – 'what do you expect from me, you're the Italian, I never went to school in Italy.'

I often wonder what she would say if she could see me now. What she would think about the sort of things I do, what she would make of what I get up to. The idea that she's watching me from up above, seeing everything and disapproving of everything that I do, as always, because I'm doing everything wrong, aren't I, Mum, that she's clutching her head, you little ninny, you really are going bonkers, or that she just takes a drag on her cigarette and rolls her eyes. I don't wish she were here dispensing advice on how I should live my life, it's not that, we never agreed on anything, she'd never been happy with me, or with anything that ever mattered to me, but still, I would like Mum to be here, just so that I didn't feel so lonely, abandoned, and at the mercy of the world. Since she died, I've been floating in a vacuum, despite Matteo and Luca, despite a bunch of friends, male and female, despite the network I have in this country, in addition to my aunt and the rest of the family in Bratislava. Without Mum I feel – I know this may sound quite corny – as if there was no longer anyone keeping an eye on me from above.

But unlike her, I'm lucky enough to be at home here. I can't imagine living anywhere but here, in Turin, or to be more precise, in the triangle of the Vanchiglia district.

I don't have to rush so much on the way back as the three of us walk down Corso San Maurizio, then down Via Napione, take a shortcut past ASL until we reach our little cul-de-sac, Via Riccardo Sineo, a stone's throw from the Po. 'Matteo, would you mind walking a little faster please, stop right there, Luca, where do you think you're going, we're not going to the shops now, no Leone sweets for you today, our house is that way, off you go', up to the third floor as our house has no lift, they've been planning to add one for a while, it's been at the top of the agenda at every housing association meeting, 'so where are we on the lift front, what's holding things up?' 'The work is about to start, it's just a matter of days', I'll believe it when I see it. I don't mind the stairs at all, I envy Chiara, she has stairs inside her flat and claims she keeps fit by running up and down them, she brags about her toned bum, says her boyfriend also rates it very highly, she says that sometimes she tries to find an excuse to run up and down the stairs, three times in a row if need be. But my sons are unbelievable, plodding up the stairs ever so slowly, dragging their feet, luckily we don't live on the fifth floor, we'd have to get up extra early in the morning because, oddly enough, they're even slower on the way down. I take out my keys, we go in and the whole menagerie that's been waiting by the door pounces on us as if we hadn't seen each other just half an hour earlier, especially the dog, my little mongrel Jackie, God knows why I've schlepped him in, as my husband never tires of saying, the cats are also in attendance, Tiger is miaowing reproachfully.

'All right, all right, no one will be left out, just wait your turn', first I have to get organized, to make sure everything is done before my husband is back, in time for the Pasolini. First of all, I must turn on the telly for the children, that's crucial, that's our starting point. 'Off with your jackets, hats, scarves, gloves, put your shoes away and chop-chop to the bathroom now, both of you, wash your hands, Luca! properly, use the soap, one quick rinse doesn't count.' I'm in the living room by now, looking for the remote, I tap in channel 46, Cartoonito, excellent, it's Blaze, I'm off the hook, they'll both sit there glued to the screen watching monster trucks racing each other, and I can take the dog for a walk. I tip the dog and cat food into their bowls, pick up the leash, 'Matteo, I'm taking Jackie for a walk, keep an eye on Luca, make sure he doesn't get up to any mischief, won't you? you're responsible for your brother, I hope you realize that'. Matteo barely nods, mesmerized by the screen, of course I know that should anything happen to my children because of the stupid dog, it will hardly be Matteo's responsibility, leaving a seven-year-old at home to look after a four-year-old unsupervised, oh well, worse things have happened, although none of the mothers I know would ever do this, most of them are perfect, at least to judge by what they tell me. Especially the ones who've never have to spend any time with their kids, who have a busy full-time job but also an au pair.

I remember the time I invited over this little girl from Matteo's nursery, he had a crush on her. Her parents came round with a present for Matteo, it made me feel bad because I had nothing for their little girl, it had never occurred to me. While the children were playing I chatted to her parents, they said they let Sofia watch TV for ten minutes a day max, she's not allowed any more, or rather, the au pair is not allowed to turn the TV on, she's not being paid to take things easy, nose to the grindstone, her job is to stimulate the development of their offspring's talents and skills, to play with her, come up with creative ideas, to draw, take her kite-flying and to clubs. Her mother doesn't come home from work until nine in the evening, the father until ten, that's what they call looking after their child, brilliant, they put her to bed, read her a story and then at seven in the morning they hand over to the au pair who takes the girl to nursery school. Oh well, you have to make some compromises in life, my children watch quite a lot of TV, as I'm the only one who's with them all the time and one or other of the boys is ill nearly all the time, so the only way to preserve my sanity and stop myself from chasing after them with a rolling pin is to park them in front of the TV at least for a little while and breathe a huge sigh of relief.

Of course, when they were still little and when looking after them consisted of breastfeeding and nappy changing, I made resolutions of every kind. For example, I swore I'd never ever let them watch Teletubbies. When I saw that my cousin in

Bratislava let her kids watch the show time and again, I was appalled by those multi-coloured monsters with huge heads chasing rabbits around a green hill and waving their little hands – Teletubbies, Teletubbies, say hello! And: Big Hug! Let's have a big hug! Let my children watch something like that? Such mindless drivel? Never! I won't let that happen! Over my dead body! And how did it all end? Any guesses? Worn out by hours of beep-beeping with Matteo's toy cars and choo-chooing with his train set, I ended up pleading with him, 'Matteo darling, would you like to watch some Teletubbies?' And there I was, dangling a cuddly, whistling monstrosity in front of his nose, 'look, here comes Tinky Winky inviting you to his fairytale land, come along', I wheedled as I took a DVD off the shelf – I had the complete box set. He was totally entranced by Teletubbies, and so was I. When Luca came along, I no longer had any pangs of conscience, he basically grew up with Teletubbies, and one day, when I took Luca down to the riverbank in the pushchair and said look, this is the River Po, Luca happily waved his little hand and shouted: 'Po! Dipsy! Laa-Laa!'

As I walk Jackie along the promenade, a word keeps buzzing around my head, decorum, I can't get rid of it, what does it refer to, what does it mean, is that what my husband and I have been doing, maintaining decorum? Is it the outward appearance of a family? Should one maintain decorum in front of the children? Will it help them grow into level-headed young men whose family won't fall apart at the first sign of a crisis? Will they remember: 'oh yeah, mum and dad had some problems but they stayed together, in spite of everything.' Have our sons even noticed that we haven't really been together for a very long time? That we don't live with each other, only alongside each other? They seem to lack any awareness of the relationships in our family. They don't think it strange that their mum and dad never kiss each other goodbye or when we come home, that we never touch. Will it ever dawn on them, or, by the time they reach the age when they become sensitive to this kind of detail, will we be the last people they'll want to think about? Are we setting a bad example? Should I overcome my reservations to set them a good example? Is hypocrisy a good example? Or would I be a better role model if I ended this marriage at last and moved out, taking them both with me? If I were faithful to myself – and to the truth? But then why are all the children from divorced families so messed up, why is it so traumatic for them? Such a big trauma that they will fight to their last breath to prevent their own family, which they have put so much effort into establishing, from breaking up? Goodness, I hope they don't end up like those people who regard infidelity as a disaster of apocalyptic proportions and give up on the idea of starting from scratch. My mum brought me up on her own, but that never seemed a big deal to me. And since my husband and I have become estranged, the word divorce has taken on a distinctly positive ring, almost like the promise of a better tomorrow. Now I actually find the idea attractive. And yet I've done nothing to make it happen. And perhaps never will.

But let's take another look at the word estrangement. My favourite word at secondary school, my *chuchu* word, as the French say. My Italian teacher was impressed that I wanted to talk about estrangement with him, or rather, alienation, ah, alienation, Kafka, a whiff of concentration camps and a dehumanized world. I used to be so articulate and clever on topics like that, I relished it all, the drivel I spouted, although I had no idea what the words really meant. Or maybe precisely because I had no idea. And look at me now – I've become alienated myself. My husband and I have been estranged for years. Sometimes I talk to Chiara about it on the phone: my husband's sole purpose in life is to nag me, there's nothing he likes better than sitting in his armchair in front of the TV and pontificating. About me, about everything I do and try to achieve. The household – 'don't get me started, the place is an absolute tip, grime and filth everywhere, it squelches under my feet, one of the cats has pissed on the carpet, the other has ripped the couch to shreds. And the mess, the stuff scattered all over the place', he never stops griping, 'the electricity bill hasn't been paid, the gas bill hasn't been paid, where in this mess am I supposed to look for those old unpaid bills now. They'll cut us off. Not to mention your work, if you insist on calling it that.'

I do, actually, because I am working too. I translate film subtitles. From English and Spanish. For ever-dwindling pay. So little, in fact, that it's more like a hobby, I'm practically working for free. Sometimes he mocks me, 'go on, admit it, you're only doing it to get noticed and be cast in a film, so you can see your name up in lights.' Only a total dickhead could come up with an idea like that. I do the subtitling at home without ever getting off my chair, it's all done over the internet, I never get to meet the director, never see any of the creatives, let alone anyone from a foreign production company. What can I say, a moron.

Once, years ago, I helped out at the Turin Film Festival, I also had a stint as clapper loader on a film shoot, but that was a long, long time ago, a memory from my earliest days. I love the cinema. That dickhead can't forgive me for loving films because he has never in his life felt passionately about anything. I have my films, he has nothing. He is constantly channel-hopping while he watches TV, can't stick with one thing. If he picks up a book by some chance, his head begins to droop after five minutes, and he lets the book slide to the floor. I doubt if he's finished a single book in the past twelve years. He has no interests, no friends, he has nothing. Just his job and me. He makes an effort at work and then he takes it out on me. And lastly – the thing that he really can't stand about me is the very manner of my existence in this world.

He says I'm round the bend. 'Lara', he says, 'there's something seriously wrong with you, do you realize what your behaviour is like, what you're doing, what kind of impression you're making on others? Cut it out, Lara, stop running around, Lara, you never get anything done around here anyway, just look at this mess, Lara, why are you letting those so-called friends take advantage, Lara, don't you get it, you have to understand that there's no point, no one will do anything for you in return, you're so naïve, Lara, you make me laugh, Lara. Lara, will you stop flapping around the flat already' – 'But how can I not flap around, if you never lift a finger, if you never help out!' – 'Shut up, Lara, slow down, Lara, forget about all those people, what are you talking about, Lara, I can't make head or tail of it, Lara, don't tell me you've gone and complained about Matteo's teacher again? Do you want the boy to get expelled, Lara? You won't listen to reason, Lara, you're like a motorbike running on empty, Lara, with its wheels rearing up, the engine is on and running, it's all roar but no movement, stop pretending that you're working, Lara, I'm the one who brings home the bacon, they're just taking advantage of you, why don't you spend some quality time with our boys for a change, Lara, do something useful at last, what deadlines are you talking about, Lara, I wouldn't be surprised if you ended up paying them for your work on the subtitles, Lara.'

'Lara, Lara, Lara', I can't stand it, why does he have to mention my name in every sentence? Just as well that he's not around much, just as well he works in Cuneo and turns up only occasionally, that's the only saving grace in this marriage. The almost permanent absence of the other person. If he spent more time here, I would have topped myself a long time ago.

I bound up the stairs, almost running, throw the front door open with bated breath, phew, everything is under control, they're both glued to their seats, thank goodness. I let the dog off the leash, 'so how was school, Matteo? don't you have any homework to do?' But Matteo doesn't hear me because Blaze is pounding across an overpass, he's beating Crusher again, the dog has nestled down in his bed, the cats make an appearance, start to rub against my legs, 'what is it you want, my dears, you've had your dinner already', from the living room I walk over to the kitchen, it's all a single open space, all that separates the living room from the kitchen is a low wall, a different kind of flooring, different tiles, different colours. From the kitchen I go to the bathroom to empty the washing machine, I started it before I went out. I hang up vests, underpants, socks and shirts to dry and I know that my husband is right, something is seriously wrong with me, I've never been right in the head, that's what my mum used to say all the time, she claimed she'd never seen a child like me. From her I took it as a cattle brand, a stain, a mark of Cain, I didn't mind so much when my mum said it, but from my husband – how dare he!

I thought it meant that I would go round the bend sooner or later. As I was growing up I tried to imagine what it might be like, being off my rocker, what form it might take, obviously what I imagined was based on the films and books I was into at the time.

I thought I would start hearing voices and that arms would come thrusting out from walls, like in Polanski, or that I'd have visions, like in Altman, I would be a stunning blonde like those actresses who go around murdering men left, right and centre, courtesy of advanced schizophrenia, or perhaps something more low-key, less spectacular, severe depression and head in the oven, like Sylvia, and if I should survive, I'd be given electric shocks, of course, and have a lobotomy like Jack, and end up spending the rest of my life, in a wheelchair in some godforsaken institution. My fantasies never quite reached the point where I was chasing someone with a knife in a wig like Norman, that seemed too funny and absurd, only when I grew up did I come across a book that really fitted me, or at least the title did, *I'm Dancing as Fast as I Can*.

Faster, and faster still, I move so fast I can't stop, everything is in motion, my body, my mind, my thoughts keep hurtling on and I can't cope with them, can't switch them off, but I'm not crazy, I've come to terms with the fact that I'll never be sick enough to need medication, I ruled out schizophrenia long ago, it usually manifests around the age of twenty, and depression would have a hard time with me. I can't imagine anything capable of over-powering me, slamming the brakes on me, pinning me to the bed or under it, even though I sometimes wish there was something, I wish I could just lie here, completely slowed down, without any thoughts, and immerse myself in the darkness, in my innermost sanctum, like sinking below the surface of a lake, but I feel that I'm just skimming along my surface, gliding along it as if it was frozen and no matter how hard I try, I can't break through the ice, I feel I can't claw my way into myself, I'm too fragmented, I can't focus on anything, on myself, can't stay in one place, hold on to one thought, analyse it, embrace it. I feel that I always take on too much at once, things that annoy me, won't leave me alone, my life is too full, some might say it's hectic but that's not it, I'm just a stay-at-home mum with two children and a head filled with nonsense, I'm well aware of that and yet, these thoughts won't let me catch my breath, I can't get a grip on them, can't come to any conclusion or take a fundamental decision, and so I try, at least, to focus on the detail, on what is evident, anything that sticks out, anything in my body that is peculiar or typical, because my body is something I can at least see and feel, at least I can say that I understand what my body is.

But I draw the line at talking to my body. When I was younger I had a friend who had the habit of speaking very animatedly to the threads and yarn that she used to make friendship bracelets, she would fasten the one she was working on to her knee with a safety pin, and in every spare moment, at the bus stop, at school, she would sit down to braid them while telling her threads off, 'where are you going, you pink one, hello black thread, there you are, I almost forgot about you, you're just what I need now, hey, you, green one, don't hide, this is where you need to go'. I used to watch her, fascinated, she was otherwise a very shy and quiet girl, but when it came to her threads she would really let herself go. Well, nothing like that has ever happened to me, I don't speak to my hands, lungs or ankles, but I do watch them, I watch them closely. I try to be aware of every detail of my body, understand how it reacts to different things, what it likes, what causes it pain and how intense the pain is and when it subsides. And yes, pain is not necessarily a bad thing, at some point it stopped bothering me, or rather, since I gave birth for the first time I've been much less sensitive about my body, what interests me more is how it copes with what's happening to it, with cuts and grazes. When I bleed I'm interested in seeing how long it takes my body to stop bleeding, how long it takes for a scab to form and fall off, I observe the wafer-thin darkened skin that's left behind, I feel it with my fingers, test it. Skin fascinates me, its self-healing qualities, our largest organ that allows us to sense and experience so much, sometimes I feel that my skin is more sensitive than other people's, that it can absorb more, even though it is getting more and more pockmarked. I don't deny it, I often scald myself while cooking or ironing, the scars remain and I can date many of them exactly, I try to ensure that my body obeys my commands, I maintain it, look after it, but as the years go by and I notice that it is losing its suppleness and pliability, all sorts of problems and deficiencies have appeared. My body will either deal with them or they will remain and I'll have to learn to live with them, but I don't mind, I'll be happy to explore new territories. I welcome new challenges, it never ceases to amaze me anyway that my body has served me well for thirty-nine years and has rarely failed me.

My mum used to say, 'even as a child there was something seriously wrong with you, you were obsessed with your body, I was in despair, when other children were attached to princesses and dolls and toy cars, you as a four-year-old would squeeze my breasts and ask where the milk had come from and why it had stopped coming, what's in there now, mummy, what's in your breasts now, what's hiding in there if there's no milk, you demanded to know, they're so big, there must be something in there, in a word, you were incredibly logical, and then you asked me, enthralled, if my milk tasted good, if it was sweet, you wanted to know whether, as a baby, you had liked it and was there really no way you could take a sip now, and whether you would ever have such big breasts one day, would you grow breasts, too, and would they bounce up and down when you walk, you constantly embarrassed me with questions like that. Your nursery school was quite far away, we used to take the tram and you would always hum this little tune, something about breasts, the pussy and the bum, – you even invented a kind of bum dance – sometimes you'd sing about farts or shit or knickers, I remember one of your little ditties, mummy has a pair of knickers, oh-oh-oh, what a joy it must be, ho-ho-ho, you'd sing it over and over again, there was no stopping you. By the way, even as a teenager, you were fascinated by turds, whenever you saw one on the pavement, your face would light up, look mummy, a little turd, hello lovely, what a lovely little turd you are! Sometimes you would jump and dance around it, sometimes you'd say hello to it, you said hello to turds on the pavement but hardly ever to our neighbours. When we bumped into a neighbour in the hallway and they'd go, hello Lara, you didn't reply, you just gave me a surprised look, who's that? no matter how many times we had bumped into them before. At the swimming pool, when you were four, you and a boy from your nursery school had a conversation about nipples, his and yours, he said you didn't have a little ball there but he did, and then at home you wanted to know why, you would follow me into the toilet, even when I had my period and could barely conceal the blood, when you saw my sanitary pad you laughed, heh-heh-heh, you're a grown-up and you still wear a nappy! When you turned twelve there certainly was no need to introduce you to the idea of menstruating, you already knew all there was to know about periods, you were interested in every kind of bodily fluid and excretion, you always wanted to see your turd before flushing it down and wave it goodbye, you laughed at me when I wiped your bum because I would end up with a smelly hand, for a long time you refused to wipe your own bum, it was yucky, you said, you used to pick your nose and pull out the bogies when people were around and while eating you'd spit a mouthful you had chewed back onto the plate to dissect it, you did that quite often, and you liked to lick sweat, not just your own but also mine! And on top of that you were a right little matchmaker. In summer on the tram you'd lift up my skirt, my T-shirt, you always tried to expose me, show me off to others, especially my navel, you were convinced that the navel was the sexiest part of the body and that's why you wanted to humiliate me in public, you laughed like crazy and shouted, mum, show this man your navel, don't be shy, come on, many times I had to threaten to get off the tram and leave you there, or that we would both get off and walk the rest of the way, you were a real disgrace, my goodness, let me tell you I've never seen a child like you, I'm amazed you ended up OK, with a family, a husband and children, that you manage to function quite normally, but let me tell you, you were really hard work.'

This is the sort of thing I keep mulling over, my mum's banging on about how I turned out surprisingly well, considering what a little weirdo I'd been, oh mum, if only you knew the kind of mischief I've been getting up to lately, if you knew what a mess I've made of my life since you died. It's just as well you don't, though I would give my entire screwed-up life to hear your voice just one more time telling me off for being not quite right in the head.

I've turned off the TV, the boys are playing with their toy cars, or at least that was the plan, let them amuse themselves on their own, let their own creativity blossom, as they say. But it seems that the TV is the only thing that can keep them under control, Matteo is whimpering and Luca is bashing him on the head with a toy car, but no, I'm not going to intervene, I've done enough intervening in their… well, let's call it their games, enough is enough, they have to deal with it on their own, they can't expect their mother to hold a safety net under them every step they take. Since Matteo is the weaker and less assertive one, he might as well get used to it, this is just the way things will be for the rest of his life. But I don't want to watch them, I've got to make dinner anyway. I turn to face the kitchen cabinets and start taking out the pots and the vegetables, a chopping board, vegetables are a must. I turn the radio on to keep me company, sometimes it makes me sad how I was never able to tell my mum that I felt very close to her and it's no good telling myself that she knew. She was unhappy and lonely in Italy and that might have brought us almost too close as she had virtually no one else in this country. My father died of emphysema when I was six, he basically suffocated, I don't actually remember him properly, but Mum couldn't move back to Slovakia with me, it was still under communism, so we stayed here and for much of the time we didn't even know anyone we could invite to dinner or have a picnic with at the Parco Valentino on a Sunday, we would sometimes take a blanket and go on a picnic by ourselves. Later, as I grew older and made lots of friends, at school and at the film studio, Mum was a bit resentful, as if secretly she wanted me to be as lonely and unhappy in this country as she was, to not fit in, which would prove that she and I were alike, and, even worse, sometimes I suspected that she was trying to steal my friends from me. This may sound absurd, but the fact is that she would chat to them, wanted to know everything about them. She would grill me about their news, show great interest in them, and in later years she went as far as to phone them regularly, meeting them for coffee and, being just as scatterbrained as me, she sometimes mistook one for another, which was quite a faux pas, and generally she behaved in such a way that I often ended up feeling embarrassed by her.

Ah, embarrassment, faithful companion of my youth! Like everyone else, I was embarrassed at primary school. For example, I had a crush on our swimming instructor who made me stand on the edge of the pool and used me to demonstrate the correct arm strokes for crawl, but I clearly remember being embarrassed even earlier, in nursery school. The other children would hug their parents and shout, 'Mum!' when their mothers came to pick them up, while I would barely acknowledge mine with a nod, I pleaded with her never to kiss me when the teachers were around, on no account was she to embarrass me like that, and out in the street I wouldn't let her hold my hand, not even when we crossed the road, that was another thing to be embarrassed about. I guess these eccentricities and peculiarities of mine must have made Mum rather unhappy, but perhaps she didn't find it all that strange, I'm half-Slovak after all, and I'm sure my Slovak relatives don't express their affection in such a showy, emphatic and robust manner as my more distant relatives from central Italy.

And now? Sometimes I think it wouldn't do me any harm if I felt some of that early embarrassment, there's hardly anything that embarrasses me now, certainly not my body. At the seaside I don't need a changing booth or even a towel, not only do I not feel embarrassed in front of my female friends but the same goes for strangers, I bare my breasts as if they were no different from my nose or arms, it's an attitude I adopted while breastfeeding, that was a major turning point, or maybe it was when I was in labour. Actually, that surreal scene as ten strangers stared into my pussy even though that was the last thing they were interested in at that moment, that was the crucial point, that trivialization of my organs and my body in the hospital, not that it has left me traumatized or hurt, quite the contrary, it's been helpful, this is nothing but a body which another body forces its way out of, the body is not sacred, the body can be manipulated any way you like, anyone can touch it and deform it, open it up and torment it, abuse it, do whatever they like to it. And if anyone else can, then why not me.

The courgette has begun to splatter in the pan, goodness, I've used a litre of oil again, it's splattering all over the kitchen, I give it a stir with a wooden spoon while I turn down the water for the pasta, but I don't put it in it yet, I let the water boil until everything else is ready. I taste the Bolognese sauce, ouch, *cazzo*, I should have blown on the spoon to cool it, I've burned my lips again, I scald myself every time I cook or iron, or do any other household chore, it's not my forte. I'm much better at subtitling than at looking after my family and cooking, and to cap it all, I never learn from my mistakes, I will keep licking the hot spoon like an idiot, as if it hadn't happened a thousand times before. Never mind, I've survived pain that was worse.

But that childhood fascination, the fascination with my own body, exploring and testing its limits and possibilities, that hasn't changed, or rather, it's been reinforced by experience. Because pain is actually what started it all.

Things didn't go too well with my first boyfriend, I don't like to think back on it, my first boyfriend struggled, he fought with my body for many months, but it wouldn't submit, it refused to expand, to let him in. He managed to deflower me eventually but I can't tell when exactly it happened because the crucial part was missing, no blood stain was visible on the bedsheet as evidence. I've never understood why, all I know is that he kept pushing and shoving as he tried to get in, thrusting away as I writhed in pain and sobbed, the silly goose that I was, what was the point of weeping, and yet I did, and as a result I stiffened up even more, 'are you in yet', I kept asking, 'did you get inside, is that it?' and he – it was his first time, too – said,' I don't know if I'm fully in, if I can go any further, what do I do now?' 'just keep at it a bit longer.' Did I deserve to be deflowered in that way, did I really? We never found any trace of blood despite all our exertions, my boyfriend probably didn't believe I was a virgin, that he was my first, but he was. I was fifteen and had never seen a cock before, my boyfriend complained about having a small one, I measured it once, seventeen centimetres. Women who place ads usually look for twenty at least, but to me it didn't look like seventeen, fifteen at most, give or take, but I said nothing because it seemed more than big enough to me. It seemed enormous, frightening and, most importantly, thick, I was convinced that it was its thickness that was the problem, the obstacle to a satisfying sex life, so instead I said that it was big and beautiful and perfect. I covered it in kisses, gave him blow jobs, just so he wouldn't suffer, but in fact I was the one who suffered, I thought it would always be that painful, that I would never be able to have normal sex. I didn't want to suffer, I wanted to enjoy it, to find my G-spot as it said in the magazines, at fifteen I couldn't imagine that pain could be appealing, that it's also a form of experience, and a very powerful one at that.

    My life can be divided into the time before I gave birth and the time after, it was a life-changing experience, having two three-and-a-half kilo *putti* pass through my privates, and in some way that initial torment stayed in my memory as a time when I could still feel everything properly, when I was still tight as a drum, but at fifteen I had no idea. After suffering for a while, I broke up with my boyfriend, replaced him with another, and everything worked much better straight away. I don't think it was only because his cock was thinner, rather it felt as if something in my body had loosened, given way, it was suddenly ready to welcome this new man – and others who followed – and I enjoyed it. I wonder if someone like him would still satisfy me physically now, after I have given birth twice, would I even feel him during sex? I really do have a sense that labour has left me wider, that I could now insert something bigger inside. Then there was the effect that giving birth had on my day-to-day life, the second time left me incontinent for a few months, I was so desperate I resorted to Kegel exercises, doing them every free minute I had, I went to a pelvic floor clinic, I couldn't think of anything else, wondering if this dreadful problem would ever get sorted, I wore sanitary pads and considered myself a write-off in social and sexual terms, but things did get better, more or less. I no longer need sanitary pads although sometimes, when I cough or sneeze, there is a bit of leakage, who knows what would happen if I gave birth the third time, I might lose control of my bladder altogether and have to consider plastic surgery.

But I'm not willing to entertain the idea of giving birth for the third time, I try to see the funny side, I know a woman who has a phobia about seeing a gynaecologist, I find that really funny, a big deal, seeing a gynaecologist! Personally, it wouldn't bother me if I had to see one every day, I'm no longer squeamish about my body, too many people, men and children, have passed through it, it's no longer a carefully guarded secret that's poised on the edge of a swimming pool, embarrassed to let her swimming instructor use her as a prop to demonstrate the crawl, I think I might let a man do to my body almost anything he likes.

Maybe that's why I enjoy watching men doing things to other women, it's a relic of my first unhappy relationship, the less sex we were able to have the more porn we watched. My boyfriend liked the softer kind, the stuff for women, featuring two girlfriends who get up close and personal, that sort of thing, sometimes a guy joins in, preferably a beefy swimming pool attendant who can't believe his luck, this is every man's dream, a threesome with two women, I wonder why a threesome with two men isn't every woman's dream? Or with three or four or a whole gang. I no longer watch women's porn, I'm into the more extreme stuff, S&M, gangbangs, orgies, DP and rough sex, I watch it with a mix of repulsion and fascination, but watch it I do . Now and then. I don't set the bar too high, all that matters is that the woman should appear to consent, I can't stand rape scenes, and it can't be interracial. I'm a racist when it comes to porn, when it comes to porn I'm all for apartheid, black on black and white on white, no mixing please. I watch men pushing women's heads down, shoving it right down their throat until they almost choke, they're gagging but they can take it, I wonder if they had something removed from their throat, how they manage physically, there must be something to it, a trick, like Marilyn Manson, who had a couple of ribs removed to perform autofellatio. But who knows what the real story was there, maybe it was just empty talk that he was spreading about himself to sell more CDs, but those women, they do it for real.

After I had my first baby, I read on some blog for new mums

that watching porn is deplorable, especially when it's done by husbands who can't understand that in the first six weeks after giving birth, or rather, for ever after, a woman has a mountain of things to worry about other than the fact that her husband's balls are about to burst. Because women have to change the nappies, of course, they have to breastfeed and agonise over which jumper to put on their baby when they go out for a walk, or what is the most suitable first solid food, mashed carrot or mashed potato. Definitely not apple or banana, in case the little darling develops a sweet tooth and refuses to eat their veggies. Never mind. Let's not dwell on it. I feel sorry for these women, as there are things I can't bear to watch either, I can't believe that they subjected themselves to it voluntarily, they must have been drugged, at the very least, in order not to feel the pain, not to feel debased, to not feel, basically. And if some woman does it voluntarily, I'd be tempted to advise her to see a psychiatrist, because it must have come from somewhere, daddy issues, an inferiority complex, or a trauma of some kind, an unresolved relationship with oneself and one's own body, I'm convinced they have some sort of a problem. But then again, who doesn't. In any case, I thank God and all my stars that I have two boys, two men, if I had a daughter I'd be terrified that someone might abuse her, that she might let some disgusting pig hurt her. I can't even begin to imagine how the mothers of those porn actresses, the mothers of those sluts might feel, I would find it much easier to take it if it was my sons hurting someone, if they appeared in porn movies, changed partners recklessly. In their case it would be regarded as a sign of mental strength and virility, they would be the top dogs, but when I tell them to come to the table because dinner is ready, when I look at Matteo with his deep-set eyes and slightly dopey expression, when I look at Luca who can't wait to eat his yummy dinner, I know that being the good boys that they are, they would never ever hurt a woman.

With my older one, Matteo, the expression 'the poor darling' always comes to mind, he's so sickly and oversensitive, I want to hug him and caress him and look after him, keep him close to me, protect him. He's such a good boy, he's trying so hard, but no matter how hard he tries, it's no use, he just can't make friends at school with those thugs, he gets on much better with girls and that obviously makes him a laughing stock, even though to me he doesn't seem effeminate at all. He has a nice face, he is slim but well-proportioned, looks quite athletic even though he's very clumsy, totally unsporty. He always does his homework and likes to draw, he's constantly drawing maps of his fantasy worlds, sometimes he comes to tell me about them and who lives in them, and I reply, uhm, you don't say, how fascinating. But if truth be told, I don't listen to him at all, I'm usually running up and down the kitchen cooking, or I'm ironing, my mind is somewhere else, it's a miracle that he hasn't noticed.

He is my son, my beloved first-born, but he is also my husband's son and seems to be the spitting image of his father. He has certainly inherited his oversensitivity, the kind that is totally alien to me and drives me up the wall. The latest is that he weeps in silence, holds back his tears and says, in a choked voice, 'I'm fine, leave me alone', and retreats to the nursery. He's realised that I can't stand his hysterics, his gratuitous crying, his constant apprehensiveness, because he knows that I will start shouting hysterically at him if I think he's making too much fuss over nothing. I tell him – 'you're a boy, a man, you should behave like a man', but that just makes him cry even more, as he sees that his mother isn't happy with him, and then I feel sorry and vow never to say this kind of thing to him again, but of course I do, after a while I say it again.

This has actually got worse recently, now he no longer complains, he just goes to his room with a hurt expression in his face and stays there for the rest of the day, sulking, because I don't understand him and I'm too strict with him. But am I really supposed to think that it's OK for my son to start shrieking with horror at the sight of a bluebottle that's flown in through an open window? Anything that flies past him startles Matteo and makes him jump, he's even frightened by the tiniest flying insects, including fruit flies, let alone dragonflies and horseflies. And the dark, goodness, he's absolutely terrified of the dark, the other day we had a power cut and he howled with fear. It was so bad that I had to fetch a torch from the cabinet and look for him by following the sound of his voice and slap him across the face to make him stop howling and scaring his younger brother. Mind you, Luca the little devil, he just laughed at Matteo. Another thing he can't stand is the sight of blood, especially his own, but mine too, whenever I cut myself, he has to look away, the other day I took him to hospital for some blood tests and had to chase him around the waiting room – of course I didn't tell him in advance where we were going, he would never have come voluntarily. To sum up, my son is a wimp, a poor, feeble little thing, but then who is there to toughen him up, when his father is even worse?

When we go to the seaside it's a total farce, my husband needs to wear sandals to go into the water, the kind that won't float off, because the pebbles might hurt the delicate soles of his feet. Meanwhile his son is screaming his head off on the beach because a bit of sand got stuck between his toes. Back in the hotel Matteo is prone to tumbling out of bed every night screaming, while his father complains that the mattress isn't as hard as the one at home and how is he supposed to get a good night's sleep on a mattress like this, and to add insult to injury, the pillow is so uncomfortable, I mean really, even the princess on the pea can't have been so thin-skinned. But I have to give it to him, my husband takes a genuine interest in the maps that Matteo draws, he listens to his son and asks him questions that are to the point, like where are the horses' stables or how does the dragon get out of the enclosure, yes, sometimes it's a joy to behold, father and son chatting in the living room.

But in every other respect it was hell when Matteo was little, he kept falling over and you could never tell if he'd really hurt himself badly or was just making a mountain out of a molehill, he always shrieked as if he was being skinned alive, he always fell right onto his face, never put his arms out, no instinct for self-preservation, and generally, he kept trying it on, complaining that something hurt here, or there was a pain there, so that I'd comfort him and feel sorry for him. He wanted me to hold him in my arms, but it's true that he was often in pain, in the three years at nursery school he always had something, one infection of the middle ear followed by another, scarlet fever followed by chickenpox, the flu by bronchitis, atopic eczema by pus in the eyes.

I clear away the pasta leftovers, serve the vegetables and the meat, top up the boys' fruit juice and make a mental list: Matteo doesn't like the seaside because of the sharks and jellyfish that live in the sea and he might drown, Matteo is afraid to put his head underwater, because he can't breathe there and seawater makes his eyes sting, Matteo is scared to get on the climbing frame because other children would push and shove him around, Matteo is afraid to go to sleep with the blinds up, because a giant might come in and eat him up, but also with the blinds down, because then it's dark and he can't see a thing, Matteo is scared to get on his bike because he might fall off, Matteo is seven and still doesn't dare go on the swings because if it goes too high he might fall off, Matteo is afraid of going ice-skating because… he might fall. Matteo is really trying hard, Matteo would really, really like to, I can see it in his eyes, this eagerness to please me, but it's never good enough for me and I always end up screaming at him, calling him a silly little klutz and telling him to man up. Damn it, he's got to pluck up his courage at last, how is he ever going to assert himself in this hostile world if he doesn't let go of mummy's skirts.

God, I wonder what sort of mother he thinks I am if he's so desperate for my approval, never dares do anything off his own bat, totally lacks initiative or courage. I'm a bossy mother, a mother and father rolled into one, hard as it is I ought to admit that I've screwed up, that I keep yelling at him, that I lack the necessary patience and empathy and say things I wish I could take back as soon as I've said them, because they may scar him for life, they may have done already. It's hard to admit that I'm not coping, I've long suspected it and I guess it's true, what Matteo is most scared of is my disapproval, of disappointing me, what terrifies Matteo most of all is me.

My younger son, Luca, he's a little dynamo, constantly on the move, ever since he was born I seem to have done nothing but chase after him, around the flat, around the courtyard, around playgrounds, I must be quite fit although running has never been a favourite activity of mine, Luca is my little ray of sunshine, Luca is always happy, a mischievous little monkey, always cheerful, lively, not just lively but also resilient. There's something about Luca that makes every old lady that we meet break into a smile, something about him that makes everyone forgive him for his mischief-making, his cheekiness, in a word, Luca makes everyone love him straight away. So much so that people always say to me, what a handsome boy, isn't he cute, even though objectively Matteo is the better-looking one, his features are more delicate, but people never react to him the way they do to Luca. There's just something about Luca, that open little face of his, that is so keen, so hungry for this world, raring to go and try everything it has to offer.

The only thing that drives me to distraction is his laziness, but make no mistake, it's quite different from Matteo's clumsiness and apprehensiveness, Luca is unspeakably lazy if you ask him to do something he's not interested in, that he doesn't enjoy. Luca can take five minutes to put on a single sock, and sometimes it's not even on properly, I catch him sitting on his bed with half the sock hanging off his foot, staring into space, or scratching his leg instead of getting dressed. He's nowhere near as studious, thorough and conscientious as his older brother, but I just can't bring myself to be angry with him, he never clears his toys away no matter how many times I say I'll never buy him a new toy again, that I will throw them all out, Luca runs away to the bedroom, Luca slips under the bed, Luca hides in a tent or runs out onto the balcony. Sometimes I worry how he will cope at school, it will be sheer hell for him, he really can't sit still for a moment, but I tell myself that he may have a bit more sense by then, calmed down a little.

Of course, sometimes also I yell at Luca, if he's too slow putting his socks on I shout at him that he'll end up in a special needs school, a four-year-old should be able to put on his own socks lickety-split, but I know that it's useless in his case, he doesn't care, and it won't leave him with any lasting trauma, we both laugh about it afterwards. Besides, he knows perfectly well that I will give in eventually and put his sock on for him, so why bother. He's sharp, as my friend Chiara says. Oh gosh, Chiara, it's the Pasolini tonight, why are the boys eating so slowly, why do they have to pick at their food like this, they should be used to my improvised Michelin-starless cooking by now, oh dear, I suspect this is another thing Luca got from me, the reliance on winging it, he keeps trying to take his trousers off without using his hands, just by kicking them off.

Luca is inventive and daring, he also has something of my chaotic disposition, he is ready to throw himself into every dangerous situation, I'm not really sure if it's always a good thing, as if he had no self-preservation instinct. When he was two he clambered to the top of a very tall climbing frame in Bratislava and I had to ask some older boys in the playground to help me get him down. Luckily we don't have that kind of climbing frame here in Vanchiglia, or anywhere in Turin for that matter. He can really let rip at the playground, he learned to go on the swings a long time ago, he will talk to anyone, and has a tendency to start brawling and won't let me help him with anything, just as it says in the handbooks. He wants to do everything by himself, apart from putting his socks on, that is, and if I try to help him out, he is quite capable of whacking me on the head. He's sure he can manage.

I thought that having him around would be good for Matteo, that it would make Matteo less of a shrinking violet, but it's had the exact opposite effect, Matteo now sits on the bench with me like a good boy, a big boy who's grown out of all that playground stuff, at the ripe old age of seven. So Luca wanders off on his own, marches up to the next bench and starts eating someone else's elevenses, I dash over to apologise, but deep down I'm pleased, I'm on the side of the cheeky little monkey: that's the way. I still remember how upset my older son was when I wanted him to go on a see-saw with another kid instead of with me, when he was playing in the sandpit I had to tell him, 'hold on to your little shovel!' because he was capable of letting go of it and handing it to some toddler who scurried up on all fours. And then he would start bawling. To say nothing of the fact that before Luca was born, I found playgrounds rather stressful myself, whenever I saw someone hurt my son, I would be there like a shot, ready to fight, teach them a lesson, even swear at those cheeky kids, so that they'd let my son take his turn on the slide. And then I'd skedaddle if their little darling went off to complain to his parents that this nasty lady had said something horrible to him. Now I'm having a ball, my son is the naughty kid, and I can relax on the bench and enjoy the sun shining on my face.

So there I am, enjoying the sunshine on my face, lost in thought, and my mind keeps churning around willy-nilly. Sometimes I insist that my older son goes out to play and can't bear it when he comes back grumbling that someone has hurt him or wronged him in some way, but I no longer intervene, I ought to trust him to deal with it on his own, but I've noticed that he usually turns to his four-year-old brother. I pretend I don't see him as he circles the edge of the playground and makes no effort to chat to anyone. When he was little, he always wanted to play with me, but now I refuse, I've given you a brother, you really can't expect me to play with you anymore. But, at the same time, I know he's not entirely to blame, I think several things have come together, my attitude, and my own faults are part of it, for sure, but much of it is my mother-in-law's doing.

There's nothing surprising about that, seeing as she is the one who brought up my husband, he too is her handiwork. When Matteo was younger she would often take him out for walks, and exerted her influence over him, 'don't run, you'll get all sweaty and catch a cold, don't run, you might fall over, don't climb that tree, you might fall off and hurt yourself, don't go there, stop running, you could get run over by a car, don't lean over that fountain, you might get wet, don't run down the stairs, you might trip and graze your knee'. She never stopped going on in this vein and sure enough, he kept falling over. Even when she stopped taking him for walks, she would ring up and tell me to take care outdoors, to look after Matteo when we're out there, in the playground, inside the flat, in the playgroup, wherever, when he's asleep too, and I would say 'yes, all right, will do'. I didn't attach great importance to it at the time, I didn't pay much attention to it, I had other things to worry about, my husband and I were just beginning to get estranged. It only dawned on me later that this may be one reason Matteo has turned out the way he has. When Luca was born, my mother-in-law didn't take him outside so often, I didn't let her exert her baleful influence on him, and she was getting weaker physically, now she hardly ever leaves the house. She sits at home in front of the TV, polishing her china and worrying. About all of us. Well, let her worry.

My mum would have made a totally different kind of grandma, I'm so sorry that she didn't live long enough, that she didn't live to see Luca. Because what's the point of beating my breast, searching for reasons and justifications and pondering if it's nature or nurture or different kinds of temperament and character. There's something I have to admit, and it's difficult, maybe the hardest thing I've ever had to admit to myself: although I love both my boys equally, I really do, I don't feel equally close to them both, I do have my preferences, there's no point fooling myself.

As I pile the plates and cutlery into the sink, there's a thought niggling away at me, something I can't put into words. I make the boys clear their toys away, Matteo is the only one who obeys of course, here I go, thinking about pain again. No matter how much I love my boys, and I really do, whether I understand them or not, whether I dote on them or not, pain is an untransferable experience, an untransferable sensation, and just as I can't protect them from so many things because they lack my experience of the world, I can't take their burden of pain away and carry it for them. I'm particularly conscious of it with Matteo, he's a sickly boy, and whenever he has the slightest problem breathing, I feel it even more acutely, precisely because my own air passages are free. When Luca grazes his knee I become aware of the childhood scar on my own knee that has long faded, when one of them is screaming with pain, like the time Matteo had an inflammation of the middle ear and screamed and screamed for hours on end, it was so bad that I wanted to die, nothing helped, not Nurofen, Cilodex or Avamys, but I didn't feel his pain, I wanted to, but I couldn't, I felt no pain, though my child was in agony and I found that unbearable, it wasn't supposed to be that way. I wish I could take all the pain they will ever feel in their lives upon myself because, as I've said before, I am used to pain, I'm often not aware of it at all, I am interested in pain. But that's the one thing I can't do for them, I've given them independent bodies, they have forced their way out of me and now I no longer have any influence over them, they are no longer connected to me, we are separate organisms whether I like it or not, anything might happen to them, anything on earth, and not only will I be unable to prevent it, but I won't even feel it physically. And that's what I find very hard to come to terms with.

Once the kitchen is more or less sorted out, once I've told Luca off for not helping his brother and stroked Matteo's head, 'Matteo, you're mummy's little angel, thank you for clearing everything away', and once I've given the boys one more thing to do, to get ready for bed, I decide to clear out the litter tray for my cats, my two Aristocats, my husband is furious when I call them that, he doesn't have a good word to say about them, 'it's the hairs, the cat-hairs, Lara, I even find them in my morning cup of coffee'. In fact, only one of the cats, Tiger, is hairy, Lisa is short-haired and both my pussycats are beautiful and noble creatures that move around gracefully, looking down their noses at us, although I have to admit, sometimes it does happen, like the other day when I took the chicken out of the oven I spotted a singed cat-hair on it, I admit that Tiger sometimes strolls across the breakfast table and might take a peek into a mug to see if there's milk or something edible or drinkable in it other than coffee, once I actually saw him trying to dig a hole in the table to bury a buttered roll, he thought it was something disgusting that needed to be hidden, all right, all right, I know, but this is all part of life, if my husband wasn't so oversensitive it wouldn't be a problem at all. But with a mother like his, how else could he have turned out, the poor thing was never allowed to mess around with his toys in his own room when he was playing. Tidiness, tidiness above all, but I don't feel sorry for him, he's on the wrong side of fifty, he's had plenty of time to get over it. When I see him running around the flat with a lint brush to pick up the hairs from the couch, the armchair, the curtains, he cuts such a ludicrous, pathetic figure, what harm would it do if he sat on a couch with some cat-hairs on it? I, on the other hand, grew up in a healthy way, in a proper mess, and it's stuck with me for life. Instead of assuming a ladylike posture while we eat, I sit with one leg folded under my bum, I don't need a hundred paper napkins to wipe my mouth after every bite, the only thing my Slovak mum drummed into me and that I still stick to is taking my shoes off when I come home, as soon as I step into the flat, so don't pretend to be the oversensitive one, while you go around spreading the mud on your shoes all over the kitchen, like a bloody Italian peasant. And, I usually add, OK, but the main thing is that your china is nicely polished, isn't it?

Never in those twelve years has he ever cleaned out the cats' litter tray, he hasn't taken them to the vet once, so he can go and stuff himself. He's not really living with us anymore, what business is it of his, how dare he criticize me for not being on top of the cleaning, say the place is a pigsty, how dared he scream at me when I brought Jackie home.

I just couldn't leave him there, he would have got run over, I told my husband I simply couldn't leave the poor thing wandering by the motorway. He looked so wretched and homeless after some swine left him on the road in the scorching heat, probably to save money on a dog kennel if they went on a seaside holiday, that's what people do, they buy a dog for Christmas and come summer they let him loose on the motorway. This was four years ago, he was still a puppy, now he's a crazy young dog, of course I know that a dog was the last thing we needed, so at first, I really tried to find him a home, I placed ads offering 'a beautiful golden-haired stray', I contacted various organisations that help find new homes for abandoned pets, but I was out of luck, out of luck being the official version for my husband. The unofficial one is that I got really attached to him and stopped looking, and when my husband realised that the dog was staying, all hell broke loose, but I said, 'fine, you go and find him a new home, and it's got to be a family, not a shelter, OK? go ahead, I won't stand in your way'. I knew perfectly well that he wouldn't lift a finger and even if he tried, he would never succeed, and so Jackie stayed, to the great displeasure not just of my husband but also the cats. But after they gave him a thrashing a few times, he stopped sniffing their bottoms.

I go over to the children's room, I catch sight of the clock on my way, my husband should be home in about fifteen minutes, time enough for a cup of coffee, but first I'll check on the boys, they're watching something on their tablet, a game of some kind. 'Luca, you haven't even taken your pyjamas out of the wardrobe, come on, chop-chop! and don't you dare make a mess here before you get washed', I go back to the kitchen, to be honest, it wasn't just my love of animals. It also had to do with A. I had just ended the affair and needed something to fill the void, anything, even an abandoned dog.

I spent that summer driving up and down the Savona-Turin motorway, with Matteo, he was only three then. It was A that I was going to see. We had met early that summer in Bordighera, he owned the hotel where my son and I stayed for two weeks, Matteo's paediatrician advised taking him to the seaside, for the whole of the summer if need be, because of the recurring inflammations of the middle ear, the sea air would do him good. So, almost as if I'd taken the doctor's recommendation to heart and tried to extend Matteo's holiday, I embarked on an affair with A even though he was pushing 55, even older than my husband. I started the affair before my young son's very eyes, we would eat out together, stroll along the promenade, swim in the sea, we even went over to Nice, not to mention the nightly trips to his flat after Matteo had gone to sleep. At first, I kept it a secret from my husband, but I was so infatuated, so hyper, that I couldn't stand it for very long, I had this absurd feeling that it was the love of my life, it must have been the sea air that befuddled my brain. Although, as a matter of fact, A also seemed quite keen, he offered me all sorts of things, he spoke of our future together, a future at a beach resort, well, what more could one ask for, and that second week of the holiday I was really living it up at his hotel, pampered like a queen, and I thought to myself, why couldn't it be like this all the time, what's stopping me, oh, wait a minute, what about the small matter of being married, with a three-year-old son? I could hear my dead mother's voice warning me, but I was past caring about my mum, or the father of my child, or even about the child, really, there was only one thing on my mind, the desire to be with A.

When I came clean to my husband, the gates of hell opened before us, it was the hottest summer of my life, almost everything burnt to a cinder. The two weeks passed, I returned to Turin, but nothing changed, I commuted regularly to see A, I was really naïve at first, I thought my husband would take care of the kid while I was away, *cazzarola*, it was his child too, after all, I thought he should also have to do his bit, but he never did, neither before nor after, let alone in this kind of situation, and when I realised that my husband wouldn't aid and abet my adultery, I simply started taking Matteo along. As soon as we left Turin I would forget about my husband's hysterics, put on Virgin

Radio, in Bordighera we had a suite on the same floor as A's flat, and after my son went to sleep I would walk over to his place and screw away with abandon, but worse than any sense of guilt was the feeling that I had wronged Matteo in the most dreadful way, that I have traumatized him for life, because I didn't manage to do my best to keep him out of this relationship.

As we drove down, I would say, 'isn't Bordighera lovely, you like being at the seaside, don't you, Matteo, you can swim in the sea, and our hotel has a swimming pool too, you can have spaghetti alle vongole for lunch every day and sausage pizza for dinner, you like that, don't you? it's better than mummy's cooking', I'd say with a laugh, 'come on, out with it, it's better than my pasta with *ciliegino* tomatoes, come on, I won't be upset, and uncle A has been so nice to you, he keeps buying presents for you as well as for mummy, we're not really used to that, are we?' I'd tease him, 'your daddy doesn't give you so many presents', and Matteo would just sit in the back seat mutely, what was I expecting, his approval or blessing even? He was around when my husband and I had rows, he was there when I held hands with A on the promenade, I don't suppose he fully understood what was happening, who that nice elderly gentleman was that kept buying him ice cream and candy floss and treated his mummy with such courtesy, but he must have sensed that his mummy had changed, that something bad had come between his mummy and daddy, and he'd say to me, with a slightly frightened look, 'but I will stay with you, won't I, mummy, we will stay together'. My infatuation was so strong that my own son was afraid that he, too, might be abandoned for this new man, I would laugh out loud, 'Matteo, sweetiepie, what are you talking about, I'm your mummy, we will always be together', then I would shrug it off, pay no attention to it, there were other things I was more worried about and interested in, I had no idea how much damage I had inflicted on his young psyche.

I seriously contemplated leaving my husband, as I found it more and more difficult to deal with his pain, with his rages, I wanted to get it over with as soon as possible, but my husband ratcheted it up a notch, he started threatening me, said he'd see to it that I lost custody of my son, the judge would give him custody, obviously, since the boy's mother had no job, no income, no flat, no savings, so how could she provide for her child, what sort of conditions would she raise the child in, and that gave me a real fright, he was right of course, I had nothing. A was well-off but I couldn't expect him to sign his property over to me, A wanted me but he wasn't the father of my child, he couldn't help me resolve the situation with my husband, and my husband kept threatening to drag me through the courts. Then he would turn on the tears and beg me to come to my senses, and assure me of his undying love. A friend who specialised in family law confirmed that in this kind of situation you couldn't predict who might get custody of Matteo, they might award shared custody if the husband expressed an interest, and that's when it suddenly hit me, I had taken it for granted that the child was mine. How could anyone possibly take my child away, I'm his mother – that's the only thing that matters, I thought, but that wasn't the case, and so it finally dawned on me that I was deciding Matteo's fate, not just mine, in fact, mainly Matteo's fate. That same afternoon I took the car and set out on the familiar route along the Turin-Savona motorway, I drove incredibly fast, perhaps subconsciously I wanted to get killed, and, who knows, maybe I actually did want to kill Matteo, who was in the back seat. I ended the affair with A, I had to tell him in person, I had to see him one last time, and on our way back, instead of smashing into a crash barrier I spotted Jackie, the little yellow mongrel wandering along the motorway, I didn't think twice, and I stopped on the hard shoulder, put him in the car, and brought him home.

Of course I despised my husband, the wimp, I had slept with another man and he didn't even slap me across the face, although I was prepared to leave him in a heartbeat and the only reason I stayed was that he threatened to take my son away. Yet he carried on as if nothing had happened, insisting that he had never stopped loving me, and all he wanted was to make me come to my senses, he begged me to return to the marital bed, I think that was when I lost any remaining shred of respect for him. I started to sleep with him again, although I had to force myself to do it, maybe I just felt that it was the right thing to do, part and parcel of staying with him, but also, since I could no longer have A in my life, I stopped caring about my body and allowed him to take it through the boring marital motions. What worried me more was that I was finally starting to realise what I had inflicted on my little son, as all his fears, anxieties and paranoias got worse around that time. He wouldn't leave my side, followed me everywhere around the flat, and whenever I was about to go out, he would cling to me as if he didn't trust me, didn't believe my assurances, he was scared that his mother might suddenly disappear from his life for good. I was unhappy, sad, depressed, forgetful and I'm sure that it was because I was feeling so miserable that I sometimes forgot to take the pill, but be that as it may, sometime in late autumn I discovered that I was pregnant again. I was so annoyed that I stopped having sex with my husband. I didn't realize that this state of affairs would last indefinitely. Luca was born in early summer and, as if by magic, he turned out to be just like A.

Christ, I really don't pay attention to my children, I reproach myself for it, and yet I can't help it, all I ever do is plonk them in front of the TV, tell them to play together, drag them out with me for walks, the most I can manage is to check their homework, I know it's not enough, I know that this is the crucial age, while they're still young, I could do so much, like teach them English or Spanish, take them to clubs or creative workshops, anything to develop their potential, that's what people do. I should be talking to them, actually we do talk quite a lot and we are close, but being the person that I am, I'm unable to set boundaries, though I no longer tell them the kinds of awful thing that I had said to Matteo during that summer with A, still, I often come out with something unsuitable, age-inappropriate, I reproach myself for failing to give them firm foundations in the world, to ensure they trust me, their mother. I have failed to stay calm and even-tempered, to instil a sense of security in them, I often yell at them, once I even hurled my slippers at Luca, OK, they're only cloth slippers, but hurl them I did, and in the heat of the moment I shouted at him to get out of my sight or I'd give him a good hiding. Not to mention the time when Matteo was still little, and I slapped him so hard that his ears got blocked. When I'm in a good mood I try, I really do, I play pairs with them for example, and they always win because I never remember where a particular picture was, but I can see how happy they are that their mother is playing with them, but it happens very rarely, usually I just focus on my chores and my menagerie and my work and their illnesses, allowing all kinds of nonsense to float freely through my mind, scraps of memories of things I screwed up or accomplished, things that happened and things that shouldn't have, at what point did I start making one wrong choice after another, sliding down this spiral, hello there, Trent Reznor, and I kept being dragged down that spiral, and I just couldn't break free.

The key rattles in the lock, here he is, both boys come dashing out of their room and start jumping up and down in front of him, not for joy but for purely selfish reasons, and lo and behold, my husband produces two Kinder eggs. Apparently it doesn't work without bribery, he has to bring something back from every business trip, to reward them for having survived, poor things, for the hardship they endured while daddy was away. I go over to the sink and rinse out my coffee cup, my husband gives me a nod from the door and walks over to the shelf where we keep the post, to check for any bills that are due, as he walks past me I look down, he hasn't taken his shoes off of course, after I spent three hours this morning spring-cleaning, is there any point in me bringing it up again, after twelve long years? and yet I can't help myself and point to his shoes without saying a word, he rolls his eyes and goes back to the door and takes them off, duh, you moron, it's because you've never had to clean the floor, last year, when I went to stay with my cousin in Bratislava for three weeks with the boys, you didn't mind living here in total filth for three weeks, you didn't empty the laundry basket once, I found the litter tray overflowing with cat litter, but that was all right by you, and still you claim that I'm the messy one. Never mind, forget it, tonight is my night out.

My husband, now wearing his slippers, hangs around by the shelf with the letters. Matteo is on the verge of tears because they opened their Kinder eggs – I saw the scene unfold – and his had a Smurf while Luca's only contained some junk, so Luca grabbed his Smurf and Matteo couldn't fend him off. Then my husband snarls, 'Lara, it says here on this card from the postman that they couldn't deliver something, how come it wasn't delivered, weren't you at home?' 'Of course I was at home', I protest, 'but the postman just doesn't give a shit, he won't ring the bell and just drops the note into the post box, or maybe', I add after a while, 'he did ring the bell but I was in the middle of hoovering and didn't hear him'. I turn on my heel to leave while my husband is swearing and cursing, 'another trip to the post office, what a waste of time, I mean, really Lara, is that too much to ask', I turn my back on him because I can't stand the sight of him anymore. This is a new thing, it started only about a month ago, I can't bear to look at him any longer. He has lost some weight lately, he sort of dried up, the lines on his face have deepened into furrows, he looks really old now, older than A did five years ago, of course I'm not getting any younger either, but I'm fifteen years younger than he is, so there, I'm not yet forty, although I only have a year to go, and looking at him I can't help thinking, I used to sleep with this man, this is the man I have tied my life to, this is the man I mixed my gene pool with. Never mind, enough of these dreary thoughts, I check, 'you haven't forgotten I'm going to the Pasolini tonight, have you?' He pricks up his ears, 'is that tonight?', I knew it, 'I've reminded you a hundred times and you've forgotten', I wave the Circolo leaflet under his nose, 'it's tonight at nine', my husband is alarmed, 'will you not put them to bed', I lash out, 'come on, what's the big deal, Matteo can wash himself and you'll manage with Luca somehow, sorry but I've been looking forward to the Pasolini for a week, I make plans to go out once in a blue moon and you act as if I went to Murazzi every night to get wasted.' Resigned, my husband says, 'all right, all right, calm down Lara, I haven't said anything', I turn to the boys, 'put the chocolate wrappers in the bin and off you go, daddy is going to read you a story tonight'. And then I lock myself in the smaller bathroom to get ready.

As I stand in front of the mirror my mind starts racing, these are the kinds of thoughts I'd rather not be thinking, but I can't chase them away. There was a time after we first met, well before A, that I enjoyed sex with my husband, but now I can't recall what it was I liked about him, just as well, I'd rather not go into the physical details, the main thing I remember is that my husband released me from the despair of my early adulthood and my immature relationships, because that definitely was a factor, it did play a role back then, he didn't seem old to me, just experienced, an experienced forty-year-old. But after the first baby, things went steadily from bad to worse, and now there's nothing, nothing at all that we share, it's a taboo subject, it's never raised, never discussed. Sometimes it flashes through my mind that he might have found someone else, he's surrounded by all these young women at work, it wouldn't bother me, not at all, but I don't actually dwell on it very much, his life and my life are worlds apart. I put on eye shadow and mascara, I hope my eyes won't start watering as I walk through town, I hope my make-up won't run in the cold as it tends to, never mind, I'll check my face in the compact when I get there. I come out of the bathroom, the boys are brushing their teeth in the other bathroom, or rather, Luca is having his teeth brushed by his father, I give both boys a kiss, wave to my husband and before I leave I mention that I'm going with Chiara, 'have you forgotten that too?' but my husband says nothing, he just waves back, 'off you go, Lara.'

I leave the house, reach the end of Via Riccardo Sineo, our quiet cul-de-sac, so far it has been spared the invasion of *movida*, although it started just around the corner and has been spreading relentlessly, several new joints have opened in the Via Napione, there's DiVino and a new hipster café, it's awfully cold outside, there's slush underfoot, my thoughts drift to summer – sea, sunshine, beach, serenity, right? no, of course not, it's A I'm thinking of, how roughly he handled me, it verged on abuse, violating my physical integrity even, it was right on the edge, where it could have gone either way, where pleasure can flip over into pain. That's right, it was in Bordighera, it was with him that I discovered how good it can be, how much I enjoy submitting to a man totally, the right man that is, sex as a systematic violation of physical integrity, maybe that's why I've always liked Pasolini. I remember how we used to go and see *Salò, or 120 Days of Sodom* at secondary school, I don't mean the one time we went to see it, but all the times we went, because none of my friends managed to sit through it the first time round, the idea was to last as long as possible without throwing up, when it got too much, we'd look away and watch other people get up from their seats one after the other and elbow their way out, into the fresh air, away from this filth. I must say I usually won, I could last the longest, I've had a strong stomach ever since I was little.

I've reached Corso San Maurizio, I should now continue to Piazza Vittorio Veneto and then turn into the Via Po leading to the Circolo, but instead I head up Corso San Maurizio, I pass small groups of young people, lit-up bars, here at least there's some snow by the kerb that hasn't yet melted, I recall the winters of my youth, we used to have huge amounts of snow in Turin, but no longer, not for the past fifteen years, now you'd have to go to the Alps for some snow, but how am I to find time for that. A view of Palazzo Nuovo opens up before me, the university, the building of my old department, and looming behind it, yes, there it is, towering high, the Mole, its outline at night never fails to take my breath away and remind me of that silly film with Roberto Benigni. I tilt my head back to see it properly as I walk, it's beautifully lit and somewhere behind it, the PPP programme is about to begin, I smile to myself, I'd love to see it, I really would, but not tonight, forgive me Pier Paolo, we'll make up for it some other time, maybe in the Massimo film club, today I have crudely exploited you, though maybe there's no need to act out this stupid little piece of theatre, it's none of his business, we haven't been together for years now, this doesn't really have anything to do with him, but still, I try to behave decently, maintain decorum, as I mentioned earlier.

The noise rises to a crescendo, more and more people are milling around, I reach Via Tarino, the whole street is throbbing with bars and music, and all that can be seen of the Mole is the tip of its tower behind the roofs. I turn my back to it and start walking down the street, past a Japanese restaurant, towards Madre Cabrini, the Catholic Institute at the top of the road, but I come to a halt two houses down, I ring the bell at a doorway next to a bar, the buzzer goes, no words are exchanged, it's the agreed time, he knows that it's me and lets me in. I cautiously look first right then left, to make sure I haven't been seen by anyone who knows me, this is the critical moment, I slip inside, now I'm safe, relieved, I run up the stairs to the first floor two steps at a time, the door is ajar, I push it and enter.

I spot him in the doorway between the hall and the kitchen, we grin at each other as I discard my hat and jacket and gloves and scarf, the sounds of *movida* coming from downstairs, it's right below us, I don't understand how he can live here, how he can take it, but he's a barman so maybe after years in noisy dives he doesn't mind anymore, but it's not my problem anyway, I don't live with him and never will. I take my shoes off, it's a must, he ushers me into the kitchen, 'well then, ready for the carnage?' and he smiles, 'but let's have a drink first'. He is leaning against the fridge, I'm not leaning against anything, the kitchen table is between us, I sip the sweet slop he's poured me, he knows that I've given up alcohol. I look around with curiosity, there's a radio on the shelf, a Basquiat poster, unwashed dishes in the sink, usually we meet in one of his friends' digs, this is only my second time in this place. 'How did you get rid of Cecilia? Are you sure she's not going to barge in on us?' He shrugs, 'she's away in Bari visiting her mother, I spoke to her on the phone half an hour ago, the only way she could turn up here', he adds, in what is meant to pass for a joke, 'would be by teleporting.' Sometimes I picture him ripping off my clothes while I'm still on the doorstep, hurling himself at me and carrying me straight to bed, that's how it's supposed to be, that's what it's like in all the films I do subtitles for, sometimes I'm annoyed that we've fallen into this calm routine, although I shouldn't complain, it's lasted a year and a half. I put my glass down and take a few steps towards him, but he walks around the table and directs me to the bedroom, 'let's do it there, have you brought everything? I've blacked out the windows already.'

We stand there facing each other, he's left the bedside lamp on, hasn't bothered to turn the photo of his smiling blonde girlfriend around, I like that, we gaze at each other close up, I still find it disconcerting, I'm still not used to how good-looking he is, although when I say that, he laughs and tells me to go and see an optician, so today I decide not to say anything. We start kissing, caressing, squeezing each other, at least it won't go to his head, why should it always be me paying him compliments anyway, I pause for a moment and pretend to give him a stern look, I even raise my index finger, 'no naughty stuff today, understood? make sure you don't do it without a condom, it's my peak fertility day, I can feel the egg aching to lodge in my womb.' He raises an eyebrow, takes a step back, and shouts in mock horror: 'get thee behind me, Satan!', I smile, kneel down, and take his prick into my mouth.

Back out in the street an hour later, I feel good, the tension has finally eased, I'm more relaxed than I have been for a long time, I'm at peace with the world, my life, the universe. I don't even notice how I got back to Corso San Maurizio, and the *movida* is still full on, its rhythm pounding away into the night, but I no longer pay any attention to the bars or to the Mole, my legs carry me of their own accord, and it feels good to have a head empty of every thought, until it suddenly occurs to me that perhaps he did come inside me just so he wouldn't have to change the sheets before Cecilia came back home from the south. It's a horrid thought, normally he takes the condom off towards the end and comes on my breasts, my face or mouth, which always leaves a small stain on the covers, and I'm always absolutely sure that I'm safe, that my period will come as usual, but today, when I felt he was about to come inside me, I actually loved it, it was wonderful, I had no strength left, but it gave me pins and needles in my hands, he is so strong when he grabs hold of me and keeps thrusting away, but he was wearing a condom. Why is my head trying to spoil everything with this insidious thought, I shake it off, it's just a thought, like hundreds of other thoughts that go around my head every day, and there's nothing I can do about it. I know that I might start awake in the middle of the night, despite being a sound sleeper, that in the middle of the night I will open my eyes with a pang of anxiety, what if I'm pregnant, but right now I'm still walking on air, I know that it's nonsense.

But then I notice that something is happening down there, I feel something leaking out of me, only slightly, but it is a leak, definitely, it gives me a fright, was he really wearing a condom? But he was, damn it, we talked about it, I saw him put it on and take it off afterwards, I try to summon up his image to calm myself down, but what if it didn't work? I can't stand it anymore, I dive into the nearest bar on Corso San Maurizio and without asking for a coffee I head straight for the toilet, phew, what a relief, it's only blood and not much of it. The bastard has gone too far again, he overstretched me, but I didn't resist, I wanted it just as much, so I mustn't complain now, it will pass, it will stop, it always stops after a while. I'm not as terrified now as I was when it happened the first time, the only problem is I don't have a panty liner on me, so I take some loo paper at least to stop the blood leaking through my trousers before I get home, before I lock myself in the bathroom and sort myself out, I come out of the toilet and quietly leave the bar, luckily it's crowded, no one pays any attention to me. I walk down the Corso San Maurizio all the way to the Po, but instead of continuing straight onto Via Napione I cross the road and head for Murazzi, I glance at my mobile, it's quarter past ten, that's about right, I hope my husband has gone to bed, he has an early start in the morning. It's getting colder and colder, the slush is starting to freeze over, but I don't care, although tomorrow I'll be risking my life on the pedestrian crossing, there aren't any people sitting on the low wall on the river bank now of course, but in the summer the place will be heaving, in the summer the *movida* extends all the way out here, one day someone will fall off this wall and get killed, and not just one person, on Fridays and Saturdays young people get totally stoned and wasted, and they fall off this wall like rotten pears, whenever we go for a walk on a Sunday we see broken beer bottles, vomit, and stains of every kind, we meet the dustmen cleaning the street, and I wonder where was the exact spot that the boy they wrote about in *La Stampa* killed himself, only a few metres from where we live. Who would have thought, such a beautiful city, the lights shining on Superga Hill on one side, on the other the Gran Madre di Dio and the blue glow of the Santa Maria del Monte Dei Cappuccini, and further on, the plane trees and Borgo Po, the nicer, quieter neighbourhood where I might one day want to live. Actually, I wouldn't, I feel too connected to our humble Vanchiglia, where I've lived since the age of nine, where young people fall off low walls and the night life never lets you sleep, ambulances wail as they speed towards the Gradenigo with a cardiac arrest or an attempted suicide on board. I lean against the low wall, the bleeding seems to have stopped, nothing serious, just our usual carnage. I stare at the dark waters, I know I should go home and ring Chiara on the way, to find out what PPP was like, Chiara who is covering for me, but I want to stay here a little longer, now that I can truly feel my entire body, as it tingles and proclaims its presence, this moment when I'm fully aware of being alive, and I know that I will let him do it again, because it is what I need. I know that I will encourage him, goad him to go further, further and further every time, until one day he will really hurt me and it may end badly, there are so many ways it can end badly, yet I cannot bring myself to put a stop to it, even though I know deep down that one day I will pay the price, a price that is much too high.

# VERONIKA

The word kept cropping up so often that Véronique started wondering if she should change her nickname but the thought of having to re-register, re-enter her address, email, age, gender, plough through all the general conditions and data protection stuff was just too much, so she gave up, Véronique remained Véronique. But she decided to find out, to take the first opportunity the next time it came up, and there it was, just five minutes later, someone called Christophe, *excite-moi, Véronique qui nique,* he let the cat out of the bag, the verb *niquer* means to fuck, tough luck, anyone called Véronique, Dominique and any other -nique has it coming. There was even this ad, *les Véroniques qui niquent, c'est pas automatique, ah-ha, ih-hi!* – but joking aside, Christophe isn't interested in a discussion about linguistics, he's after something different, let's get it on, Véronique darling, since you've picked such a fitting nickname, but Véronique is bashful, Véronique doesn't know how to get it on, Christophe has to guide her, she lets him guide her hands on the keyboard, on her body, the body would be preferable but the computer is in the living room, her mother is around, watching the news, so they stick to the keyboard, Véronique is learning new vocab, *sucer, avaler, sodomiser, ta chatte mouillée,* it makes Véronique laugh but Véronique controls herself, doesn't burst out laughing because mother, the gravity of the situation, someone on the TV is stealing, lying, killing, shooting, dying, giving birth to quintuplets, meanwhile Véronique is being a good girl, quietly making progress with her lesson, exercise number one, change these sentences according to this example – *suce-moi: je te suce, lèche-moi: je te lèche, ça te plaît?: ça me plaît.* Ah oui, Véronique likes that.

Rico the trucker has a big red truck, Véronique is impressed, she finds red trucks incredibly sexy, much sexier than green or blue or grey ones. Véronique pictures a pristine truck, free of the dust of motorways, roads, petrol stations, just a clean red truck, without any horrible texts or images of a cow licking a happy farmer, a busty blonde proffering biscuits, no ads, nothing, just a taut blood-red canvas, thirty tons of cargo and Rico the romantic at the wheel.

His name is David, her new friend David is from Nancy. Véronique dashes over to take a quick look at the map, where on earth is that, she knows nothing about Nancy but she knows quite a lot about David by now, for example, he keeps using all kinds of smileys, now he winks at Véronique, then he sticks his tongue out, then he rolls his eyes in amazement, David is serious, David didn't open their first chat by asking for a blow job, it doesn't even come up later on, David just chats with Véronique in the normal way – school, girlfriends, parties – Véronique also tells him about her school, her friend Svetlana, her mother, their chats are a bit tedious, but after a few days he teaches her to make smiley faces, she remembers only two: a happy one :-) and a sad one, :-(,

Véronique forgets the others but Véronique is all right with that, two emoticons will do for her, she's not demanding. David sends her his picture, Véronique notes that David is good-looking, *un beau garçon*, David sends her five happy emoticons in return, David is pleased that Véronique likes him even though he has a girlfriend, he loves his girlfriend, of course he does, but I have to tell you, Véronique, when I was young I used to be a fattie, I was sweaty and smelly, the other kids laughed at me, a sad face, Véronique commiserates, she sends him a sad face too, followed immediately by a happy one because David is good-looking now, he's no longer fat, he even has a girlfriend, as he said, David also sends a smiley, two smileys, but he sticks to serious subjects, when he was at secondary school, every time he went up the stairs the other students would push and mock him because he would huff and puff, he struggled to climb the stairs, they were really mean to him, shouted at him, that's why he lacks self-confidence to this day, Véronique doesn't know what to say so she sends three sad smileys and tells him she's sorry, *désolée, mon pauvre petit David,* David nods and adds that he's very shy but at the same time he's happy to have found such a wonderful friend in Véronique, and Véronique is also happy to have found a wonderful friend like David, an orgy of smileys.

How about a photo?

Will you send me a photo?

Do you have a photo?

Come on, send me a pic.

Hey, so where's that photo?

I'll send you my picture if you send me yours.

What do you actually look like? I want your picture!

Momo is in love with her, Momo's full name is Mohamed, he keeps saying how much he loves her, truly, madly, insanely.

Momo lives somewhere in Kabylia, in the desert, infertile soil, red-hot sun of course, Momo is cooped up all day long in a tiny mixed-goods store sweating and writing poems, which he sends Véronique with a dedication, Momo raves about her beauty, in his poems he compares her to a shining star in the sky, he lives in the desert so the sky must look very different from what she sees on Šoltésova Street in Bratislava, Momo sings the praises of her soft velvety skin, Momo is in raptures about her blue eyes, Momo wishes he could run his fingers through her silky wavy chestnut-brown hair. Every now and then Momo hints that it's about time that Véronique sent him her picture as he longs to set eyes on the shining light of his days but also, Véronique suspects, his imagination may have its limits, Véronique finds Momo a bit boring, she's bored by his poems as well, one evening she read one of them out to her mother, to boast that she's found someone who sends her love poems, but they must have lost something in translation, Véronique's hands trembled as she held the sheet of paper, Véronique broke out in a sweat realising how embarrassing this was. Her mother just chuckled, I bet he's copied them from some book, that Arab is just sweet-talking you. Véronique knows her mother is right but nevertheless, Véronique imagines Momo sitting at the till all day long writing and rewriting his love poems, crossing out stanzas and dreaming of her heavenly beauty.

Sahib is a body-builder, or at least the picture he sent her shows a body-builder. Véronique isn't sure, she took a good look at his huge biceps, no, this sort of thing really doesn't turn her on, Sahib on the other hand is turned on all the time, or at least wants to be turned on, *mon bébé, excite-moi, bébé, tu me tailles une pipe? bébé, avale,* Véronique consents, Véronique always says yes at first, she kneels down in front of him, yes, she gives him a blowjob, yes she's loving it. But as soon as she tries to change the subject, like what have you been up to today, Sahib, where do you actually come from? Sahib logs off without saying goodbye, unceremoniously, he just logs off, only to log back on a few days later with the same or a very similar request, oh, *mon bébé, je veux lécher ta chatte,* and Véronique replies on autopilot, without giving it much thought, she tells him what he wants to hear, while Momo waxes lyrical about her neck and David sends sad and happy faces.

Ali has a beautiful voice, that's the first thing Véronique notices as she picks up the phone, she is more aware of his voice than of what he's saying until Ali gives a nervous laugh and Véronique comes to her senses, what, what did you say? Ali repeats what he said, he says it surprised him that Véronique has given him her phone number straight away, that's unusual, girls are normally more wary about that, at least in Paris where Ali lives, Véronique is taken aback for a moment, is this Arab suggesting that she's a slut because she hands out her phone number willy-nilly? Véronique is walking down Vazovova Street, she's on her way home from an internet café, she stopped there to log into the chatroom because recently her mother has been limiting her access to the internet to one hour a day, but let's face it, one hour is way too little. Véronique tries to imagine some Arab guy whom she's given her phone number arriving from Paris to harass her, rape her, kill her, Véronique realises what an absurd idea that is, Véronique shrugs, so what, she will give her phone number to whoever she likes, and besides, Ali is the first who's asked, Ali was the first to call her, and it's not just Ali's voice she loves but also his laughter. Véronique's laughter, on the other hand, is quite shrill so she sits down on a bench in Martin Benka Square, this is going to take a while, she wants to delay the moment she reaches the stairway in her block in Šoltésova Street, Ali is giving her an account of his life, he lives in Paris or rather, somewhere near Paris, in Melun (Véronique will have to check the map again), he rents a small flat there, he's a lift salesman. Véronique guffaws hearing that, a lift salesman! a travelling lift salesman! now there's something she'd like to know, how do you go about selling lifts, ding-dong, hello, can I interest you in a brand new lift, we have a special offer on this month if you place your order by the fifteenth, Véronique is laughing, Ali is laughing too, he hasn't taken offence, although he goes on to explain to Véronique, sounding a bit reproachful, that selling lifts is no laughing matter, sometimes he can't sell a single lift for days, weeks, even months, his employers don't find that funny either. Of course, Véronique nods, of course she understands, and what does Véronique actually do, where does she live, where? never mind, the place name doesn't ring any bells with Ali, he promises to call Véronique again because Ali prefers talking on the phone to online chatting, and before he puts the phone down, he asks Véronique for her landline number, just in case, it's less expensive, and Véronique gives him her number, she's entitled to talk to her friends on the phone, whatever her mother says, she's over 18, after all, so there!

Fatah is a journalist, he is serious about Véronique, he emails her after reading on her profile that she lives in Slovakia, because Fatah is planning to travel around the post-communist countries this summer and write a report for his weekly paper, a Slovak connection is just the ticket. Véronique agrees, summer is a long way off, it's only the beginning of spring now, the first buds have only just appeared on the trees, the first snowdrops have started to pop up in the woods at Železná studnička, summer is still so far away, she's not afraid, she can't really think that far ahead. Véronique relishes her newly-gained confidence, she promises to be Fati's guide, she'll show him everything, there's no greater expert on communism than Véronique who was seven years old in 1989, she will tell him how in Year 2 they were suddenly told to address the teacher as Miss instead of Comrade and they managed all right, it was their parents who kept getting it wrong, she will tell him about the taste of Pedro chewing gum, she can't remember what it tasted like but she'll think of something, it might have been strawberry-flavoured, yes, there's nothing more boring than strawberry flavour. She'll show him around the Petržalka housing estate, Petržalka is always a huge hit with foreign visitors, Véronique doesn't give a shit about what Fati ends up writing for that rag of his, she's much more interested in his flowery French, his long subordinate clauses, Véronique is interested in Fati even though in his photo he looks like a boring pen-pusher, no, Véronique hasn't sent him her picture, Véronique hasn't sent her picture to anyone yet, she doesn't want to send old photos in which she weighs ten kilos more than today, but she hasn't had time to have new pictures taken, of her face, body, smile, but it looks like she will have to find the time because her new friends are getting ever more insistent and annoying.

Especially Didier the skier, he's been begging for her picture non-stop, almost as if he wasn't interested in anything else. Didier the skier has sent her three photos of himself already, all of them on skis, with snow and mountains and somewhere in the distance, halfway down the slope, there's Didier in a ski suit, Didier in a bobble hat, Didier is fit, even fitter than David, although of course Véronique would never tell David, she couldn't cope with the deluge of sad faces that would surely follow, but Véronique can't help it, even though Didier is a silly name, it keeps reminding Véronique of tits, but his face, he has this lovely baby face, regular features, bright blue eyes, sometimes she wonders how this tender baby face can possibly go with his chats, in which he keeps saying that he'd love to have anal sex with her.

After about eighty requests she finally decides to take the plunge, Veronika is standing in the bathroom, her mother is out, her mother is at work, her mother is running errands, her mother has gone to the shops, her mother is gone. Veronika has set the self-timer, she takes a sideways glance at the mirror to check what she looks like, is it a flattering angle, but then she thinks no, this won't do, she looks like an idiot, she is smiling like an idiot, she *is* an idiot, she doesn't want to disappoint her friends, they would think I've wasted a month chatting to an idiot like this, I've written poetry for this idiot, an idiot who can't manage more than a couple of smiley faces. Veronika makes a couple more attempts, posing, flashing broad smiles and subtle smiles, she lets her hair down, ties it up again, she even puts on a little make-up, she's still not happy, Veronika thinks hard, then she remembers Svetlana, Svetlana likes taking pictures, Svetlana could take some good ones of her, except that Svetlana would never agree to that, her friend disapproves of her new internet pals, Svetlana takes every opportunity to try and talk sense into her, to talk her out of it, she would deliberately make her look awful in the pictures, or she might make her swear she'll never send these pictures to the Maghreb or wherever. Véronique rejects the idea, she banishes the thought of Svetlana, she'd like to do something that will surprise her new friends, her friends have been waiting for so long that a run-of-the-mill picture – a face, a body, a smile – would disappoint them, what's needed is something original, bold, unexpected. Veronika climbs into the bath, Veronika has had an idea, all it needs is a little determination and a bit of acrobatics, a nervous chuckle, what if her mother came home just now, that's all she needs, Veronika leaps out of the bath, runs to the hallway, locks the door, then she places the camera on the bed next to the big mirror on the wardrobe, Veronika tries out this and that, she's in a frenzy, a creative frenzy, when she's got through a whole roll of film she gives a sudden shudder, has the heating gone off or what? Veronika gets dressed in a hurry, turns the key in the lock, sits down to Belgian literature and a cup of tea gone cold.

The response is overwhelmingly positive, Rico the trucker says he'll definitely stop by if he ever passes through Bratislava, he and Véronique will have a shag on the mattress in the back of his lovely red truck, Sahib the bodybuilder seems happy although he doesn't have very much to say, he's probably not the visual type and prefers the written word, *ah, mon bébé, suce-moi*. The picture she's sent Momo the poet was a bit more coy, she has to leave something to his imagination, but obviously that was all he needed, he immediately asks Véronique to send him a letter of invitation, that's the only way he can get to Europe and now that he's been ravished by her heavenly beauty, he absolutely has to come and take her in his arms. Ali the lift salesman says he'll give her a ring in the evening, she hasn't sent a picture to her friends David and Fati the journalist, their relationship is based on something else, but she definitely will one day, her face, her smile, but not right now, she doesn't feel like it now because she's just opened a message from Didier the skier, he is in raptures, Didier says she's beautiful, incredibly beautiful, he loves her, now he's more determined than ever to have anal with her, she absolutely must send him more pictures like this, he needs them, he's begging her, he wants more.

Véronique is all smiles, she's feeling so good that she sends her picture to a total stranger with whom she's been chatting for five minutes, he shoots her a message back straight away, you want me to get a hard-on? Véronique crows with delight, it's so easy, so easy-peasy to meet a man, to engage, attract, captivate, to start a relationship, and what's most incredible is that here, in the chatroom, all the men find her beautiful, something that has never happened to her in real life.

And it's not just starting a relationship that's easy, it's ever so easy to get engaged, almost natural, automatic. Véronique is in her mother's office, her mother is teaching, she's giving a lecture somewhere in an auditorium nearby, explaining something, in despair over her thick foreign students, Véronique is in the chatroom, she's lost count of how many Arabs she's got engaged to in the past two hours, five or six maybe, and their names? how can she remember all those names? but the last one, he stands out, his name is Nico and he comes from Algeria, it's a bog-standard opening gambit admittedly, routine stuff, a description of positions and activities, but then they get chatting and Véronique discovers that she's on the same wavelength as Nico. They tease each other, they have a laugh, they wind each other up, Véronique takes an instant liking to Nico, Véronique loses track of time, Véronique immediately agrees to yet another engagement, but it's soon obvious that it was a mistake to mention six other engagements that day, it turns out that Nico is the jealous type, he demands that she call off all the other engagements, Nico wants Véronique all to himself, Véronique is his *bb*, no one else's, she's his little girl, he insists on that, he absolutely insists! Véronique laughs, she agrees, she will get rid of them, get rid of all today's new paramours, she doesn't give a toss about them, they can all get lost, Véronique promises to be faithful to Nico to the grave, Véronique imagines her life in Algeria, her life with Nico although she doesn't even know what Nico looks like but that's a detail, an insignificant, negligible detail, Véronique is walking down Meursault Beach blinded by the sun, she throws herself into the waves, just at that moment her mother storms into her office, she's knackered, visibly aged, it's terrible, she collapses onto an armchair, these Arabs are terrible, they can't divide eight by two and they've come to this country to study integrals.

There seem to be an awful lot of truckers here, thinks Véronique, it looks like every other one man here is a trucker, there's Rico of course, he's always waiting at some border or other, for a cargo inspection or something like that, Véronique wonders what there is to inspect all the time, Véronique is not an expert. But there's also Thomas, a Belgian guy, he says he's as hard as a rock, Véronique writes back – *je jubile!* Thomas also likes her photo, he says he'll print it out and have it on the dashboard of his truck, that way they will always be together, Véronique and Thomas, Véronique will criss-cross Europe, she loves the idea but only until Thomas sends her his picture, my God, Véronique covers her eyes, she can't believe it, even though he did warn her, he did say he was no Robert Redford, but this? as bad as this? and she has sent her picture to someone this hideous? She'll be driven all around Europe by this hideous creature? He'll be showing her off to his pals at motorway stations? Jesus, she's really crossed the line this time, she quickly logs off, she hadn't seen him in the chatroom before, she hopes she'll never bump into him again, no more bumping.

But then another unpleasant thing happens later that evening, her phone rings, a twelve-digit number, she picks up, there's a guy at the other end, he introduces himself, names a place, it doesn't ring a bell but Véronique pictures a map in her mind's eye, a place somewhere in the Middle East or somewhere like that, the guy says she shouldn't be doing things like that, he knows what she's like and he's sorry. Véronique doesn't understand, what is he sorry about? the guy says he's sorry that a young lady is into this kind of stuff, what kind of stuff?? sending people photos like that, sending her phone number to strange men, Véronique breaks out in a sweat, Véronique wishes she could slam the receiver down but for some strange reason she can't, she hears herself blabbering into the phone, no, you're wrong, I haven't been sending my pictures to everyone, the guy says sadly, you should be ashamed, young lady, and hangs up, he's the one who hangs up on her.

Ever since she's started handing out her phone number to all and sundry, her mobile has been ringing at all hours, three a.m., five a.m., all kinds of men leaving messages on her voicemail, background noise, noises from Africa, she hears words, talking, coughing, sighing, laughter. Véronique wakes up a wreck every morning, Véronique picks up the phone half asleep in the middle of the night, she says something but by the morning she forgets what she said, she just finds a log of received calls, numbers with strange country codes.

Ali the lift salesman rings regularly, almost every other day, he calls the landline, Véronique has started taking the phone into her bedroom at night, she runs the cord under the door and prepares for his call with a blanket and a cup of tea. Sometimes Ali says he'll ring but then he doesn't, Véronique falls asleep crouching by the door, curled around the phone, her mother comes first thing in the morning, wakes her up and makes her go to bed, turns the light off, on a few occasions she cut off the call, her cruel mother has just cut Ali off, hello, who's that? I can't understand you, stop calling this number, *please don't call again!* The next day Véronique and Ali have a good laugh at her mother's expense, she's obviously not coping mentally, she's evidently not fallen under the spell of Ali's mellifluous voice, her mother can't stand Arabs, she makes no secret of it, Véronique has given her a piece of her mind, called her a racist, a nasty xenophobe, intolerant. Her mother, in turn, has told her off several times, know why they're all Arabs? it's because decent people are at work during the day, or spending time with their families, they're too busy to be glued to a computer all day long chatting to young women! That's not true, Véronique yelled back at her, they're not all Arabs, there's Didier! Rico! David! Thomas! and others, too! Although she obviously knows that most of them *are* Arabs, eighty per cent of people who contact her in the chatroom are Arabs, the Badrs, Ahmads, Jamils, Mohameds, Abdels, Karims, Omars and Ali, of course, the lift salesman from Melun, who phones from his brother's office because it's free, and if he can't make the call, Véronique phones him, and happily chats to him for an hour, without thinking of the consequences, the looming phone bill, it feels so good to talk to Ali that she forgets about everything else, they can easily spend an hour talking, laughing, reminiscing, planning their future. Ali is the one she's established the most stable relationship with, when she puts the phone down she can't remember what they talked about all that time, what issues they discussed, she just remembers the odd snippet, Ali has a Hungarian ex, Véronique a mother *qui me fait chier!*, bores her shitless, and perhaps that's how it should be, why should people who are in a relationship always have to talk about earth-shattering stuff, isn't it enough to share trifles, platitudes, everyday worries, Véronique is planning to visit Ali in Paris, Melun that is, in the summer, Ali will show her all kinds of things, Véronique can't wait to see Ali's studio flat.

David's sister has died, Véronique learns one morning in Obchodná Street, lately she's been going to an internet café in Obchodná, it's in a courtyard, it's very cheap, Véronique has spent nearly all her money on the internet, on chatrooms, relationships with French and Algerian men, Véronique is in shock, not about the fact that David's sister has died, people do die, Véronique knows that, she's not a child anymore, she's in shock at the fifteen sad faces at the end of David's message, it reads *ma soeur est morte* :-( :-( :-( :-( :-( :-( :-( :-( :-( :-( :-( :-( :-( :-( :-(, why fifteen, Véronique wonders for a moment, it's absurd, the whole thing doesn't make sense, how can you end a sentence like this with an emoticon, but still, Véronique can't stop thinking about the number, how did David arrive at this number, are fifteen sad faces sufficient to express the enormous grief he feels? do fifteen sad faces prove that he loved her very much, or do they suggest that he is relieved in some way that he no longer has to share a room with his annoying sister who's been bringing boyfriends home at night… or something like that, or is fifteen a totally random number, David goes on and on, he tells her how it happened, two days ago his sister decided to take a nap in the afternoon, said she wasn't feeling well, something with her stomach, and she never got up again, cardiac arrest, she was only thirty-two, Véronique would like to commiserate with David but she can't, she can't manage a single emoticon, she's simply incapable of typing out a sad face so she ends the conversation in a hurry, finds an excuse, any excuse.

That day Véronique picks a new nickname, she registers as François, Véronique is now François, František, Franz! Véronique knows that every time she goes online, at least ten Arab men respond to her female nickname, men who are looking for casual banter, a one-off. Véronique has noticed the predominance of male nicknames, women are few and far between, women are rare and highly sought after in the chatrooms. There are days when she enjoys that, but not today, today she's not feeling like all that *lèche-moi, suce-moi* and all the rest of it, come on, make me come, in addition she needs a break from chatting to some of her friends, she prefers to wait for David's grief to subside by at least ten sad faces, around five would be bearable, and there are some men she doesn't feel like talking to at all, like the hideous Belgian trucker Thomas who keeps begging her for more nudes. The only one Véronique feels like talking to is Didier the skier with the baby face, Didier may have also begged her for photos but at least Didier is fit, Véronique is happy to send some pictures to Didier, more and more photos, and no, Véronique is not ashamed of being shallow, Véronique fancies Didier, Véronique is a little bit in love with Didier, Véronique is flattered that he likes her pictures, that he finds them helpful, that they turn him on. Véronique has a pretty good idea of what use he puts them to but that's not all there is to their relationship, Didier has also been telling Véronique about himself, his family, his city, without any smileys, and that has impressed

Véronique, Didier wants Véronique to come to him, not to his house, his parents wouldn't allow that, he wants Véronique to come to Auxerre, book into a hotel and Didier will come and visit her after school, Véronique finds his naïve and cheeky ideas rather amusing, in fact, she wouldn't mind visiting him because Véronique has started to really like this boy, that's why she has decided to seek him out in the chatroom, posing as François. She posts a message on the public forum, anyone seen Didier today? she doesn't have to wait long for an answer, someone by the name of Nuredin says – *dégage, pédé!* – get lost, you fag!

Brush up your French? I can't believe you said that! her mother looks as if she's about to have a heart attack, lately she's had that look every time she and Veronique have a fight, all because of her new internet friends, Véronique has just explained to her that her French has improved by leaps and bounds over the past two months, slang, abbreviations, pronunciation, everything, but her mother doesn't want to know, she just goes on shouting – I would understand it if you wanted to go to France to brush up your French! spend two months as an au-pair! or in a summer camp, the kind that young people go to these days, looking after the disabled, picking up litter, building walls! but this? wasting days on end exchanging emails with some layabouts? what is it you talk to them about anyway, I would really like to know!

Véronique doesn't understand what Fati is on about at first, he is delighted that at last she too has realised that their attachment is growing stronger by the day, he's known for a long time that they have a bond, but she was the first to articulate it, he admires her courage, but for him, well, basically, it's mutual. What? what's he talking about? what does he want? Véronique has to re-read his message twice before it dawns on her, before she remembers that she ended her last message with *mon amour, je t'aime*, Jesus, he's taken it at face value and has now gone all melodramatic. Come on, this is her standard sign-off, she says it to everyone, *mon amour* has become just a meaningless phrase for her, she opens the folder with the photos of her sweethearts, pulls up Fati's picture, examines his face trying to find something positive, something attractive, but she can't help herself, he's a pen-pusher, a bureaucrat and a pen-pusher with a grey, nondescript face, this Arab has no mojo, unlike many of the others, Ali, Nico and the rest, although he might be the one who is the most educated, with the widest horizons, best manners, so now what? Véronique doesn't waste much time pondering this question, she might as well get engaged to him too, one fiancé more or less, same difference, Véronique writes back, *oui, mon amour*, no one can beat Véronique at declaring love in French, Véronique doesn't even have to make an effort, it comes automatically, she attaches some pictures and sends off the message, forgetting about it instantly. The reply comes the same evening, Fati's affection has burst all bounds, Fati can't wait to come to Bratislava and hold her in his arms, Fati bares his soul, he confesses to his new love that he hasn't had a serious relationship before, just dalliances, *amourettes*, but Véronique is something else, he feels that this relationship will last, he feels that she's the love of his life, no one has ever said to him the kind of things Véronique has said, no other woman has awakened the real male in him and, to top it all, Véronique is so beautiful, he can hardly believe his luck. Véronique reads intently, Véronique sips her tea in the internet café and mutters to herself – holy crap! Fati concludes his fervent declaration by asking for her phone number, Véronique pings back her mobile number, it might be more expensive, but she's reserved the landline for Ali.

Yannick the car mechanic is a recent discovery. Véronique likes the fact that he calls her *ma princesse*, it's true that Véronique is *ma puce* for Didier and for Ali she is *ma biche*, but let's face it, a princess is better than a flea or a doe. Yann lives somewhere in the Massif Central, he works in a garage, when he sends his picture, Véronique studies it on the living room computer, fascinated and as her mother walks past on her way to the armchair and her TV news, she remarks resignedly, so now you're friends with druggies as well? Admittedly, Yannick looks a bit weird, there's a kind of yellowish-green tinge to him but surely that's just the lighting in the garage, his body seems all contorted, but Véronique finds that when she stares at him really intensely, after five minutes he starts to look gorgeous, Véronique imagines herself living somewhere in central France and helping him with his work, always covered in oil and petrol, wearing overalls, but still, a princess! Véronique promises Yannick she will come and cook him nutritious meals every evening, Yannick laughs and tells her to cool it, to slow down, *ne t'emballe pas trop vite, ma princesse*, life in the mountains is hard and I'm no *prince charmant*, Yannick is not trying to pull her, he doesn't want her to be disappointed later, and of course Véronique is instantly hooked.

Up till now Véronique has only done this sort of stuff in writing, even with Ali Véronique hasn't gone as far as doing it on the phone, but now the phone rings, it's Sébastien. She only met Sébastien in the chatroom half an hour ago, Sébastien has asked for her phone number, Sébastien has dialled her number and he's now asking Véronique to turn him on, Véronique is doing her best, she is shy, she stumbles, he has to coax it out of her although she mastered the necessary vocab long ago, but not like this, live, it's not working, she can't do it, so Sébastien takes the initiative, Sébastien gives Véronique instructions in that sleazy French accent of his, what, how and where she should caress, lift, lick, rub, insert, but mainly moan, why aren't you moaning? Véronique emits a half-strangled moan, then slams the phone down.

The next day Véronique is back in the chatroom, talking to someone called Francine, which is strange in and of itself, Véronique doesn't usually talk to women, except sometimes by accident, a foreigner studying French who needs someone to help with her homework, that's happened a few times, Véronique spent a whole night discussing *subjonctif, indicatif, passé composé*, but Francine wants a proper chat, Francine wants to discuss her boyfriend, she tells Véronique about their open relationship, they had a threesome with a female friend the other day, then again a threesome with a male friend, not to mention a foursome with a married couple, then there was a party that got out of hand so that, by the end, five of them were sprawled across one another on the bed licking and fingering each other. Véronique begins to yawn wondering what Francine's final count might be but then, out of the blue, Francine suddenly says, but you weren't too bad on the phone either last night, were you? Véronique, a lump in her throat – what are you trying to say? If you tried a bit harder you could go a long way, Véronique – what's that supposed to mean, is that you, Sébastien? Francine – of course not, I've told you I'm Francine and I heard you moan yesterday, it turned me on, Véronique doesn't even log off, Véronique just switches off the computer.

What? you haven't told your mother about our engagement? fumes Véronique, screaming and shouting at Fati on the phone. Véronique continues, first you're all mon amour, *mon amour, je t'aime tellement, ma douce et tendre*, you're good at that, but when push comes to shove… Véronique is taking the piss, Véronique is having fun, but Fati may not have noticed, Fati is blinded by the seriousness of their relationship, Fati is bending over backwards to explain, his hundred-year-old mother suffering from dementia somewhere in Algeria, buried under a burqa, his mother has never heard of Central Europe, Slovakia, let alone Bratislava, this kind of information would only confuse his mother. Véronique dials it down, having to listen to Fatah's excuses makes her cringe, promise me you will tell her before our wedding day, will you? Fatah is laughing, Fatah agrees, of course, I will tell her before our wedding day, don't worry, her relationship with Fatah has taken off lately, there have been phone calls, pictures, even letters by snail mail, Fati has taken to writing Véronique old-fashioned letters, not infantile poems like Momo who works in the convenience store, but real letters declaring his love for Véronique, confessing his feelings, and Véronique won't be outdone, she dumps all sorts of intimate information on him, pouring it over his head like bucketloads of dirty water, her depression all last autumn, her sense of powerlessness, Fati listens intently, he is perceptive, sympathetic, supportive, Véronique tells him she finds it hard to talk about it but as her boyfriend he is entitled to be informed of her dark past. Véronique is lying through her teeth, nothing is easier than talking about the past, romantic, tragic, she'd find it much harder to speak of the present, to explain away her twenty other fiancés and other horrors, his aged Algerian mother is not the only one who'd get confused but Fati would too, with his undying love and earnestness.

Do you know how long mine is? Véronique laughs, she sends a jolly smiley, Rico, you idiot, you've told me a dozen times already! Rico hesitates, and every time you gave a different size, adds Véronique and Rico pings back – that's only because the real size *de ma bite* would blow your mind, that's why I tried to make it a bit smaller, I didn't want to frighten you, Véronique – oh I'm so scared already, Rico is happy, Véronique – but if it's that big how do you even fit into your truck's cab. Rico cracks up – I can manage, don't worry, Véronique – well, thank God for that, so where are you now? Rico – on the Spanish border, my cargo is being checked, I may have to spend the night here, Véronique – oh, so far away, the other end of Europe, Rico – don't worry, one of these days I'll pass through Czechoslovakia too, Véronique – I doubt that, she wonders if she should add: you'd need a time machine for that, but then she thinks better of it, Rico wouldn't understand anyway, Rico insists – just you wait, I will come to Czechoslovakia and then you'll get to see it with your own eyes! Véronique – I'll see your red truck, great, I look forward to it, Rico – but I meant *ma grosse bite*, Véronique laughs – enough already, stop it now, please.

An earthquake has hit the north of Algeria, 6.7 on the Richter scale, hundreds of casualties, people jumping out of their windows, the seaside resort of Boumerdes is devastated. Véronique reads in horror, she quickly goes to the chatroom and fires off messages to her boyfriends and fiancés to make sure they're all right, are they alive, were they anywhere close? The first to reply is Sahib the bodybuilder, don't worry, *bébé*, I'm here, we're badly shaken, I'm urgently in need of a pick-me-up, how about a quickie, Véronique smiles, Sahib is obviously all right, he's at it even between aftershocks, she ends the chat without saying goodbye, a couple of other Algerians reply, others don't, Momo hasn't written, maybe he's offended. He's been asking her for a letter of invitation for a month now and she's refused, the gushing stream of poems has dried up, he's probably latched on to some other European woman, a more understanding, responsive, obliging one, although Véronique doubts that any other woman could compare with her, at least when it comes to heavenly beauty. Half an hour later Véronique signs out, more or less reassured, most of her fiancés have survived, some are bound to get in touch later. When she stops to check her messages on her way back from Uni she finds one from Nico, he is livid, he's been nearly buried by the earthquake but hasn't heard a word from his fiancée, she hasn't bothered to ask if he's alive, if he's ok, if his house hasn't collapsed on top of him, she obviously doesn't care that his cousin is being dug out from the rubble as he writes, that's it, he's breaking off their engagement with immediate effect. Véronique is sorry, it's true that Véronique has completely forgotten about Nico but now that he's got in touch, she realises how much she cares about him, it was so stupid of her to lose him just like that, he's such a nice guy, one of her favourite fiancés, she's lost him because of the earthquake, because she's so scatterbrained. She makes a last-ditch attempt to make up with him in the chatroom a few days later, when she finally sees he's online, but Nico is dead serious, *laisse-moi en paix, stp*, he refuses to communicate with her anymore. Véronique sighs and leaves him alone, leaves him to dig out his cousin from the rubble, Véronique isn't all that sorry, in fact Véronique is laughing. Yannick the car mechanic has just sketched out a plan for their life together in the mountains, Véronique has to be ready to get up before six in the morning, be in the garage by seven so she can pass the tools to Yannick who will be squeezed under a car, the thought makes Véronique laugh, a princess with a tool belt, Véronique no longer regrets breaking up with Nico, Véronique is absolutely fine with it.

The relationship with her friend David is back on track, David is no longer grieving for his dead sister, every now and then David sends her a happy smiley, sometimes even lots of different jolly smiley faces, like when he describes how he went to a party and got pissed out of his head, David lives a busy student life, he goes to chalets, plays board games, smokes weed and keeps breaking up and getting back together with his girlfriend, who is also a student, every time they break up David tells Véronique how sad he is, how he regrets that she is so far away. David is convinced that if he and Véronique lived closer to one another, if they went to the same school, they would be an item, they'd get on like a house on fire, they'd make love like wild beasts, David sends angry faces because Véronique lives in some godforsaken hellhole in Central Europe, Véronique is flattered, this nice blond boy, always stoned, is so into her. Véronique decides to reward him, she will surprise him by secretly learning to type some new emoticons and send them to him, how do you do a winky face? Sometimes when David feels depressed he asks Véronique to tell him what he's doing wrong, why his girlfriend Valérie keeps messing with him, Véronique is a woman, Véronique must know, but Véronique doesn't know shit, Véronique always tells him he's an *adorable mignon* and *beau gosse* and Valérie is a stupid goose if she fails to see that, David is happy and grateful for her words, then David tells Véronique that she's as beautiful as the morning dew and he loves her *à la folie*, at this point Véronique usually signs out and waits for David to come to his senses again, this is the point Véronique usually thinks that this boy is a real stoner.

At first her mother tries to talk sense into her, tries to understand what's got into Veronika, this dependence on internet chatrooms and Arabs, Veronika is doing nothing except going online, writing, giggling insanely at the computer screen, her mother wants Veronika to stop and think because if Veronika stopped and thought for a moment she'd realise that her behaviour isn't normal, that it's not right, but Veronika doesn't stop and think, Veronika starts yelling, it's all for her French! her mother has no idea how much it's improved! how fluent she's become! now her mother is shouting too, and what about the pictures I've found, they also have something to do with French? they also help you improve? improve in what way exactly? Now Veronika loses it completely, how dare she snoop around her computer! go through her folders! betrayal, deception, misappropriation! Veronika is fuming, she's exploding with embarrassment and humiliation and fury, Véronique locks herself in her room for the rest of the evening, she calls Ali on her mobile, tells him everything, has a good moan and a cry, Ali comforts her, Ali makes light of it, Ali tries to see the funny side, he makes Véronique feel better, he makes her smile and then even laugh, Ali is relieved to have his good old Véronique back. Ali invites her to Melun, to his studio flat in the suburbs, she would finally be rid of her annoying mother, Véronique accepts, Véronique promises she'll come in the summer, definitely, Véronique ends the call feeling much better. Veronika opens the door into the hallway, walks over to the kitchen, her mother is sitting at the table doing some marking, she raises her eyes from the papers, 'I bet your phone number and photo is posted on every telegraph pole in Algeria.'

Rico writes – *alors, mon bébé*, I'll be passing through Czechoslovakia two weeks from now, your town, Bratislava, is on my route, what do you think, eh? shall we get it on? Véronique – I don't believe you, Rico – sure thing, I'm coming and we'll fuck, Véronique – *c'est une blague?* No, it's not a joke, he has a delivery in Poland, he'll make a small detour to combine business with pleasure, Véronique hesitates, then she sends him her mobile number, Véronique is gripped by a fever, Rico is coming, Rico, her truck driver! she'll be making love to Rico in the back of his truck! her fever subsides as soon as she logs out, Rico must be just having her on, as always.

Didier the skier is really pissed off when he finds out, when Véronique comes clean, Didier the skier was naïve enough to think that Véronique was wearing white knickers in some of the photos, and now this, a betrayal, a dirty trick, Véronique has admitted that she's retouched some of the pictures, she's whitened out some parts of the pictures that seemed too explicit, pictures where her legs were spread too wide, she didn't dare send them to anyone. Didier feels betrayed, Didier demands that she immediately resend all the pictures undoctored, Véronique laughs – I'm not sending them, screw you! Didier threatens her, he'll cut off contact, he'll never talk to her again, he'll forward her photos to others in the chatroom. Véronique is laughing, go on, send them to whoever you like, I don't care, Véronique won't be easily intimidated, who does Didier think he is. Didier dials it down and starts to explain, to flatter, the pictures are not as gross as Véronique thinks, Véronique mustn't think of it as gross, it's a beautiful thing, the most beautiful thing ever, Didier cannot imagine anything more beautiful, Véronique thinks about it, how do you know it's beautiful if you haven't seen it, if it's retouched?

Didier is rattled again, how dare she mock him like that, he starts typing in all caps, VÉRONIQUE, IF YOU DON'T SEND ME THE PICTURES, I'LL START TO DOUBT THAT YOU'RE SERIOUS ABOUT OUR RELATIONSHIP. As she reads this Véronique laughs so uproariously that everyone in the computer room in Obchodná Street raises their eyes from their combat games, Véronique wipes away her tears, Didier is roiled by doubt, she writes *oh-là-là !* and disconnects.

Veronika is sitting on a low wall by the Danube with Svetlana, Veronika asks, Svetlana, do you like trucks? Svetlana, without the slightest hesitation, I do! Veronika – what about red ones? those really long ones, with a trailer? Svetlana – those are the best, Veronika – they're great, aren't they, Veronika is happy, Svetlana is thrown slightly off balance, another long silence, they sit there cracking pumpkin seeds, waiting for their next class.

It's actually quite sweet, thinks Véronique, she has only met this boy earlier today, his name is Patrick, they had a little chat, exchanged a few messages, there was some dirty talk of course, Patrick asked for her phone number, Véronique gave it to him, now Véronique is sitting in the internet café, Véronique is waiting, the phone doesn't ring, she waits a little longer, then she writes, why aren't you calling? Patrick is embarrassed, I didn't know it was an international number, I can't afford international calls, Véronique – tough, you don't know what you're missing, Patrick – why, are you good? Véronique doesn't reply, why waste energy, he's not a good catch.

There are fifteen sad faces, Véronique has counted them at least three times, fifteen sad faces, exactly the same number as his dead sister and her cardiac arrest merited, David's girlfriend has walked out on him tonight, this is obviously a tragedy on the same scale as the death of a sibling, if only they hadn't broken up and got back together some twenty times before, but David swears blind that this time it really is for good, Valérie found out that he'd cheated on her, Valérie discovered the other one, not Véronique, Véronique might be the third or fourth or umpteenth, this wasn't a virtual person but a real one, a student from another class, Valérie had solid proof so David had to come clean, Valérie knows no compromise, she's dumped him. Valérie took all her stuff with her, Valérie has taken back the presents she'd given him once as a token of her love, a ladybird mug, a cushion with her photo, the porn, David is devastated, all alone in his parents' flat, alone with the internet and the chatroom, now he's sending sad faces to Véronique, he might be a bit drunk or high, who knows, he says Véronique is the only one he has left now, his most loyal friend. Véronique goes – what do you mean, and what about the other one, the one with whom you cheated on Valérie? At long last, David sends a happy smiley, oh yes, nearly forgot about her :-) but then he starts moaning again, he feels sorry for himself and sends a sad face, nothing has changed, ever since primary school everyone has been out to hurt him, he's still the fattie that anyone can kick with impunity and they do, he loved Valérie so much, how could she do this to him, so heartless, a heart of stone, *cette connasse de merde* ! Véronique thinks that he's bit OTT but it's a delicate moment, probably not a good time to tell her friend he's talking gibberish, that he's going too far, that he seems to lack self-awareness and other home truths of that kind. Anyway, it's not just Valérie, Véronique is also fed up with David and wonders if she should follow her example, in a word, Véronique is thinking of bailing out, the only thing actually bothering Véronique is whether she too would also merit fifteen sad faces if she suddenly disappeared from his life, would David also be so heartbroken if their friendship ended?

The envelope looks somehow different, it doesn't bode well, the envelope is twice as big as usual, Veronika has found it in the letter box, it was folded in half to fit in, Veronika climbs the stairs very slowly, only on the third floor does she dare open the envelope and take a peek, Jesus Christ, she quickly closes it again, ten thousand! She has made ten thousand crowns' worth of phone calls over the past month?! that can't be right! surely it's a mistake! Veronika is trembling, surely it can't be that much, but then she remembers Ali, the hour-long call to his French mobile, and a few other phone calls, only slightly shorter, and then there's Fati, in fact, she now recalls all sorts of people and starts to believe it. She has to find some explanation, some acceptable reasons, but when her mother comes home from work and she hands her the envelope, there's no need for an explanation, her mother understands straight away, she is furious and starts screaming like mad, Veronika has never seen her in such a state, she should have guessed that Veronika would make calls to all those Arabs, Veronika promises to pay it all back, her mother shouts that this is not the point, the point is that she's completely lost the plot, that she has no awareness whatsoever of her behaviour and her actions. Veronika locks herself in her room to get away from her screaming, Veronika has an inkling that the shit will really hit the fan when the mobile phone bill arrives.

Just then her mobile beeps, I'll be with you in Czechoslovakia in two days' time, Rico.

Veronika is sitting with Svetlana on a bench in Primaciálne Square, it's Wednesday evening, it's still light outside because it's June, Svetlana is licking an ice cream, listening to Veronika holding forth as usual, Veronika in raptures about her impending adventure, the big love story that's about to have a happy ending, on the platform of a truck, in a muscular embrace on a mattress. Eventually Svetlana pipes up, so if I understand it right, you're going to meet some guy and the only thing you know about him is that he drives a red truck and wants to screw you, Veronika is taken aback, that sounded so harsh, but Svetlana goes on, she doesn't ease off, has it ever occurred to you that he might not be alone? Veronika doesn't understand, what do you mean, not alone? Well, truckers usually travel in pairs to take turns, one sleeps while the other is at the wheel, then they switch places, that's how it's done. But Rico has never mentioned a second guy, Veronika objects feebly, he travels alone, but Svetlana finds that hard to believe, I'm sure there will be two of them, Veronika, I bet that when the other guy sees you like this, in this tight tank top showing your tigerprint bra, all made up and your hair all nice, I bet he'll want to have a go too, have you thought of that? hasn't that occurred to you? all right, but at least you should think about it now, is that really what you want, isn't it too risky, do you want to end up raped and stabbed somewhere in a wood near Ovsište... Veronika listens intently but she just can't grasp what Svetlana is on about, what risk she is talking about, it's Rico, the funny young guy who's been flirting with her for months and who thinks Veronika is beautiful, it's just Rico! not some serial killer or rapist! She wants to shout at Svetlana to disabuse her of that notion, but all she says is, but Rico is my friend, Rico wouldn't do that to me, Svetlana frowns, what do you mean – your friend, you really think that some truck driver is as good a friend of yours as I am? Veronika doesn't know what to say, she just manages to stutter something confused, but that's a totally different kettle of fish, no comparison, but yes, she does consider Rico her friend, and not just Rico but also David and Didier and Yannick and Momo and Ali and Fati and Nico, actually, not Nico anymore, and others too, Svetlana can't begin to imagine how close she's become to all of them over the past few months, Svetlana gets up abruptly, tosses what's left of her ice cream into the bin, go ahead then, get closer to your friends, your truck drivers and whoever else you like, good luck to you! She turns on her heels and walks off towards the Polish Institute without a goodbye, Veronika stays on the bench and watches Svetlana leave, she doesn't turn back once, but Veronika doesn't do anything to stop her either, she just sits there, then she hugs herself for a moment, it's getting colder.

Veronika criss-crosses the city centre, it takes some imagination, some invention to vary routes in this small space of a few square metres, these ten streets or so of the Old Town, it's gone dark, the shops are closed, only cafés and pubs are open. Veronika glances at the shop windows, she stops for half an hour in Prašná Bašta for a cup of tea, then at Verne's for a coffee, Veronika is blissed out, she's a woman now, or rather, she is about to become a woman courtesy of a man who will phone her any minute, a man who is on his way to meet her, who desires her. Yes, Veronika tells herself happily, he's a real man, not some adolescent with his voice breaking, over the last few months Veronika has matured enough to attract real men, and not just any old men but truckers! Veronika is on fire, she imagines Rico's strong hands as they grip the wheel, her waist, spread her legs, Veronika doesn't know if she's scared or excited by the prospect, she's trembling in feverish anticipation. She goes down Panská Street again, heads for the Cathedral, then up the unlit Kapitulská Street towards St Michael's Gate, when she reaches the Austrian Institute there's at last a beep on her mobile, Véronique tries to control her trembling hands, she resolutely takes her mobile out of her bag and reads the message, I'm about to cross the border. She repeats the words out loud: I'm about to cross the border.

# RECENT TITLES PUBLISHED BY JANTAR

---

### The City of Torment *by* DANIELA HODROVÁ

Translated by Véronique Firkusny and Elena Sokol

An intoxicating, personal journey through 1,000 years of European culture where history's losers bite back. On one level, a family and generational novel, conveyed through the complex voice of a first-person female narrator whose subjectivity becomes elaborately intertwined with the main protagonist, Eliška Beránková (Lamb). Eliška/Daniela is searching above all for her dead father, but also for her dead mother and ultimately for herself.

ISBN: 978-1-914990-01-4

### The Birds of Verhovina *by* ÁDÁM BODOR

Translated by Peter Sherwood

A gripping portrayal of a totalitarian society in all its irrationality, absurdity and implacability, simultaneously provoking laughter and shuddering in the reader. Home to nine hot springs, Verhovina used to be rich in natural beauty, yet it has become a wasteland, with only a few dozen inhabitants left. Trains to Verhovina are scarce; the timetable has been cancelled. One day, even the birds disappeared from the region.

ISBN: 978-1-914990-03-8

You will find many more amazing books on
**www.JantarPublishing.com**